The Chaos Machine

by Jim Hamilton

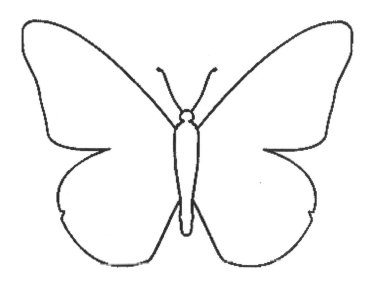

ISBN-13: *978-1537112596*
ISBN-10: *1537112597*

*Dedicated to my wife, Linda,
and my three wonderful children:
Nelson, James, and Sarah.*

*Special thanks to Jean
for her proofreading
and valuable feedback.*

*Frontispiece butterfly by
Jessica Love Mear.*

*Cover art and internal
artwork by the author.*

Contents

5342 BC - NW Persian Gulf Delta

On a high hill overlooking the northernmost end of the sea, Mardu sat gazing out at the wide expanse of water. The sky to the southeast was just starting to fade into night and the night light was already up in the sky to the east. He had been sitting on an outcrop of rock watching the day light descend to the ground when his attention was caught by something that flared in his peripheral vision. He had turned to see what it was and stared, fascinated, at a new light in the sky. At first, it appeared to be like the other night specks in the heavens, but as he continued to watch, it was clear that it was growing steadily brighter. So absorbed was he in this spectacle that he almost collapsed in fright when, in the space of a few heartbeats, the new light swelled in size with a roar like a hundred winds and slammed into the sea only a few thousand strides away. Without even thinking about it, Mardu reflexively turned and ran screaming down the far side of the hill looking for his brother.

Itok was building up the fire inside their tent when he heard what sounded like the largest and most fierce sandstorm imaginable. Almost before he could even wonder what it was, it stopped just as suddenly and was followed by a silence that somehow seemed much quieter than normal. He went to the doorway and looked out to the south and east seeking its source.

"Itok! Itok!" Mardu yelled.

Itok saw him in the distance and went running to meet him.

"What's wrong, Mardu? Are you okay? What was that terrible sound?"

Mardu was nearly out of breath by the time he came to a halt in front of his brother and he had to take several deep breaths before he could speak.

"It fell into the sea, Itok! One of the night specks fell into the sea!"

"You're not making any sense, Mardu. What are you talking about?"

"I was sitting on the hill watching the day light fall to ground and one of the specks grew and grew until it was the size of a mountain and it fell into the sea. That was the noise you heard."

Shaking his head in disbelief, Itok said "I think you must have fallen asleep or hit your head. This wouldn't be the first time you came up with some wildly improbable tale to impress everyone."

"If that is so, then what was that noise? You said you heard it too!"

"True enough."

"Come with me, Itok. I want to go back and see if there's any sign of it still. I was so frightened that I turned and ran and didn't stop until I got here."

"It's almost night, Mardu. By the time we get there we won't be able to see anything. Come on back to the tent and help me fix something for us to eat. We'll look for your fallen speck at first light."

Mardu started to protest, but he glanced around at the deepening dusk and realized that his brother was right. It would have to wait until the light of a new day. "Okay, little child, let's go fix us something to eat."

Itok smiled at his older brother, "You're just jealous of my youth, old man."

The two walked back to the tent where they fell into the evening ritual they had practiced now for many years. After a simple but filling meal, Itok and Mardu sat in front of the fire and said very little. At one point, the fire popped and spit an ember out of the pit.

Mardu pushed it back into the fire with the fire stick. "That's just what it looked like," he said. "Maybe that's what the night specks are. Big balls of fire in the sky far, far away. And tonight, one of them jumped to the ground."

Itok grunted, "And maybe the night and day lights are big balls of fire as well?" He rose up and went to his corner and laid down on his reed mat. "Goodnight, my crazy brother."

After a bit, Mardu got up and went to lay down on the mat in his own corner. "Goodnight, Itok," he said, but Itok was already fast asleep. Mardu laid down and closed his eyes, but sleep did not come to him as quickly as it did for his brother. He kept replaying the scene that had happened so quickly over and over in his mind. Again and again he saw the speck as it fell into the sea. For just a moment it looked like it had actually stopped as it touched the surface of the water and then just sort of slipped in with hardly a ripple. Or perhaps he imagined that part of it. He tried to recall what it looked like, but all he could clearly remember was a bright round light that nearly blinded him. It was much later when he finally drifted off into a fitful slumber.

+ + +

In the morning, Mardu arose before Itok and went outside. Already it was getting light in the east and he went back inside where his brother was just getting up.

Itok grimaced, "I can see that there's going to be no rest for us until we go see your speck."

"It fell into the water," Mardu reminded him. "There may not be anything left to see."

"That may well be. Grab your things and let's get going. We'll eat when we get back."

As was their practice, they had both slept in their robes and needed only to fasten their plaited belts about their waists and don their sandals. Itok raised one eyebrow inquisitively, "Since when do you need both your club and your knife?"

"You weren't there, Itok. It was like nothing I've ever seen before. Who knows what we might find?"

Itok didn't answer but headed out the door. Mardu ran to catch up and then settled into a comfortable walking pace beside him. They said very little until they crested the hill between their farm and the sea. At the edge of a short bluff they stopped and looked out over the calm waters.

"I don't see anything," said Mardu, obviously disappointed.

"That doesn't mean it didn't happen," replied Itok.

"I know what I saw, but I was hoping that there would be something to show you, something to prove to you that it really happened!"

"It's okay, Mar, I believe you. I don't know why, but I really do."

The two brothers stood and looked out across the sea as if expecting something to show itself. To show a sign. To show that Mardu hadn't simply dreamed or made the whole thing up. After a while, Itok squinted into the eastern sky, "The day light is a hand above the hills. I think it's time for us to get back to the farm. There's work to be done. Come on, Mardu, I'll cook us some breakfast."

Mardu took one more long look at the sea and then turned to his brother, "You're right. There's nothing here to see. Let's get going." He started off down the side of the hill without waiting to see if his brother was following him.

Six Months Ago - San Francisco, California

Allen's alarm clock chimed at 6:30 AM letting him know that another day had begun. He sat up and swept his sandy hair out of his eyes. Suddenly he remembered yesterday's press conference and leapt out of bed to turn on the news. Flipping through the channels, he found one covering the stock market and waited to see if his announcement would generate any excitement. As it turned out, he didn't have long to wait.

Video Announcer: *"From Silicon Valley's genius billionaire comes yet another advancement in computer technology. Yesterday afternoon, Brookstone Heuristics Corporation announced a revolutionary design in scalable datastore architecture that they claim will allow near-infinite expansion of widely disparate datamarts into one seamless storage system. "Imagine everyone in the world hooked up to one giant disk drive" says CEO Allen Brookstone, when asked to describe the advance in layman's terms. "This technology makes it possible." Wall Street certainly seems to like what it heard as Brookstone stock was up nearly twenty percent only minutes after the opening bell and is still climbing."*

Allen didn't need to hear any more. "Hot damn!" he thought, mentally giving himself high fives. He had hoped that, at best, the stock wouldn't suffer, and that, at worst, it might not drop too much, but this exceeded his wildest dreams. He knew that he had another lion by the tail, but he wasn't sure he could convince the rest of the world. Maybe the investors were becoming more savvy these days. His last "advancement" had almost bankrupted the company before it caught on and made them more money than any other endeavor. He had been raked over the coals in a number of ways during that time and was prepared for it to happen again. Maybe things are different now. "One can only hope," he thought wryly.

Allen turned off the news and went into his bathroom. He turned on the shower, stripped off his pajamas, and waited a moment for the water to heat up before getting in. While he shampooed and washed himself, he hummed tunelessly and thought about all the things he had to take care of today. The stock market's reaction to his announcement was the icing on the cake. It was going to be difficult enough to pull this off without worrying about the finances at the same time. There were times he longed for the old days when it was just himself alone in his little crackerbox apartment living off of Ramen noodles and Kraft macaroni and cheese and cranking out exquisitely elegant computer code for operating systems. The code was everything and everything flowed from the code. Life was so simple back then.

Allen shook his head. "Don't go there," he said to himself, "That was then and this is now." The reality was that tens of thousands of people now depended on Allen to keep their paychecks coming and millions more depended on him to keep their stock investments healthy and productive. "Maybe after this I should think about retiring," thought Allen, but he knew it would never happen.

He turned off the shower, stepped out, and toweled himself dry. Wrapping the towel around his waist, he started the water running in the sink and looked at himself in the mirror. He saw a middle-aged man staring back at him with hazel eyes, short hair, and a day's worth of Don Johnson stubble. "What the heck," he thought, turning off the water. He was already chomping at the bit with the desire to get into the office and dive into the things that warranted immediate attention, so he impulsively decided to save time and skip his shave. The stock market surge had surprised him, but he had planned for that eventuality and, as a result, needed to put two strategies into motion as soon as possible. He crossed over to the intercom next to his bed and pressed a button.

"I'd like to leave in about ten minutes or so and would love to have some breakfast on the way. Thanks."

He released the button and walked into his closet to pick out his clothes. Thinking about the old days had put him into a rebellious frame of mind, so he decided on a pair of faded jeans and a polo-style shirt with the corporate logo on the pocket. Slipping his bare feet into his hemp sandals, he looked at himself critically in the full length mirror. "Not bad, for a forty-nine-year-old dude," he said out loud. He smiled at himself briefly in the mirror and decided that he really hadn't changed that much since his college days. He still had a fairly trim figure that looked good on his six-foot frame and his hair was greying just a little around the temples. In the old days, some women had volunteered that he was "not bad looking." Nowadays, of course, they all swore that he was the best looking man they'd ever met. He tried to picture himself with long hair pulled back into a pony-tail, but he didn't quite succeed. "It's true what they say," he thought. "You really can't go back." He sighed and walked over to the elevator. The doors slid open and he stepped in and punched the button for the roof. The doors closed and when they opened again, he stepped out and was pleased to see that the helicopter was already waiting. He ducked down, crossed the landing pad, and climbed into the passenger compartment. Inside was a well-appointed executive cabin with a small table set between two rows of plush seats. Buckling himself into the center seat facing the front, he grabbed the headset off the wall and placed it over his ears.

Toggling the mike, he said to the pilot "I'm ready to go any time you are," and toggled off.

The door closed and he was suddenly enveloped with the silence afforded by the extra sound-proofing that had been installed. He smiled at the young woman sitting across the table from him.

"Good morning, Sunshine. What do you have for me this ay-em?"

"That depends, Your Highness. Do want business or pleasure first?"

"Pleasure, of course," he smiled.

"In that case, I have scrambled eggs, bacon, cinnamon toast, and orange juice for your delight." She pointed to the tray in front of him and lifted the cover. "And, needless to say, your daily double-dose of espresso."

Allen picked up his fork and attacked the scrambled eggs. "So how's business?" he said between mouthfuls.

"I can deduce from the fact that you're wearing jeans that you've already seen the morning financial news. Suffice it to say that any of the short term concerns you had about capital have vanished. However, all of that will be short-lived if the demonstration next week doesn't go as planned. The Directors are getting a little concerned that it's not quite ready for primetime yet."

"It will be." Allen reached into his shirt pocket for his memory chip and tossed it to her. "I fixed the two remaining bugs in the routine. Give this to Jeff and he'll take care of the rest." He grinned, "Don't worry, everything will work as advertised."

"That's what I told them, but they're not going to rest until they see it working with their own eyes."

"Yeah, yeah, I hear you. What's next?"

"The phones have been ringing off the hook with everyone wanting more information. The press, investors, even two members of congress. So far, all we've said is 'No comment.'"

"I'll bet that really pleased the members of congress." He smiled. "I think we need to have another press conference. Something where I can answer specific technical questions with specific technical answers. As you know, the stuff I spewed yesterday came from Marketing. 'Sell the idea without getting technical' they always say. Well, sometimes, when you're in a high-tech business, you have to get a little technical. How about 1:00 PM? That should give you enough time to set it up and let them know about it and yet have it early enough to easily make the evening news on the east coast."

"No problemo. I'll take care of it."

"What else? If it's not incredibly urgent, I don't want to hear about it until we get to the office."

"Well, in that case, that about wraps it up." She turned in her seat and ignored him as she spoke into her own mike, occasionally poking at her tablet with its stylus. He knew that she was making the arrangements for the press conference as well as probably warning everyone that he was wearing jeans and sandals today. He smiled at the thought as he continued to eat his breakfast.

By the time he was done with his meal and had exchanged a little more light-hearted banter with his secretary, the helicopter landed on the roof of the Brookstone Building. They climbed out, strolled across the roof to the waiting elevator and went in. One floor down, the doors opened up into a large waiting room that was empty except for a row of comfortable looking chairs along one wall and a large circular desk with a nameplate that said "Cassandra Stevens."

As they exited the elevator, Allen said "Call a meeting of the Board for eight o'clock and confirm that everyone will be there. Then join me in my office."

"Yes, Sire."

She walked around the desk and sat down at what she liked to think of as her Command Center. With capital "C"s. She jacked her tablet into its docking cradle and started tagging the board members.

Allen walked on past her desk to the left, opened one of the double doors that led to his office, and went in. The door closed softly behind him. He walked across the large room with floor-to-ceiling glass windows that looked out over the Valley. He sat down behind his own elaborate version of Cassie's Command Center. He, too, thought of it with capital "C"s. From here he could tap into the world and ride the information super-highway like one of Gibson's Console Cowboys. That all sounded so corny now. Once upon a time, there was only a handful of the elite that were well-versed enough in the arcane lore to bear that proud mantle of honor; today there were billions of them spending their days jacked into the web.

Allen touched his desk screen and scrolled down through his in-box. Nothing that couldn't wait. He brought up the project folder for Pandora and flipped to the section he had ready in case things heated up quickly. He printed a baker's dozen copies to the printer in the conference room where Cassie would distribute them to the directors around the table. He got up from his desk and walked over to the door to his private bathroom in order to freshen up a bit before he left for the meeting. He opened the door, walked in, and went over to the sink. It wasn't until he looked in the mirror that he saw the man standing behind him.

With a start, he turned and blurted out "How did you get in here?"

The man smiled and said "Please don't be alarmed, Mister Brookstone. My name is Wyatt Earp and we need your help." He reached out as if to shake hands.

Allen's mind was momentarily overwhelmed with surprise and consternation and he reflexively grabbed the man's extended hand in response. And then everything went black.

+ + +

Cassie finished text-blasting the directors and made a final note in her tablet. She took it with her as she entered Allen's office. Since he wasn't at his desk, she assumed he was in the bathroom and sat in one of the over-stuffed chairs facing his Command Center. She smiled at their private joke over the "CC"s and thought about how that was one of the many reasons she really liked working for the guy. Unlike some of the other assholes she had worked for, Allen was actually a human being and acted like one. At least most of the time. He was old enough to be her father and he sometimes treated her like the daughter he never had. She had no illusions about anything more ever developing between them and, as a result, had developed an almost motherly affect where he was concerned. Inside the big bad man was still an insecure little boy.

Cassie suddenly realized that Allen still hadn't come out of the bathroom. She stood up and walked over to the door and knocked loudly. "Everything okay in there?" There was no answer. She put her ear to the door trying to hear some sound from within, but there was none. She knocked again more loudly. "Allen? Is everything okay?" Still, there was no answer. Cassie was now getting a little apprehensive. "Maybe he passed out or slipped and hit his head," she thought. "Or maybe worse."

She knocked once more and yelled, "I'm coming in Allen. I hope you're decent."

Cassie slowly opened the door and peered inside. Not seeing him anywhere, she entered the large room and looked around.

"Allen?" she asked tentatively; but she could already see that he wasn't there.

Puzzled, she left the bathroom and went behind Allen's desk thinking that maybe he had fallen to the floor. He wasn't there either. Growing thoroughly alarmed, she walked the entire perimeter of the office and looked into the bathroom again. She looked up at the ceiling, but couldn't see any way he could have left by that route. And it didn't seem likely that he might have crawled out through the two-inch wide vent in the wall. She went back into the other room and studied the ceiling there as well before returning to her desk. Cassie wasn't quite sure what to do next. All she knew for certain was that: (1) Allen had gone into his office and (2) he hadn't come out, and (3) he wasn't in his office or bathroom. Maybe she somehow missed him leaving? Maybe he had waited by the door and had slipped past her without her noticing? "That's what happened!" she thought. It wouldn't be the first time he had tried to duck out and go AWOL.

Cassie sat down at her Command Center and opened the window for the security cameras. She selected the one for her office and scrolled back fifteen minutes earlier and hit "play." She watched as she and Allen got off the elevator and he entered his office. A few minutes later she saw herself get up and go into his office as well. Five minutes later she watched as she came out again. No sign of Allen. Frowning she pulled up the video for his office. Normally, she wouldn't look at this feed without his permission, but she felt that this was a special circumstance. She cued it up and hit "play" and watched Allen stroll in and sit at his desk. A few minutes later she saw him get up and go into the bathroom. Cassie continued to watch until she saw herself enter the room and sit down. There was nothing more to look at since the bathroom itself had no video camera.

"He went in and he never came out," she said to herself in disbelief.

She sat there for a few minutes gathering her thoughts and then got up and went over to the elevator. When the door opened, she went in and pushed the button for the next floor below. A moment later she walked down the hall to the conference room, opened the door, and went in to where the directors were sitting around the table waiting expectantly for Allen to show up.

Cassie nervously faced the Board of Directors of the Brookstone Heuristics Corporation and said, without preamble, "Houston, we have a problem."

5342 BC - NW Persian Gulf Sea Floor

Altair cursed himself for the umpteenth time for not replacing the dilator valve. Lonni had warned him two jumps ago that it was ready to blow anytime. If only they weren't so damned expensive. They had finally saved enough to at least get it rebuilt after this jump, but now it was a moot point. And he had no one to blame but himself. Unfortunately, his procrastination had put his six crew members in jeopardy as well. It didn't help any that they reassured him that it wasn't his fault. They knew that there wasn't enough money to do anything about it until they delivered their current cargo and received their payment. They had rolled the tetragons one too many times and had come up death-eyes.

Altair allowed himself one more sigh of regret before focusing on the problem at hand. Problem being that they were now stranded on an unknown planet orbiting an unknown star in an unknown system in an unknown galaxy in some god-forsaken corner of the universe. It is said that when you jump through the folds in space-time, you are simultaneously passing through every point in the universe. Lose your dilator valve in mid-jump and you can come out literally anywhere. Ferta was still running the calculations, but if they had popped out anywhere remotely near civilization, she would have pinpointed it by now. The reality was slowly sinking in that their odds of being rescued were pretty much equal to zero.

On the bright side, however, they had come out of the jump in orbit around a planet in a system that was an eerie mirror of their home world of Shoomar. Not being a cosmo-theorist, he didn't quite understand Ferta's explanation of how that, without a dilator valve to absorb or provide a net flow of energy, entropy guaranteed that they exited the jump in a gravitically neutral location. In other words, some other place in the universe where the masses and relative positions of nearby bodies were identical and, those that were much further away, nearly so. One moment they were in orbit around Shoomar and the next moment they were in orbit around this planet. This system had the identical layout of their home system including an asteroid belt and a couple of gas giants. Most of the stars were in the same relative positions as the ones he was used to seeing in the sky, even though they were not the same ones. The planet itself was the same size as Shoomar, but it had different continents and oceans and hence looked quite unlike home. The moon, however, looked just the same and it sent shivers down his spine when he first glimpsed it through the viewport.

Regardless of the reason, the fact that they had found themselves in a slowly decaying orbit around a possible place to land was a stroke of good fortune. With only their limited attitude jets and no space-tug to move them into and out of orbit, they would have otherwise been doomed to live out their lives in space drifting in some remote void. Thanks to Sparta's ingenuity and skill, they had actually managed to land a space-faring vessel onto the surface of a planet without cracking up. It was indeed unfortunate that this incredible feat would never make it into Tooley's Book of Universal Records.

He tapped the comlink in his left ear and spoke:

[Author's Note: In striving to be as accurate as possible, the events described herein were translated directly from the original (and un-edited) Captain's logfile. What Altair said out loud in Universal sounded like: "SŪ NŪ-WÅ TÅ-MÂ-SO ÂK-TÅ WÅ-NŪ." It doesn't help much if this is translated literally as "Everyone group-meet {place?} {time-period?}". Since Universal nouns, times, and measurements have no direct referential translation into our language, I have exercised my literary license and have henceforth translated them into equivalencies that are more familiar to the reader. In other words, Altair said: "Hi everyone. Just a reminder that we're meeting in the mess hall in ten minutes." - JH]

He reviewed the list in front of him with a critical eye. Now that they knew that they were castaways, they might as well get on with ensuring their self-sufficiency. With this in mind he had asked the crew to take a fresh inventory of items on-board. He already knew what should be there, but he wanted to make sure that they didn't overlook any potentially useful items. Once more he reflected that it could be much, much worse. If Sparta hadn't figured out how to get them down intact, they would right now be searching for one another on the surface after their escape pods grounded. And they would only have had those items that they could carry with them in the pods. Their ship and all of its resources immeasurably improved their odds of survival.

Altair stood up from his desk, picked up his notepod, and went out into the brightly lit corridor. As he approached the lift, the doors opened up in anticipation and he strode inside. As the portal closed behind him he commanded "Mess Hall." Almost instantly, the doors opened again and Altair walked out into the eating area where his crew sat around the large round dining table waiting for him. It was evident that he had walked into the middle of a conversation that had stopped abruptly with his appearance. The crew glanced at each other apprehensively. Altair knew what lay behind their anxiety and hoped to avoid a direct confrontation.

"We were just coming to look for you, Captain," said Mirta. "We thought that maybe you had gotten lost."

Altair laughed wryly, "As a matter of fact, I *did* get lost. Unless Ferta has figured out where we are, perhaps?"

His lame attempt at humor broke the ice and most of the tension dissipated around the table. Ferta smiled, "Yes and no. Do you want the facts or just speculation?"

"Both, actually. Start with the facts first."

"Locally, we're up to our eyeballs in muck about 30 meters below the surface of a saline body of water. Globally, we're about a third of the way from the equator toward the pole on a planet that tilts quite a bit more on its axis than Shoomar. Systemically, we are located where Shoomar would normally be this time of year relative to the sun and the other planets. Universally, I can only state as fact that we are not in the two-thirds of the universe that has been explored." She grimaced slightly, "That's pretty much it for the facts."

"And?"

"Speculatively speaking, I think that we're lost. I mean, really, really lost. I think that we are so lost that the distress signal we've been broadcasting will not be picked up for millions of years, if ever."

"And I think that you're only confirming what we already knew in our hearts. It's pretty clear that we're here, we're not going anywhere, and no one's coming to look for us. We're on our own. Castaways! We need to accept the fact that this planet is now our new home. This is where we're going to spend the rest of our lives, one way or the other." Altair looked at everyone in turn around the table, "Are we all in agreement?"

One by one, they slowly nodded their heads.

He smiled at them with all the earnestness he could muster and said, "We've all complained from time to time about how boring things are.

Well, things are not only no longer boring, I suspect that they're going to become even less so as we go along."

Their laughter was reassuring to Altair. It was important to keep their spirits up.

"As you well know, Cap'n, we always love a challenge," grinned Tommi.

"Well, we've certainly got one now." Glancing down at his notepod he continued, "Any change in the ship's status since last night? Power? Life support? Shields?"

Lonni spoke up, "Nothing's changed. It looks like we're in pretty good shape, all things considering. I've also confirmed that we do indeed have replacement parts for the secondary converter and the O2 stabilizer. By this time tomorrow, that odd smell in the air should be gone completely."

Altair smiled, "That's good news, at least." He glanced down at his notepod, "Having secured our immediate environment, I think that the next thing we need to do is to assess our external environment for possible threats to our safety. Ideas, anyone?"

Mirta spoke up, "I've been analyzing the data from the scans we made before we, umm, landed, as well as the limited information coming from the signal beacon we left in orbit. There is abundant life here, but the most advanced technology on the planet is exercised by nomadic tribes using rock, stick, and bone implements. There are no centers of commerce and no evidence of metallurgy of any sort. This level of pre-civilization is normally off-limits to Universal visits until the inhabitants minimally achieve interplanetary travel. Even then, First Contact is limited only to Ambassadors and their appointees."

Altair raised his left eyebrow inquisitively, "And the point you're trying to make is ... ?"

"Technically speaking, under Universal Law, we should avoid contact with the natives until they develop interplanetary travel and we're cleared by the Universal Embassy."

"And how long do you suppose that will take?"

"Using the data that we've collected so far, I ran a number of simulations based on comparisons with other primitive planets with parallel development. The best of them indicates that it will be about 40,000 years or so before they will make a trip to their moon. Worst case: never."

"Never?"

"Some species are simply not sustainable. Something in their environment changes too quickly or drastically to survive. Climate, disease, disappearing food supply, but to name only a few causes. Others survive long enough to develop technology ahead of their socio-development and end up killing themselves off with massive war or global poisoning." She continued, somewhat apologetically, "I wish I had more detailed data to work from. Given the right information, I could provide a more reliable projection."

"Meanwhile, we're just supposed to sit here, keep to ourselves, and patiently live out the rest of our lives on the ship?"

"Exactly. Technically speaking."

Altair smiled at Mirta, "That's twice now that you've used that phrase."

"I'm not really sure that the Universal Law applies here. We're clearly outside the known universe where it has jurisdiction. However, the principle rules of First Contact are based upon a few million years of experience and should not be treated lightly."

"But it wouldn't hurt anything if we gathered more information about this planet and its inhabitants? Detailed data that would allow you to provide a clearer picture of where we are and what we're up against? At the very least, it might allow us to pick a place that we can settle and not disturb the local folks for some time." Altair grinned without trying this time, "I love our ship like the wife I never had, but sometimes even a happily married man has to take some shore leave for a little R & R."

There was laughter from everyone around the table.

Rolli spoke up, "How do you propose getting this information, Captain?"

Altair was afraid of this. There was no point in avoiding the issue since Rolli brought it up. He knew that the quartermaster was already one jump ahead of him.

"You're in charge of the cargo, Rolli, isn't there a shipment of exploratory probes destined for Traxtor IV?"

"Yes, there is." He frowned, "I hope you're not seriously suggesting that we should use them?"

"Well, yes, I am."

The look that passed amongst his crew was not lost on Altair. He knew what was coming and hoped that he could convince them that this was the right thing to do.

Lonni spoke first, "You want us to open the cargo in transit, Captain? I mean, we've done some pretty dicey things before, but by-passing a few silly tariffs here and there is an entirely different thing from opening the cargo–that's downright immoral! Not to put too fine a point on it, but if word of that ever got out, our reputation would be ruined forever. Not to mention being blacklisted by the Guilds."

Altair once again tried humor to soften the impact of his words, "Do you suppose the Guilds will still keep us when they notice that we haven't paid our dues for a while? All kidding aside, our failure to appear in orbit around Montregor has already been noted and we're now officially listed as a Bad Jump. If they don't hear from our signal beacon within another thirty days, our cargo will be written off and paid for in full by the insurance companies. The customers won't be happy, but they'll get their money back. Another thirty days after that and any assets we left behind will be sold off to recoup the balance of the mortgage left on the ship." Altair let that sink in for a moment before he continued, "I think that in these circumstances, if there's something in the cargo that can help us survive, that we should not only be willing to use it, but also that we're actually entitled to it."

The crew struggled with this. They knew that he was right, but it went against every fiber of their being as lifelong freight haulers to even think about touching the cargo. It was a core belief handed down through generations of haulers from Shoomar. They were Universally known for it and their very livelihoods had always depended on it. Everyone knew that if it absolutely had to be there on time, you used a Shoomaran freighter.

Altair knew that they would come around. He also knew when to ease up on his crew. "I need to hit the fresher. Talk it out among yourselves while I'm gone." He pointedly took his notepod with him as he left the room and went down the short hallway to the washroom. Whatever they had to discuss they would do so more freely if they knew they weren't being recorded. He washed his hands and splashed some water on his face. After blowing dry, he exited the room and returned to the table.

Mirta spoke up, "We've decided that it's okay, in these circumstances, to open up the cargo if it's absolutely necessary. However, we would like to wait a hundred days before we do so. It's well known that if a Bad Jump isn't found in one hundred days, it never will be. We'd hate to break the seals on our cargo only to have Folkways Tours discover our beacon on one of their junkets to 'New and Un-Explored Frontiers.' After one hundred days, no one would blame us for scavenging the cargo for our survival needs. But only for those things that are absolutely necessary, of course."

"Of course. If I didn't think it was necessary, I wouldn't have brought it up. Since it's been twelve days since we jumped, then we all agree that we can at least open up the crates for the probes in eighty-eight more days? The sooner we get them deployed, the sooner Mirta can start collecting some meaningful data."

Sparta looked quizzically at Altair, "We're all kind of curious as to how you plan on doing that, exactly. Seeing as how our launch tubes are buried beneath a ton of silt."

"As I recall from my days as an explorer ..." Altair began. A spontaneous groan emanated from everyone around the table. Tommi rolled his eyes in an exaggerated movement to make sure that everyone saw him doing it. Unfazed, Altair continued, "As I recall from my days as an explorer, these probes are small and light. Light enough to float. I was thinking that we'd just pile a bunch of them in the dorsal airlock, open it up, and let them float to the surface. From there, we shouldn't have any problems getting them on station."

Lonni nodded slowly, "And all we have to do is install a drain in the airlock beforehand and we can flush the compartment to the storage tank when we vent air back into the airlock. Nice, Captain," he said admiringly, "I can tell that you've put some thought into this."

"Why, thank you, Lonni. The sooner we get them deployed, the sooner we can get some shore leave. And once we've got a drain fixed up in the airlock, I figure that we can come and go as we please using the EV suits."

"Eighty-eight days it is," said Rolli. "I wouldn't mind getting off the ship for a stroll-about myself as well."

Altair smiled inwardly at the nods of assent from the others around the table. He knew his crew well. But that was only natural considering how many years that they had lived and worked together. If only they had not ended their careers with a Bad Jump forever tarnishing Shoomar's near-perfect record. If it weren't for that, he would have been quite pleased with everything otherwise. Like Lonni said, they truly loved a challenge.

Six Months Ago - Mount Ararat, Turkey

Allen was dreaming about an eagle soaring in the air. As he watched from afar, the eagle slowed down and stalled out in mid-flight. Suddenly it was falling to the ground, faster and faster, coming right at Allen. Allen tried to reach out to catch it, but it was just beyond his reach and he dove for it like an outfielder's desperate attempt. As he fell to the ground, he rolled over and looked up. Where he expected to see the sky, he saw the familiar ceiling over his bed and slowly realized that he had been dreaming and was now suddenly awake. Allen glanced at his alarm clock which declared it was 9:29 PM. He sat up and ran his fingers through his tousled hair. He looked around his bedroom and couldn't recall how he had gotten there. He shook his head, trying to clear the fog that seemed to be slowly dissipating. Gradually the recent events began to come back to him in fits and starts. He had gone to the office and there was a man in his bathroom and now ... now he was back in his own bed in his own house? Still in his jeans and polo shirt? That part was still a blank. It didn't make any sense at all. He was still struggling with reconciling his memories to reality when the door opened and a vaguely familiar man quietly entered.

"Hello again, Allen," said Wyatt Earp. "I see that you're awake already. I trust that you had a restful respite?"

"Who the hell are you?" Allen asked. He leaned over and yanked open the drawer to his bed-side table and reached inside. "Where's my gun? What did you do with it?"

"Your Glock is in your bed-side table drawer in your room," said the man as he walked over to the curtains and drew them back to reveal a million-dollar view of the Pacific Ocean.

"What are you talking about? This is my room!" Allen exclaimed.

"We thought that we would provide you with accommodations that would make your stay with us more enjoyable." He raised his hands as Allen started to protest, "It will all become clear after you speak with the Chairman. He's very anxious to see you. I'll be back in a half-hour to take you to meet him. You might want to take the opportunity to freshen up." He walked back to the door and opened it to leave. This time Allen noticed that the hallway beyond the door looked nothing like the one that should have been there. He was slowly accepting the fact that this wasn't his house, after all.

"Wait!" Allen yelled after him. "I want to know what's going on ... right now!"

Wyatt stopped in the doorway and turned, "I'm very sorry, sir, but I'm under strict orders. I've already said too much. You'll just have to wait until you talk to the Chairman." He turned again and left the room, shutting the door softly behind him.

Allen sat there for a moment digesting everything. He climbed out of bed and went over to the door. He tried the knob and was not terribly surprised to find that it was locked. He went over to the elevator and pressed the call button. The button flashed and dinged, but the doors didn't open. Allen went over to his desk and picked up his cell phone, sliding it open. No service. He flipped on the TV and scrolled through several channels. Nothing but snow. Next he tapped the keyboard of his computer and was rewarded with the password box of his screen saver. He typed in his password and the familiar sight of his desktop appeared. The red icon flashing in the corner of his screen confirmed his suspicion that his network connection wasn't working.

He understood that this was not his bedroom and that this was not really his computer. But a quick scan of the drives showed the files and folders he would have normally expected to see. He opened one experimentally and saw that it was, indeed, one of his files. This was growing more and more bizarre by the moment. Somewhat in a daze now, he wandered over to the window and looked out over his garden and his pool. In the distance was the Pacific Coast Highway bounded on the far side by the Pacific Ocean itself. Allen looked around the room and went over to the bookshelves where he picked up a solid brass bookend that depicted Atlas holding up the Earth. Hefting it in his hand, Allen ran toward the window and threw it as hard as he could. It hit the center of the window with a loud bang and bounced back at Allen, narrowly missing his bare foot. He wasn't sure, but he thought that there was a brief spark where the bookend had hit the glass. Or whatever it was.

Allen glanced at the clock. He still had nearly twenty minutes before Wyatt returned for him. He shrugged and decided that he would follow the advice he was given. His normal pragmatism settled around him while he went into the bathroom to splash some cold water on his face. After studying himself in the mirror for a moment, he decided on a quick shave as well.

He had just finished re-dressing--choosing a nice pair of gray slacks, polo shirt, and brown loafers--when the door opened and Wyatt entered the room again.

"Ah, I see that you are ready. Very good. If you will follow me, I'll take you to see the Chairman now."

He turned and stepped out into the hallway. Allen toyed briefly with the idea of overpowering him, finding his way out of here, and calling the police. As a generally non-violent person, however, the thought didn't linger and Allen followed Wyatt through the doorway. The hallway was surprisingly short, extending about ten feet to the left and right. It was off-white and softly illuminated with indirect lighting. Wyatt took a couple of steps across the hallway, opened the left half of the double door there, and held it open for Allen to enter. As he crossed the threshold, he stared around in amazement at what appeared to be his own office on the top floor of the Brookstone Building over-looking Silicon Valley.

The door closed behind him as he gaped at the view outside the windows. He was suddenly startled as a distinguished-looking elderly man arose from the couch to his right and said, "Hello, Allen! It's so good to meet you in person. I know that you've got a lot of questions and I'll do the best that I can to answer them. Please have a seat and let's get acquainted." The man gestured at the chair opposite the low coffee table and sat back down on the couch. He looked at Allen expectantly.

Allen was taken aback by all of this. His brain was nearing overload and he took a deep breath and sat down in the chair. "Who are you? Why have you kidnapped me?" He glanced again at the windows, "And where the hell am I that makes it look like I'm at home across the hall and yet miles away in here?"

The man smiled at Allen, "My name is Chairman Hazeltine. We desperately need your help. And we are a little over two miles below Mount Ararat in Turkey, although to explain how we provide the convincing views, I'll have to defer to one of our technicians for an explanation." He peered intently at Allen, "Would you like for me to summon one now?"

"Uh, no. Not right now."

"Good! I was hoping that you had more pertinent questions. There will plenty of time for details later."

Allen's curiosity was getting the best of him. He wasn't quite sure why, but he didn't feel threatened by this odd man and he wanted to know more. Allen sat there for a few moments waiting for him to continue.

Finally, when it became apparent that he was waiting for Allen to speak further, he said, "Why do you desperately need my help? And why kidnap me? You obviously look like you can afford to hire my firm outright. Why not just ask?" He frowned, "And are we really two miles underground?"

Hazeltine answered, "Once I explain our problem, you will understand why we had to bring you here in such an unorthodox manner. None other would have sufficed." Hazeltine stood up and walked to the middle of the room and began pacing back and forth slowly. He stopped and faced Allen, "I've planned this little speech for some time, but now that I try and say it, I find it difficult because our conversation is without precedent." He paced for two lengths and stopped again. "I am the Chairman of a secret organization located in the lava tunnels that burrow deep beneath Mount Ararat. There are three-hundred of us living and working here. We have isolated ourselves from the rest of the world so that we can carry out our research undisturbed." He smiled apologetically, "I'm afraid that sounds a little melodramatic, doesn't it?"

Allen replied, "Since you ask, yes, it does. But let's say I'm buying it, for now, since I haven't seen anything to contradict you." He looked quizzically at Hazeltine, "What exactly is this research of yours? Human clones or something?"

Hazeltine laughed, "Not exactly. What do you know about Chaos Theory?"

Allen looked bemused, "Which Chaos Theory? Do you mean the pretty little fractals? Or the so-called Butterfly Effect? Or water rolling off the back of Jeff Goldblum's hand?"

"None of the above. I want to hear what you know about Chaos Theory."

Allen replied, "I think that the name itself is a misnomer. In my opinion, what we label as Chaos is actually a very orderly interaction of particles that has progressed throughout the universe since the Big Bang. We can't work with so much detail so we try to analyze and categorize the outcomes with broad strokes." Allen furrowed his brow in thought, "Personally, I think that if you could take a snapshot of every particle in the universe along with its physical and dynamic attributes and store them in a computer, you could then 'roll forward' the interactions of the particles and predict their behavior. In theory, you could predict the future. In practice, no computer is capable of storing or processing so much data as to make this feasible. As a result, in lieu of detail, gross approximations are substituted with the resultant gross outcomes. Our current climate models are a good example of this. It has become a Holy Grail, of sorts."

The Chairman grinned and slapped his knee, "I knew it! You're just the person we need!" He leaned forward in earnestness, "I want to show you something that only a handful of people have ever seen. I have dedicated my life to its development and it's exciting to be able to share it with someone that can understand what it is and what it is not." From his shirt pocket, he pulled out what looked like a remote control for a TV or DVR player. "The effect is a bit unnerving the first time you experience it. You will probably feel like you're falling, but it's just an illusion. No matter what things look like, you're still sitting in that chair with your feet on the floor." He smiled as he thumbed a button on the remote, "Hold on to that thought and you'll be fine."

Even forewarned, Allen gasped as the room disappeared and he appeared to be floating in space high above the surface of the Earth. He gripped the arms of his chair as he stared down to where he could feel his feet on the floor, but where there was clearly nothing there. He suddenly realized that he was holding his breath and exhaled slowly.

A now disembodied Hazeltine spoke, "We are looking at the Earth from 175,000 kilometers away." Concern entered his voice, "Are you okay, Allen?"

Allen was slowly calming down and had released his death grip on the chair arms. He volunteered, "I take it that this is the same technology that provides the realistic views outside the windows?"

"Yes, although those are clipped to seamlessly blend reality with virtual reality. What we are looking at now isn't clipped so you are enmeshed in the virtual reality itself."

"So it's not real."

"Not in the physical sense, no. But perhaps in the philosophical sense ..." his voice trailed off.

Allen wasn't quite sure what he meant by this. He raised an unseen eyebrow at Hazeltine and waited for him to elaborate.

"Here, let me show you what I like to think of as my Google-Earth-On-Steroids-Power-Point-Presentation." He apparently did something with the remote and Allen found himself falling toward the planet at incredible speed. In spite of himself, he gripped the arms of his chair in alarm. As the horizon rose up around him, the Earth turned beneath them until they were falling towards the western part of North America and the California coast. At an apparent height of a mile or so, they slowed and began descending toward what Allen immediately recognized as the public beach near his home. As they neared the ground, Allen was startled by the resolution of the imagery and was so mesmerized by how real everything looked that he hardly noticed that they had come to a stop. For all intents and purposes, he appeared to be sitting in a beach chair looking out at the ocean while a number of families enjoyed themselves around him. The effect was so real to Allen, that he instinctively leapt up to intercept a beach-ball that had gone awry and was painfully rewarded by his shins hitting the unseen coffee table in front of him. He yelped and sat back down in the chair again rubbing his legs as a small boy ran right through him after the ball. He heard Hazeltine's voice reminding him that they were still in his ersatz office and, as he spoke, the world froze around them. The room transparently re-appeared while the beach around him faded slightly so that he was able to clearly see Hazeltine sitting across from him. "So what do you think?" asked Hazeltine.

Allen sat there slowly composing his thoughts. He could still see the ocean with its frozen waves and the beach with its sunbathing statues while clearly sitting in his office. Or Hazeltine's office. Or wherever. Both looked real and yet not-real at the same time and it was impossible to tell which was the reality. Allen was disoriented by the effect and unnerved by the thought that he had possibly gone mad. Maybe the helicopter had crashed and he was actually in a coma in a hospital ward or something. Or maybe he was dead and this odd little man was God who was toying with him for some unfathomable reason.

"So what do you think?" repeated Hazeltine.

Allen shook his head hoping that the physical movement would trick his psyche into clearing his mind as well. "I think that's the most incredible thing that I've ever seen, Mr. Hazeltine." was all that he could muster.

"Why, thank you, Allen. I had been led to believe that you were hard to impress," came the reply. "And please, call me Hazel, since that's what my friends call me. I do hope that you and I are going to become good friends. I truly do."

Allen sat there with so many thoughts buzzing through his mind, the questions outnumbering the answers, that he found himself being helplessly inundated in a flood of the familiar and the unfamiliar. Hazeltine stirred him from his funk "You haven't asked anything about how you got here, how long you've been here, or what's happened to your company and your friends in your absence." He lifted the remote and the room disappeared again. A moment later the beach scene literally jumped into motion as the frozen scene was suddenly replaced with a slightly different one. The father and son playing ball nearby were now a good fifty yards away. The sand castle that was pristine and proud a moment before was now partially melted from the incoming tide. "Reality continues on while we're paused; we're back in real-time now."

Allen frowned at this, "Real-time?"

"Yes. What we're looking at is the ultimate virtual reality. It's critically important that you understand that this is not a recorded event, but is happening right now on the other side of the planet."

"How is it being recorded? And transmitted? Not to mention displayed?" Allen wanted to know.

Hazeltine fended off his questions, "It's not really important. I'll have one of the techs fill you in on it later. I promise. But, for the time being, you must accept that it's real." He sounded truly concerned, "It will help you more easily accept the next part of my presentation. Relax and remember that you're still sitting in the office chair." Having been forewarned, Allen was better prepared for the effect when he appeared to float up from the beach and hover maybe a quarter-mile high overhead. The Earth rotated slightly westward and Allen recognized his office building as they drifted over it and descended toward the top of the building. Or at least toward the virtual representation of it, he reminded himself. He was expecting that they would set down on the roof, but instead, they continued on through and into his office. Hazeltine had oriented things so that the virtual office was aligned with the real office and Allen had a strong sense of déjà vu that disappeared as he took in the two men present in the room with them.

"Are you guys finished in here yet?"

Allen spun around at the sound of the familiar voice and exclaimed "Cassie!"

He fully expected the three of them to turn and look at him, but they appeared oblivious to him as one of the men answered, "Just about. Give us another ten minutes and we'll be through."

Cassie glared peevishly from the doorway. "Well, make it snappy. The Board is waiting to hear from your boss and she doesn't want to tell us anything more until she talks to the two of you."

"I'm sure that you understand we want to do as thorough a job as possible. Besides, our boss won't stand for less." He softened a little, "We're almost done and if I know Special Agent Williams, she won't keep you waiting much longer."

Cassie gave an exaggerated sigh and left the room. The room froze while Allen could still see her silhouetted in the doorway and Hazeltine appeared as a ghostly figure again. "What's going on, Hazel? How did you record this?"

"It's not recorded. I tried to explain that this is real-time. It's now four hours since you were, umm, 'summoned' here and the FBI has been brought in to investigate your disappearance."

Allen stared at Hazeltine, still not quite comprehending everything he had just seen and been told.

"This, my friend, is our Chaos Machine."

January 13, 1929 - Los Angeles, California

The bedroom of the small apartment was dimly lit by the afternoon light bleeding through the curtains covering the window. The room was currently occupied by a young man sitting in a chair next to the bed where an old man stirred restlessly beneath a light coverlet. The young man waited expectantly for the old man to awake. As if on cue, the old man opened his eyes and looked about the room, his gaze settling on the person next to the bed. "Who are you?" he asked, his voice rasping loudly with the effort of speaking.

"My name is Gabriel and I've come to witness your death."

The old man didn't seem particularly perturbed by this. He smiled slightly, "It can't come soon enough. It seems like most of my life was spent seeking it, but it never came. All those years of one danger after another, to be reduced to this," he gestured at himself on the bed. "If you've come to kill me, get on with it. I think I've waited long enough."

Gabriel smiled back, "I'm not here to kill you. Quite the opposite. You were always so good with faces, do you not remember me?"

The old man raised himself up feebly upon one elbow and peered at him intently for a moment. Slowly, a look of recognition and surprise lit up his face, "Your hair was a little longer, but I remember you now. But that was nearly fifty years ago! You should be an old man by now. Like me." He fell back on the bed, "You probably saved my life, you know."

"Yes, I know."

The old man coughed wrackingly several times before he continued, a faraway look in his eyes, "It was a couple of hours before we were going to get our horses and ride out of town for the showdown. You came to my door and told me that they were going to ambush us when we went to get the horses and that, if we hurried, we could head them off before they were in place." He coughed again. "We accosted them in the street and had it out with them right then and there. If it hadn't had been for you, we would have probably been gunned down at the stable."

Gabriel nodded in confirmation, "All four of you would have been killed and Tom McLaury would have eventually extended his influence over the entire Arizona Territory. By 1906, he would have amassed a substantial military force comprised of nearly 50,000 Indians, Mexicans, Southern Secessionists, and mercenaries. During the tumultuous year following the San Francisco earthquake, his forces would have moved west toward the coast and captured San Diego along with the shipyards housing much of the US Pacific Naval Fleet. By the time the Great War rolled around, America would have expended so much of its resources battling the new nation of Aztlán that it would have been unable to participate. As a result, Germany would have taken over all of Europe and its citizens, including one by the name of Albert Einstein."

"The scientist?"

"Yes," continued Gabriel, "the one and the same. Only he would have worked to assure world domination for Germany and, by 1939, would have developed a weapon of such enormous power that it would have eventually led to the destruction of the entire planet in 1942." Gabriel paused for a bit to let the statement soak in, "However, you killed McLaury and none of that happened. Or will happen."

"That's quite a story, young man."

"Yes, it is. Many people, as they near death, wonder what it was all about and whether or not it was all worth it. You single-handedly saved the planet. I just thought that you should know that before you died."

"You say that as if it were true."

"It *is* true, every word of it," Gabriel said. "I did save your life, you know. And I'm here to save it again, if you so choose."

"What do you mean?"

Gabriel glanced at his watch before continuing, "You will pass away quietly, with no pain, in a little over five minutes. Your wife, Josie, will return from the pharmacy shortly thereafter and discover your body."

The old man grimaced, "Death will not be cheated. There is no alternative."

"Actually, there is. I can save you from death and restore your health and promise that you will have a long and productive life ahead of you."

"What's the catch?"

"We want you to come work with us. You will have to leave everything you know and love as if, in fact, you had really died. We will make you very comfortable and take good care of you in exchange for an occasional task."

"Who is 'us'?

"I represent a secret organization that is intent upon saving mankind from extinction. It's basically a matter of self-preservation: if mankind wipes out the planet, we all go with it.

"And what sort of tasks would you be having me do?"

Gabriel said earnestly, "Your part in our effort would be similar to what I'm doing now. To go out into the world and locate people and bring them into our organization, if necessary. Much like you did as a U.S. Marshal."

"*Deputy* U.S. Marshal."

"As you say, a deputy U.S. Marshal." He glanced at his watch again. "You've got a little over two minutes to make up your mind."

"So, how does this work?"

"If you're willing, I give you an injection that will render your cellular functions immobile for 48 hours. During that period of time, you will, for all intents and purposes, be dead. Shortly before your body is due to be cremated, we will switch it with another body and take you to our headquarters." He grinned, "Our hideout, if you will. Once there, we will restore the functionality of your cells and repair the defective ones. In a few days, you will wake up and feel like a twenty-year-old again. Barring any unforeseen accidents, you should live another five or six hundred years after that."

"I don't believe it."

"Then take a chance. What have you got to lose?" Gabriel smiled sardonically, "Except for your life."

The old man laid still for a moment considering this. Finally he said, "Okay. But if I find out that you've lied to me, I'll track you down in this afterlife of yours and make you pay dearly for it."

Gabriel laughed softly, "So be it." He withdrew a small silver device from his vest pocket and placed it against the man's carotid artery where it made a short hiss as it delivered its organic cocktail throughout his body. "I'll see you on the other side, Wyatt."

The old man never heard him as he had already lost consciousness. His heart slowed and all of his bodily functions ceased, one by one. Gabriel moved the chair back away from the bed and took one more look around the room to make sure that nothing had been disturbed. As he heard the front door open, he squeezed the device in his pocket and vanished without a sound or a trace. Moments later, the old man's body was discovered by his wife, who fell across the bed, sobbing loudly.

5342 BC - NW Persian Gulf Sea Floor

Lonni bumped his chin-plate and announced, "I'm ready when you are, Mirta."

He was suited up in one of the EV suits and standing in the dorsal airlock waiting for the outer hatch overhead to dilate. He had spent the better part of the past week installing a drain in the room and modifying the air handlers to convert the airlock to what he now referred to as the waterlock. He had cycled the tiny room twice to test its operation. The first time, he irised the hatch a little too quickly and was somewhat surprised at how fast and forceful the water shot through the opening. When the lock was full of water, he opened the hatch the rest of the way and then shut it again. The drain was then opened and air pumped back into the room until all the water had been purged. The drain was then closed and the excess air bled back into the system until it was equalized to normal pressure again. For the most part, the test went as planned. He had not, however, expected the small aquatic creature that was left flopping on the floor of the lock. The purged water had been isolated in a separate system to prevent any possible contamination and a thorough analysis was made to determine if any harmful chemicals or pathogens might be lurking there. Once it was determined that the saline water was mostly harmless, he entered the lock and removed the now dead marine animal which proved to be organically compatible with their metabolism. Tommi fried some of the meat from the creature and tried to get them to sample it. He claimed it possessed an interesting flavor, much like the bandas back on Shoomar, but no one else was adventurous enough to follow his example.

He was stirred from his reverie by Mirta's voice in his headset, "I'm opening the outer hatch."

Lonni stood against the wall, away from the center where the water would first stream in under pressure. Before the iris had even opened enough to allow the water molecules in, the outer field had snapped through and lined the inner surface of the lock making it topologically outside the ship. As the hatch opened wider, water rose in the small enclosure and Lonni felt the buoyant force of the suit which was offset by the heavy belt strapped around his waist. He had immersed the empty suit in the second test of the waterlock and was satisfied that the modifications he had made would allow it to function in an underwater environment. As the water rose over his head and filled the room, he felt weightless for the first time in many months. When the room was nearly filled, Mirta fully dilated the hatch, releasing the last of the air still trapped inside. Lonni pushed off from the floor and floated upwards through the outer door.

"So far, so good," he spoke into his throat mike.

He swam slowly upwards savoring the experience. When he finally burst through the surface of the water, he looked around in the darkness lit by the full moon and clicked over to night vision. He wished he had figured out some propulsion mechanism for the suit, but for the time being, he would simply have to swim to the shore. He reflected that the exercise would certainly do him no harm. Resolutely, he unhurriedly set out for the distant land's edge. He had enough air and water for three days, if need be, and he expected to only be gone an hour or so at most. As he neared the shore, he picked a likely sandy beach on which to exit the water. He gained a footing about three meters out and walked onto the beach. He slowly turned a full circle and scanned the deserted landscape around him. Seeing nothing but swampy reeds, scraggly trees, and a few large boulders, he walked in the direction of the slight rise in front of him. He reached the highest point of the low hill and took a small food container from his belt. Opening it up, he removed the small dark-gray cube contained within and placed it on a large rock where it could have an unobstructed view from all five of its exposed surfaces. He carefully sealed the lid back on the container and returned it to its pouch on his belt.

He spoke into his mike, "We should be up and running on this end."

Ferta answered, "I'm receiving 99% signal strength on both audio and video. There appears to be almost no attenuation due to the water."

"That sounds good enough for me. I'm heading back now."

He looked carefully around him again and walked back toward the sandy beach and into the sea. He clicked his visor to navigation and set off back toward the ship where he swam down and through the still open hatch of the waterlock.

"I'm back in the lock and ready for purge," he said.

"Stand by for purge," came her reply. Almost immediately, the hatch began irising shut. When the water was drained and the air pressure restored to normal, Lonni left the compartment and delivered the food container to Mirta for atmospheric analysis. They would know soon enough if they could safely breathe the air or not.

+ + +

Mardu's heart was pounding. He thought it would explode in his chest. He had been unable to sleep, still troubled by the sight he had seen the week before, and had walked up to the hill overlooking the shore. While staring out across the moonlit sea, he had seen a disturbance on its surface, much like the bubbles of marsh gas that sometimes sprang up underfoot. He had sat and waited for something more to happen and, just when he was about ready to get up and walk back home, he saw the creature rising from the water barely fifty paces from where he sat. He instinctively leapt down behind the boulder he had been sitting on and peered out through a narrow crevice. He saw the shining figure walk towards him and stop just on the other side of the boulder. Mardu closed his eyes and scrunched down as much as possible to avoid detection. He was afraid it would smell his fear or hear his wildly beating heart and know that he was there. Even after the creature had walked away, Mardu lay in stillness, trying to calm down. He cautiously peered out through the crevice again in time to see it entering the water and disappearing. When his adrenaline had ebbed and his heart began beating more normally again, he got up and quietly eased his way down the hill. He walked slowly the rest of the way, thinking about what he had seen, and wondered how he was going to tell his brother. He had quickly tired of hearing Mardu tell the story over and over again to whomever would listen. When he entered the tent, he was careful not to wake Itok as he lay down on his mat and fell into a troubled sleep for the few hours left until first light.

+ + +

Itok shook his brother for the third time. "Last call, Mardu. Breakfast is ready. It's time to get up and get to work."

Mardu groggily shook his head and sleepily sat up. "Okay, you can stop now. I didn't get much sleep last night."

"Again? I know, I know. You couldn't stop thinking about it. Again."

The events that had occurred a few hours previously swept over him in a flash and he was fully awake in an instant. He had to tell his brother, no matter how skeptical he might be. "You're right. I couldn't sleep last night because I was still thinking about what I saw last week. I know that I've told a lot of wild stories about what I've encountered in the desert or seen swimming in the sea. I admit that they've all been things I made up to try to make my life seem more exciting than it is. But this time I really saw something, something I didn't make up!"

"I told you that I believed you. I really do. You've never been worked up like this before."

"So would you believe me if I told you that I went back last night and saw a monster come out of the water?" asked Mardu.

"I'm not sure. Is that something that you're likely to tell me?"

"It came up out of the water and walked right over to me. I hid and waited until it went back into the water and then came home." Mardu went on, "I was afraid to even tell you because I know that you're never going to believe me."

Itok sighed. It would be easier to call his brother's bluff than to argue. "Tell you what, let's eat breakfast and then go look for some sign of your monster."

Mardu was incredulous, "Do you really mean that? I'm sure we'll find something!"

"We'll see."

+ + +

As they neared the hill, Mardu stopped his brother, "Maybe we shouldn't go on. Maybe the monster has come back."

Itok looked skeptical, but decided to humor him, "How about we walk over that way where we can get a good view of the sea first?" He set off without waiting for an answer. While they were detouring a considerable distance from their destination, they were able to eventually see the shore and the sea side of the hill. "I don't see any monsters."

Mardu pointed to a spot along the shore, "That's where the monster came up out of the water and then went back in." He started walking and then broke into a jog as he got closer to the site. "Look, Itok!" he said excitedly, pointing at the ground. Itok had continued his normal walking pace and drew up a few moments later. He stared at the impressions in the sand without saying anything. They were unlike anything he had ever seen before. He carefully stepped next to one and pressed his weight down on his foot to leave his own impression and then stepped back. His footprint clearly revealed the woven pattern of his sandal. He looked from it to the larger footprint beside his. It, too, clearly revealed a pattern, but it was crisscrossed with fine lines that appeared as if they had been carved with exquisite care. Itok knew immediately that this was not something Mardu could have fashioned. Or anyone else that he knew, for that matter. His eyes traced the footprints up the hill and began to follow them to see where they would lead.

"Do you believe me now, Itok?" exclaimed Mardu as he followed close behind.

"I'm not sure what I believe, at this point," his brother replied. He continued up the hill and stopped before the large boulder Mardu had previously visited. Mardu ran up behind him and stopped next to him. They both stared at the dull-gray object sitting atop the rocks.

"What do you think it is, Itok?"

After a long while, Itok said thoughtfully, "I think that the gods and goddesses watch over us from above. I think that maybe one of them fell to the ground to visit us. I think perhaps you saw Nammu come from her new home and return back again. And I think that, possibly, this is her gift to you."

Mardu's mouth fell open. He hadn't thought about it like that. But it all made sense. He had been the one to see her fall into the sea. He had been the one who had seen her come out of the water. She had come straight for him, hadn't she? Nammu, the goddess of the sea, had brought him a gift! He stepped forward and gingerly picked up the cube. It was lighter than he thought it would be. He examined it closely and shook it near his ear and looked at it again. All the faces but one had the same dull-gray look. The other had some black markings on it that looked like they had been carved into the surface itself. Perhaps they had been graved there by Nammu herself?

Other than its curious shape, it appeared to be somewhat like a stone. Like some sort of specially carved talisman. Mardu started to hand it to Itok so he could look at it as well, but Itok drew back.

"I think that it's for you alone, Mardu. She revealed herself to you on two occasions and left this for you, not me."

Mardu said nothing, but carefully placed the talisman in his pouch. "Let's go home now, brother. Somehow, having proof that I'm not crazy has greatly settled my spirit. Perhaps I won't feel such an urge to try and convince people anymore."

"No," laughed Itok, "Now you'll just pull out your gift from Nammu."

The two brothers headed back to their home quietly discussing what they had found.

+ + +

Tommi found Ferta in the galley. "I think that something's wrong with the video feed from the remote."

Ferta glanced up from the sandwich she had just finished preparing, "Why do you say that? I just checked on it a little while ago and watched the sun come up. What an amazing sight! So much like Shoomar that I forgot for a moment where we are."

"Well, it's not working now. I was passing by the comm room and thought I'd take a look. The monitor screen's totally black. Nothing showing at all."

"That's odd."

"That's what I thought, so I came looking for you."

She plopped her work of art down on a plate and grabbed a napkin, "Let's go take a look, shall we?" They headed out the doorway together towards the lift. Once in the comm room, Ferta could immediately see that the screen was indeed dark. She carefully placed her plate down and sat in the chair in front of the console. "That's odd."

"You already said that."

"The signal's showing full strength." She fiddled with some knobs and frowned at the display. "Everything's working fine, it's as if it's totally dark outside."

"But that's impossible. Do we have any audio?"

"Good question." Ferta toggled on the sound and was startled to hear voices speaking in an unknown language. They were somewhat muffled but were clearly coming from at least two people communicating verbally with each other. Ferta and Tommi stared at each other and then back at the sounds coming from the speaker. Ferta flipped a switch and spun a knob until, suddenly, an image jumped onto the screen. She stopped and flipped another switch and then panned the view around until settling on the two natives walking toward the remote. They watched them approach the remote and then pick it up. As one of them dropped it into his pouch, the screen went dark again.

Ferta was the first to speak, "Well, so much for observing the rules of First Contact." She looked at Tommi, "We had better tell the others."

Six Months Ago - San Francisco, California

Cassie looked at herself in the mirror. She was in the washroom down the hall from the conference room and was trying to pull herself together before going into the briefing. She had managed to marshal her emotions up to a point about five minutes ago, when she had finally run out of things to do. With her mind no longer occupied with immediate tasks, the morning's events had suddenly washed over her. She was literally worried sick about Allen's disappearance and had run into the restroom thinking that she was going to vomit. As she had leaned over the toilet, holding her hair out of the way, she had begun crying uncontrollably as she spasmed for several minutes with wrackingly violent dry heaves. When she had run down a bit, she had glanced at her watch and realized that she only had a few minutes before the meeting. Now she carefully dried her eyes and touched up her nominally sparse makeup and slid back into her executive mode. "I can do this," she told herself, but she had to repeat it several times before her mind would believe it. As she entered the hallway, she encountered Vivian Williams on her way to the same destination.

"Are you finally coming to tell us what's going on?" Cassie asked. "I can't keep the Board in session forever. They're already impatient enough as it is." She smiled, "I'm sorry to be such a nag, but imagine a dozen spoiled children that have just been told that recess is cancelled."

Special Agent Williams smiled back, "Don't worry about it. To answer your question: yes, I'm ready to give you a summary of what we know. I will also be telling you what we plan to do and what is expected from the Board of Directors. It's critical that we work together from this point forward."

They came to the door to the conference room where Cassie held it open for the agent and then followed her into the room. She still felt a little shaky on the inside, much as she had when she first announced that Allen had vanished four hours earlier. However, to all outward appearances, she was fully composed and strode confidently over to the head of the table.

"Gentlemen, I'd like to introduce Vivian Williams. She's the FBI agent I told you about who's been assigned to head up the task force that will be looking into Allen's disappearance. I know that we all have questions we want answered, but I respectfully suggest that we allow Special Agent Williams to provide her summary before peppering her with questions. Agreed?" There were nods of assent from around the table.

"Fine. Fine. Just get on with it!" growled Cliff Greeley, clearly not happy for a number of reasons.

"Well, then," said Cassie, turning to the agent, "Please tell us what you've learned."

As the FBI agent strode over to the head of the table, Cassie stood back and assessed her feelings about her. They were both about the same height, but where Cassie had long naturally blond hair, Vivian's was cropped short and a shade of coppery red that fit her name. Her athletic build was attired in a rather sophisticated navy-blue business suit that consisted of a jacket over a plain white blouse and a knee-length skirt. Her badge was clipped to the lapel of her jacket and she had the ubiquitous earpiece that seemed to be de rigueur for her profession. Cassie had heard more than enough stories about the FBI's incompetence to cause her to wonder whether or not this woman knew what she was doing. So far, however, she had been very impressed with the agent's handling of the situation. She was curious to see if she would continue to be so self-assured in the presence of the Board.

As the agent placed her briefcase on the table, she faced the twelve men around the table and said "I understand that you have many other things you need to be doing, so I'll get right to the point. As you already know, Allen Brookstone, one of the most influential people in America, has vanished without a trace. While the FBI does not normally get involved with a disappearance until it is clear that a kidnapping has occurred, I was personally asked by the U.S. Attorney General to take charge of this investigation due to the individual involved." As she finished this last sentence, she punctuated it by popping the latches on her briefcase, the noise surprisingly loud in the quiet stillness of the room. She opened the briefcase and removed a yellow legal pad and held it up for all to see. The top half of the page was crowded with notes, but the bottom half was blank. "This is everything I've been able to ascertain about Mr. Brookstone's disappearance so far. As you can plainly see, it's not much. This is not as much due to the fact that I've only been working on this for three hours, but indicative of how little there is here to go on. The facts are very few. What we know for sure is that at 7:36 AM, Allen Brookstone entered his personal washroom and closed the door. At 7:43 AM, Cassie Stevens opened the door and discovered that Mr. Brookstone was not in the bathroom. My technicians have verified that the video footage has not been tampered with and that, other than the door, there are no other exits from the bathroom. We took additional time to bring in acoustic imaging equipment to confirm that there are no secret panels, hollow walls, hollow floors, or other unseen anomalies in the room's construction that might have permitted another way in or out. A review of the video footage going back to the previous evening shows that the last person to be seen entering the bathroom was the janitor at 10:54 PM last night. At 10:56 PM he is seen exiting the room. I called his house and had his wife wake him up so that I could find out if he had noticed anything unusual about last night's visit. He said that he saw nothing unusual and that he had washed the sink and placed a new bar of soap in the dish. He was concerned that he had done something wrong and I assured him that we were simply trying to figure out when someone's cell phone might have been left in the bathroom." She looked around the table and said "I'm afraid that I only identified myself by name and implied that I was calling on behalf of Mr. Brookstone. I didn't want to have to explain to him that his CEO is MIA until we coordinate the release of this information."

"So, basically, you really don't know any more than we do," interjected Thomas Woolward. "I think I speak for all of us when I say that I'm glad you've confirmed that the bathroom was cleaned properly. I can rest easy now." This was followed by snickers and smiles from the others seated around the table.

Unfazed, the FBI agent waited until she had their attention again and then spoke evenly, "I merely wanted to confirm that there should have been a bar of soap in the bathroom. Wherever Allen Brookstone went, he apparently took the soap with him."

+ + +

"I've had enough!" exclaimed Allen. "I demand that you let me go back there right now! They need me!"

The scene froze with the FBI agent's mouth open as she started to say something else. The room dimmed and the office came back into view again. Allen had joined Hazeltine on the couch and their view of the room was aligned such that they appeared to be sitting at the back of the conference room.

"But, we're not done yet," pouted Hazel. "I still haven't had a chance to explain why we need you."

"I don't care why you need me at this point. I've put up with your shenanigans long enough. I don't know who you are or why you're doing this, but my company needs me and I want to go back there right now!"

"I'm afraid that it's quite impossible for you to leave at this moment. Please allow me to continue my presentation and, when we are done, I'll let you decide if you want to stay or not." Hazel smiled in earnest, "I give you my word."

Before Allen could reply, the conference room seemed to rise up around him as they slowly dropped down two floors to the press-room. Hazel manipulated the control so that they were facing the podium from the middle of the room. He did something else with it and the room came alive around them as the office disappeared from view. Allen watched in amazement as his audio-video technician ran into the room and then became a blur as he swirled around the podium and then the lights became brighter and more blurs filtered in and out of the room. Finally, everything seemed to slow down back to normal just as Cassie and Jeff Rogers walked up to the podium. Allen looked around him at the now nearly full room of reporters and cameras. The clock on the wall showed one o'clock while only a moment ago it had been a couple of minutes past noon. He started to say something but was interrupted by Cassie's voice.

"Ladies and gentlemen of the media, welcome to Brookstone Heuristics Corporation. We had originally planned to have Allen Brookstone provide more information about our new product, but he was unavoidably detained at the last minute. However, we have Jeff Rogers, our head of Research and Development, who will be providing answers to any technical questions that you might have. Without further ado, I give you Jeff Rogers."

Cassie stepped back and to the side as Jeff walked up to the podium to address the audience. His face was illuminated from time to time by the flashes from the numerous cameras.

"I'm proud to announce that BHC has completed development and testing of a revolutionary new way to merge disparate data storage systems into one coherent model. We will be giving a demonstration of this on Saturday and invite all of you to be present. As Mr. Brookstone indicated yesterday, our new product is near-infinitely scalable. It is not

only capable of linking together every data storage medium currently in use on the planet, but it can also handle more than one million times that many media storage devices."

Jeff suddenly froze before he could continue and the press-room scene faded from view entirely. Allen appeared to be back in his office again. "That's enough, for now," said Hazeltine. "We need to take a break from the virtual world and wait a bit for reality to catch up."

Somewhat dazed, Allen said "I don't think I understand. What just happened?"

"I think that you *do* know. You said it yourself, earlier. I just showed you the logical outcome of events that will transpire in a little under an hour from now." Hazeltine grinned, "I've shown you the future and in a little while we'll watch the news broadcast at 1:00 PM to see how accurate I was in doing so."

He stood up and stretched. "Come with me and let's go get something to eat, shall we? Your stomach is still on California time and you should be getting hungry by now." He started for the doorway, but stopped when he realized that Allen was still sitting on the couch. "Please humor me just a little longer, Allen. After we watch the press conference, I only have one more thing to show you. And after that, if you still want to leave, we will have you back in your office before the afternoon is out."

5342 BC - NW Persian Gulf Sea Floor

Ferta's comlink came alive in her ear, "Hey, Ferta, if you want dinner to be ready on time, you're going to have to let go of some of your precious little CPU cycles. Unless you want me to whip up some nutripaste?"

Ferta sighed, but smiled inwardly at the same time, "Sorry, Tommi, I completely forgot what time it was. I've got 97% of it done anyway." She tapped a few times on her keypad. "There, I've pushed the job down into the background where it'll stay until it's finished."

"Thanks!" came the reply. "I still don't see what the big deal is. I mean, we lost a remote, but it's not like we don't have any more of them."

"You get dinner ready and I'll fill everybody in on it after we eat. Then I think you'll see why it's such a big deal, okay?"

"Okay," his cheerful voice filled her ear, "I have my own surprise for everyone as well. I'll see you all in a few minutes."

Ferta turned her attention back to the console and watched the last two-minute sequence of the summary she had put together. She had patiently combed through every second of the av-feed for the last two weeks and had finally managed to translate almost all of the conversations that had been recorded. By going back and forth through the narratives, she was eventually able to program the linguistic module with the basic phonemes she had identified and it had mostly worked out the rest on its own. Lacking a handful of nouns with no reference, the LM was now able to fluently translate from the natives' language into Shoomaran. Given a few more hours, even running in background, she expected it to be able to translate from Shoomaran into the natives' language as well. She stood up and stretched and realized that she had been at this for nearly six hours without a break. She hadn't thought to ask Tommi what he was fixing for dinner, but she was famished. She picked up her notepod and headed out the doorway toward the lift.

+ + +

Altair beamed at Tommi, "I was more than a little leery about eating this at first, but I can honestly say that it was one of the best meals I've ever had!" Nods of agreement came from everyone around the table.

"I knew that if you'd just try it, you'd like it," answered Tommi. He had fixed a seafood dinner from the marine life that had found its way into the waterlock during Lonni's outing. Working from stored templates of the original raw meat, he had experimented with different cooking processes until settling on the one that had produced the meal that they had eaten tonight. In addition to their favorite vegetables, he had made them each eat a piece of the soft marine animal as well as chunks of the hard-shelled one. The sauce was made of standard Shoomaran spices, but it blended with the exotic preparation in a fashion that caused an explosion of pleasure from the palate. "I've added them to the selector so that you can have them any time that you want."

Lonni spoke up, "I think I'm going to open the waterlock again and see what else we can catch. If these two dishes are any example of what's available, I can hardly wait! This is the first really new addition to the food store in as long as I can remember."

"I'll second that," said Mirta.

"And I'll approve it," smiled Altair. "Just make sure that we don't end up eating something that will kill us or make us all sick."

They all laughed as Tommi turned bright red. Although many years had passed since that time when one of his culinary experiments had sent them all to bed for several days, it was always brought up again whenever he tried to get them to try something new.

Ferta waited until the laughter had died down, "Not to change the subject, but I brought along a little after-dinner entertainment." She reached down and picked up her notepod and placed it in the middle of the table. She glanced around at the others and saw that she had their full attention. "Up until now, I haven't really had much to share with everyone. As you already know, it's been nearly two weeks since the two natives discovered our remote and took it with them back to their home. Since then, they've shown it to many others and it has clearly been at the center of many animated discussions. Without knowing what they were saying, however, we really haven't been able to ascertain the impact of its discovery or learn much about these people." She smiled wryly at everyone, "I'm afraid that I have both good news and bad news. The good news is that I've been able to translate nearly everything that's been said within reach of the remote. The bad news is that we've opened a veritable Cartigan's Container here."

Altair started to speak, "Oh, it can't be all that bad ..." but he was stopped by Ferta's raised hand.

"I know that some of you pooh-pooh the sanctity of First Contact, but we created the Laws in the first place for a reason. What I'm about to show you is a compilation of feeds that I've put together to demonstrate the impact our little remote has had on these people." She tapped her notepod as she raised her voice, "Lights!" The lights went out and each of the crew were presented with a view of the two natives as they initially approached the remote. Ferta continued, "Before I start this short presentation, I need to give you a little background information. The natives in this area are primarily migratory farmers. They raise animals for food and plant various grains for crops that they later harvest. Without even the most rudimentary scientific knowledge, they attribute everything that happens that they don't understand to the actions of various gods and goddesses. For example, they believe that storms that come in from the ocean are sent to them by Nammu, their goddess of the sea. Sometimes the storms are beneficial and help their crops. Other times they flood the area and wipe out their homes. As a result, she is seen as a mostly benevolent goddess with a temper." Ferta smiled, "If it wasn't so misguided, it would almost be amusing." She went on, "When the native, whose name is Mardu, first saw Lonni come up out of the water, he thought that he had seen a sea monster. However, his brother Itok came up with another explanation."

Ferta started the projection and it began playing the scene that each of them had already witnessed several times. However, this time the audio was translated into Shoomaran and they were finally able to understand what was being said by the two natives.

Mardu: *"What do you think it is, Itok?"*

Itok: *"I think that the gods and goddesses watch over us from above. I think that maybe one of them fell to the ground to visit us. I think perhaps you saw Nammu come from her new home and return back again. And I think that, possibly, this is her gift to you."*

Ferta paused the presentation, "The belief that Lonni is their sea goddess Nammu takes on its own life as Mardu begins to show the remote to anyone that will listen. Apparently, he is well known for his tall tales, but this time he has proof of his encounter. The next scene I'm going to show you occurs about a week later at a gathering of most of the natives in the region." She started the player again. The current view faded to black and built up again showing several rows of natives that appeared to be sitting in a circle around the remote. As the view panned around, it became apparent that the remote was being held aloft by Mardu as he spoke to the others.

Mardu: *"Behold! I bring greetings from Nammu, the goddess of all that really matters! She has shown herself to me and has given me this token of her appreciation of all that I am! She is watching over us and listening to us even now as I speak! She will bring an end to the drought that Enki has caused and she will make the sea rise up and water our crops again! Let her hear what you want and she will provide!"*

Crowd: *"Rain! Rain! Rain!"*

Mardu: *"That's it! Let her hear you all the way to the bottom of the sea where she has made her new home!"*

Crowd: *"Rain! Rain! Rain!"*

The view faded out and Ferta tapped the pause control again. "The region is undergoing a severe dry spell and their crops are failing. Thanks to Mardu, they think that Nammu is going to save them. Last night they gathered again, but they are getting tired of Mardu's empty promises." She started the projector again.

Mardu: *"Behold! I bring greetings from Nammu, the goddess of all that really matters! She is watching over us and listening to us even now as I speak! She will bring an end to the drought and she will make the sea rise up and water our crops!"*

Native: *"You've been saying that all week now, Mardu. But when is she going to bring the rain? My family and I can only carry so much water from the river and every day that goes by I lose more of my crop. I'm beginning to think that you don't really have any influence with her. You promised she would bring us rain if we gave you things and we did. Now you either get her to make it rain or we want everything back ... and then some."*

Crowd: *(angry murmurs)*

Mardu: *"I understand your impatience, but just give her a few more days and I'm sure she'll save our crops! She is Nammu!"*

Native: *"Two more days, Mardu, and then I want my lamb back if it hasn't rained by then. Without my crops, I'll be needing everything I have to survive the winter."*

Crowd: *(more angry murmurs of assent)*

Mardu: *"Don't worry! She won't let us down!"*

The scene faded out as Ferta again paused the presentation. "Our carelessness has caused this poor braggart to be placed in a very awkward position. Granted, he brought it on himself, but he really believes that Nammu is listening to their pleas and will do something about it."

Rolli interrupted, "Who is Enki? He mentioned that Enki had caused the drought."

"Enki is their god of the sun. According to their beliefs, he raises the sun in the morning and carries it across the sky to the other side of the world. Enki and Nammu constantly argue over how often the sun will shine and how often it will rain." She frowned, "Last night, after the gathering of the natives broke up, Mardu went into his tent and prayed to our remote to make it rain." She started the projection again and the image of Mardu appeared somewhat ghostly in appearance. "I've displayed this scene using infrared since it's almost in total darkness."

Mardu: *"Nammu ... I know that you can hear me. You have to help us. If you don't make it rain soon, they will tear me limb from limb. Why did you show yourself to me if you're not going to help us? Am I a fool to believe in you even now? I saw you come out of the water and then go back in again. I have taken such good care of your talisman that you gave me and have made your presence known to many. Please, Nammu, tell me what to do!"*

Mardu began to weep softly, his body shaking slightly as he did so. Ferta spoke up, "Lights!" and the room was once again illuminated as she shut off her notepod.

"That's the saddest and most pathetic thing I think I've ever seen," exclaimed Sparta. "Oh, the poor man!"

"Exactly," said Ferta. "The question is, what do we do about it?"

"What do we do about it?" asked Mirta. "Are you serious? We can't do anything about it! It's unfortunate that we broke protocol by allowing them to find the remote, but we can't do anything else to interfere. Don't you think that we've already done enough?"

Altair spoke up, "Did you have something in mind, Ferta? Are you seriously suggesting that we should make it rain for them?"

"Yes," she replied. "I think that we owe it to Mardu."

"Making it rain is easy," said Lonni. "It's mostly my fault that they found the remote in the first place and I wouldn't mind helping to set things right, if I can."

Ferta spoke again, "I move that we provide a nice rain for these people and help make sure that they don't starve to death for lack of it."

"But what about the Laws of First Contact?" asked Mirta, clearly worried.

"I don't think that we're bound by them since we're obviously well beyond their jurisdiction." Ferta paused to let this sink in and then continued, "While I understand that finding the remote obviously didn't cause or otherwise alter their weather conditions, I don't think that I can idly stand by and watch them die knowing that all they need is a little airborne moisture."

Lonni laughed, "I always wanted to be a goddess!"

Six Months Ago - Mount Ararat, Turkey

"How is any of this possible?" Allen asked Hazeltine. They were sitting at a table on the outdoor patio of Frère Jacques with the Eiffel Tower in the distance. Below them, the Seine flowed slowly by while picturesque white boats meandered upon the surface of the waterway. "I've given up trying to make sense of anything you've shown me in the last few hours. I think I'm finally starting to totally lose my grip on reality."

"Oh, I don't think it can be all that bad," smiled Hazel. "You don't really believe that we walked down the hallway and exited in Paris, do you?"

"Almost. If it weren't for the fact that I can see the Seine, but can't smell it, and I can see the sun, but can't feel its warmth, I could easily believe that it's all real. Or perhaps a very vivid hallucination. My favorite theories, so far, mostly revolve around lying in a coma somewhere, or maybe an exposure to some incredibly potent hallucinogen, or perhaps I'm simply dead and gone." He looked askance at Hazeltine, "If it's the latter, I can't decide if you're God or Satan."

"You're a man of science, Allen. It is a given that sufficiently advanced science is indistinguishable from magic, is it not? I promised you earlier that I would have one of our technicians explain everything to you. To be perfectly honest, sometimes it looks like magic to me, as well." He pointed to the table top. "For example, our food processor."

Allen frowned, "I don't follow you."

"Here, I'll demonstrate." Hazel placed his hand on the table and spoke, "Order!"

A dis-embodied voice replied, "Welcome to Frère Jacques, Chairman Hazeltine. It is indeed an honor to have you here. What will you be having?"

"I'll have the surf and turf, please."

"Very good, sir. Anything else?"

"Yes, a bottle of Bordeaux with two glasses."

"Very good, sir. Anything else?"

"That's all. Please provide the wine and glasses now and hold the rest for five minutes."

"As you wish, sir."

As the voice finished speaking, a bottle of wine appeared in the center of the table flanked by two delicate crystal glasses. Hazeltine pulled them toward him, poured half a glass of wine and set it down in front of Allen. He filled the second glass half full and raised it, "Here's to our new friendship and the hope that it will be a long one!"

Allen numbly picked up the glass, sniffed it, and took a small sip. He smiled for the first time in more than an hour, "That's fantastic!" he exclaimed. He reached over and picked up the bottle to examine it closer. It was an 1811 Chateau d'Yquem that was well-known for its bouquet and flavor. He took another sip. "I didn't think that there were any bottles of this left. Rumor has it that the last few that were found had all turned to vinegar." He looked about him and reflected on how such a simple thing could jolt him from his nearly catatonic stupor. "Everything else around us may be fake, but this is real enough."

"So go ahead and order something you like. I think that you'll find the food here is of similarly exceptional quality."

Allen suddenly realized how hungry he was. The two small sips of wine had not only awakened his taste buds, but acutely sharpened his senses. He felt the now-familiar rush of questions bubbling up again looking for answers. Hesitantly, he placed his hand flat on the table and said "Order!"

The same dis-embodied voice answered him "Welcome to Frère Jacques, Mr. Brookstone. It is indeed an honor to have you here. What will you be having?"

More alert now, Allen noticed that the voice had a slight French accent. "I'd like a bacon-ultimate cheeseburger," he said, somewhat sarcastically.

"Very good, sir. Would you like an order of season fries with that?"

Allen was surprised. He hadn't actually expected an affirmative reply. "Yes, that would be fine."

"Very good, sir. Will there be anything else?"

"No, thank you."

He had barely finished the "thank you" when a plate appeared in the middle of the table with what looked like a hot and juicy burger from Jack in the Box and a small pile of seasoned curly fries. Not only did the food look enticing to Allen, but the smell was almost overwhelming. He picked up a french fry and popped it into his mouth and chewed it slowly. He then picked up the burger and bit into it. He didn't recall the last time a bacon-ultimate cheesebuger had tasted so good. When he had finished chewing, he looked at Hazeltine and said, "Okay, I don't really believe in magic, so I'll ask again, how is any of this possible?"

"As you have already seen, our organization possesses very advanced technology. We are able to manipulate matter on an elemental level in a number of ways that have many useful applications. The food processor, for example, is basically a Xerox machine. We store a molecular template of the original in our repository and can subsequently create a perfect replica by combining the appropriate atoms according to the template." Hazeltine paused as his food appeared in the center of the table. "Ahh, my favorite!" He pulled the plate toward him as he continued, "The convincing scenery around us is based on a slightly different application of the same technology. As you know, a movie or video is a sequence of static pictures shown very rapidly so that the mind perceives them as continuous." As he spoke, he began to cut into his food. "The boats moving along the Seine are virtual constructs generated from the repository of the original template. Like the food processor, but on a larger scale. The real-time view of the FBI briefing, on the other hand, was generated from the raw feed as it entered the repository." He paused to place a large chunk of lobster in his mouth and smiled as he savored its flavor.

"I think I understand," said Allen. He had already polished off the cheeseburger and was working on his fries. "And the press conference we saw? More of the same technology?"

Hazeltine paused before his next bite, "No, that's a little bit different. As you've already surmised, we can't project what's not yet in the repository." He bit into the piece of medium rare prime rib.

"You called it your chaos machine. If I assume that you can store all of this into some vast repository, as you call it, then I can also assume that you can predict the future interaction of those same particles with some degree of certainty?"

"In a nutshell, yes." Hazeltine raised his voice slightly, "CNN, please!"

A view-screen of some sort appeared above the center of the table in front of Allen as he finished his last french-fry. It looked a lot like a flat-screen TV, but without the TV. Allen's attention focused on it as he heard his name mentioned:

First announcer: *"... just been informed that Allen Brookstone will not be at the press conference which will start at any moment. We now take you live to the headquarters of the Brookstone Heuristics Corporation in Silicon Valley."*

Second announcer: *"We are here live at the Brookstone Building in Silicon Valley as the press secretary is walking up to the podium. All of Wall Street is waiting on pins and needles to find out more about their new development announced only yesterday."*

The screen cut to Cassie at the podium with a banner display that read "*Cassandra Stevens - Press Secretary - BHC.*" The screen filled with her face as she began to speak:

"Ladies and gentlemen of the media, welcome to Brookstone Heuristics Corporation. We had originally planned to have Allen Brookstone provide more information about our new product, but he was unavoidably detained at the last minute. However, we have Jeff Rogers, our head of Research and Development, who will be providing answers to any technical questions that you might have. Without further ado, I give you Jeff Rogers."

Allen watched in fascination as the entire press conference unfolded exactly as he had seen it before. As near as he could tell, other than the different point of view afforded by the network camera, it was identical in every way.

"Seen enough?" asked Hazeltine.

"It looks just like what you showed me. How do I know that this is really live and not just pre-recorded? For all I know, you set the whole thing up ahead of time."

"You're just going to have to trust me on that, Allen. Surely, by now, you can see that we have technology you're only just beginning to appreciate. I don't know any other way to try and convince you that our Chaos Machine can accurately predict the future, but you must believe it is so." Hazeltine looked intently at Allen, "You simply must!"

"Why is it so damned important for me to believe that?" Allen glared at Hazeltine for a moment and then relaxed a bit. "Okay, okay, I believe you. Can we get on with the explanation of why you need me and when I can go home?"

"As soon as I finish my meal, we'll go back to your office for the grand finale." Hazeltine raised the bottle of wine and added a generous amount to Allen's near-empty glass, "Have a little more, I think you're going to need it."

Allen watched the CNN broadcast as he wondered how Cassie was taking his disappearance. She looked good, he thought. He wasn't worried about her being in charge while he was away, but he was worried that she had no idea where he went or if he would ever be back. Allen frowned at the thought. For that matter, he didn't even know if he would ever be back at all. Hazel seemed intent on keeping him here and, at times, seemed somewhat maniacal. Again, almost automatically, his self-preserving cloak of pragmatism settled around him as he sipped the last of his wine.

In a few more minutes, Hazeltine burped loudly and sighed, "That was a rather good meal, don't you think?"

"How did you know that I like Jack in the Box?"

"I know many things about you, Allen. Which is why I firmly believe that you alone can help us." Hazeltine pushed back away from the table and stood up. "Come, let's go see what the future holds for us."

5342 BC - NW Persian Gulf Delta

"Mardu! Awaken!"

Mardu groggily woke up at the sound of the voice, "Itok? Is that you?" He looked over at his brother's side of the tent where he lay sleeping.

"It is Nammu. I have brought the rain that you seek," spoke the feminine voice. It appeared to be coming from his pouch lying beside his head. He sat up and suddenly realized that it was lightly raining outside. He could smell the damp moisture in the air and was instantly wide awake. He scrabbled at the cover to his pouch and reached in to pull out his talisman.

"Is it really you, Nammu?" he asked of the cube.

"Yes, Mardu. I have heard your prayers and have sent the rain."

The voice was clearly emanating from the talisman he held in his hand. "I knew that you wouldn't let me down!" he exclaimed. "Why did you wait so long?"

"It was a test of your faith in me," came the reply. "I had to be sure that you would continue to believe in me long after the others had lost faith."

"How can I not believe in you? I saw you fall from the heavens and later come to me out of the water." He turned the cube around in his hand, "Where are you? Are you inside of this?"

"The talisman you hold in your hand is my meme. It is linked to me so that I can see and hear all. I have chosen you, Mardu, of all of your tribespeople to carry my meme and to obey me without question when so commanded. You have passed the first test of faith, but there will be more to come. Will you willingly be my loyal servant?"

Mardu didn't know what to say. He had grown used to the idea that Nammu had chosen him alone from among his people, but he hadn't actually expected to be talking to her like this. After all, Nammu was a goddess and she had been worshipped by generation after generation of his people. And now she was asking him if he would mind being her servant. Mardu's chest swelled with pride, "Of course I will be your loyal servant. I will do as you ask without question. What is it that you want me to do?"

"For now, go out and enjoy the rain. Tell your people how I heard their prayers and how I have sent it over the objections of Enki. Tell them how I have come in order to look after my dark-haired people so that you will prosper."

"Oh, I will! I will!" said Mardu.

"I will always be listening and watching. Sometimes I will respond and sometimes I will not. You must be patient and have faith that I am here."

"I understand."

"Now go and tell your people. My people. Our people!"

"I hear and obey, Nammu!" Mardu waited for a reply, but there was none. He slowly became aware of a growing noise coming from outside of his tent over the soft patter of the raindrops hitting the parched soil. As Nammu's last words echoed in his head, he began to wonder if maybe he had dreamed it. He stared at the talisman, the meme she had called it, still in his hand. He stood up, donned his robe and sandals, and went outside where the rain fell on him. The noise he had heard was the joyful cries of his friends and neighbors coming toward his and Itok's tent.

"Mardu!" came the cries. "It's raining! Just like you said it would!"

Mardu clutched the meme tightly in his hand as he strode forward to greet them.

+ + +

"Our people?" Altair raised his eyebrow quizzically as he looked at Ferta.

"Okay, okay, so maybe I got a little carried away there, but I think we have his attention," she replied.

"We have his attention, alright," said Tommi, "and now he's going to be expecting us to solve every little problem that crops up from time to time."

"Would that be such a bad thing?" asked Mirta.

Lonni spoke up, "I don't see how it's helping us any. I don't think we should have gotten involved."

Sparta laughed, "Well, you're a fine one to talk. You're the one that said you could make it rain in the first place."

Altair looked around the crowded communications room and inwardly sighed. It was interesting how the three female crew members had so quickly taken to Mardu while the three males were generally opposed to continue helping him. They had carefully prepared a script for Ferta to follow, but she had deviated quite a bit from it about halfway through. Oh, well, it was certainly the most interesting thing that had happened since they had grounded and he was quickly growing bored with the never-changing daily routine. He intuitively knew that helping these people would keep everyone from growing bored as well and, to that end, he felt it was worth supporting. Rules of First Contact be damned.

"Let's see what's going on with Mardu," said Sparta. "I can't wait to see how his people react!"

"Our people," said Ferta as she turned back to the console and fiddled with the controls for a moment. They were rewarded with a reasonably steady image of the crowd around Mardu as he was speaking to them.

Mardu: *"Nammu has sent the rain as we asked. We must have a great feast in her honor for bringing us the rain!"*

Crowd: *"Praise Nammu! Praise be to Nammu!"*

Ferta sighed and smiled contentedly, "My people love me!"

The Chaos Machine

Six Months Ago - San Francisco, California

Cassie waited nervously in the interview room. She had accompanied Vivian Williams to the local FBI office housed in a sedately shaded office complex in order to answer some questions. Cassie had seen enough cop shows to know that she was now a person of interest and she noted that the room she was sitting in looked remarkably like the interrogation rooms on the shows with the one-way mirror and camera. Outwardly, she remained calm, but inside, she was afraid. Afraid of what the FBI might want and afraid of what might have happened to Allen. She sat and waited. There wasn't much else she could do at this point.

She didn't have long to wait. Vivian entered the room a few minutes later accompanied by a man of medium-build in a tailored gray suit. Noting the earpiece in his left ear, Cassie immediately assumed he was another FBI agent.

"Hi, Cassie, this is Field Agent Bill Treadway. He will be sitting in with us as I ask you some questions."

"Is he the good cop? Or the bad cop?"

Vivian laughed, "I think you've been watching too many cop shows. We're both bad cops, of course." She smiled as she watched Cassie's reaction. "Just kidding," she said.

Cassie laughed, "As long as I know who's who."

Agent Treadway spoke, "For record-keeping purposes, this interview will be recorded. Do you have any objection to that?"

"Of course not, I want to do anything that will help us find Allen."

"Very good," he replied. He signaled to someone behind the mirror and touched his earpiece. He turned to Vivian, "We're rolling."

Cassie sat impassively as Vivian rattled off the time, date, case number, who was present in the room, and the purpose of the interview. Cassie noted that she didn't refer to her as a person of interest, but as the last person to see Allen Brookstone before his disappearance. Finally, Vivian spoke to Cassie directly, "I need to start out by getting some background information. This will help us to better understand Allen's possible frame of mind leading up to his disappearance. To begin with, how long have you known Mr. Brookstone?"

Cassie thought a moment before replying, "A little more than five years now."

"How did you first meet?"

"I answered an ad I saw in The Economist. It said that they were looking for an exceptional individual to be the personal assistant to the CEO of a large international corporation. I don't recall all of the details, but as I read further, I kept thinking that the particular individual they were looking for was me. It was as if I had been asked to describe myself and what I did best. There was only a P.O. box to write to and it wasn't until I received a request for an interview that I learned it was with BHC."

"I take it that you got the job?" asked Vivian.

"Yes. Allen conducted the interview himself and, from the moment we first met, it was like we connected on several different levels, somehow. I found out later that he had received almost 3,000 applications, but that I was the only one he had chosen to interview."

"That sounds a bit odd, to me, considering the importance of the position," said Agent Treadway.

"Well, since you put it that way, yes, it does. You have to understand that Allen Brookstone is something of an eccentric. The application for the job consisted of a hundred-word essay describing why I wanted to work for him. He said that when he read my essay, he knew that he had found the person he was looking for."

"That must have been one heck of an award-winning essay," smiled Vivian.

"I guess so," replied Cassie. "Two days after the interview, Allen contacted me himself and told me that the job was mine if I wanted it. By that time, I had thoroughly researched him and his company and learned the fate of his previous ten assistants." She hesitated, "I wasn't entirely sure I wanted the job at that point, but I figured it wouldn't hurt to at least give it a try. The rest, as they say, is history."

"Some people seem to think that there's more to your relationship than just the boss and his secretary," said Treadway.

"What do you mean?" asked Cassie suspiciously.

"Well, let's see, according to your file here, you're twenty-eight years old. You first started working for BHC at age twenty-three. Now, only five years later, he's mysteriously disappeared and you're left in charge of a multi-billion-dollar corporation."

"I'm not sure I like what you're implying." Cassie frowned at Vivian, "Bill's the bad cop, isn't he?"

Vivian didn't laugh this time, "I must admit that I find it a little odd myself. I spoke briefly with each of the board members, but they all deferred my questions to you. When we inquired who was officially in charge during Allen's unexpected absence, they all said that you have his full proxy vote in all matters."

"Yes, I take care of things for Allen, that's my job."

"No offense, but taking care of things as a secretary is usually limited to which seat to sit in on the plane or confirming luncheon reservations. When a CEO is absent, they usually name someone on the board to make decisions in their absence." She paused and slid the file from Agent Treadway to herself. She quickly flipped to a page and glanced at it for a moment. "Allen Brookstone personally owns 75% of the preferred voting stock in BHC Capital which, as you know, wholly owns the other corporations that comprise BHC overall. With Allen out of the picture, you are now essentially in charge."

"Well, yes, I guess that's one way of looking at it, but that's only until he gets back." Cassie sounded defensive, "I'm not exactly a secretary, Vivian."

Agent Treadway asked, "Is there any romantic angle between you and Allen that you might want to tell us about?"

"Now I'm getting offended. Why are you so interested in me? How is this helping to find out what happened to Allen?"

"Is there?" he prompted.

"A romantic angle? Absolutely not. We have a synergy that I can't explain that has worked exceptionally well over the years. We think alike, we work alike, it's as if we're cut from the same cloth. But romance? Sex? Not in the picture." She glared at Vivian, "Do I need to get a lawyer in here?"

"If you want a lawyer, you're certainly entitled, although I want to make it clear that you're not a suspect. However, as you know from watching all the crime shows, we look for three things: motive, opportunity, and means. I don't yet know by what means Allen disappeared, but you alone stand to gain financially and, not to put too fine a point on it, you were the last one to see him before he disappeared." She looked calmly at Cassie, "Do you want us to take a break so that you can call your lawyer?"

"No," said Cassie, clearly exasperated. "I don't have a lawyer and Allen would have a fit if he thought that I couldn't handle a simple FBI interview by myself. Special Agent Williams and Field Agent Treadway," she glanced up at the camera mounted in the corner, "and anyone else who happens to be listening or watching, I don't have time for this right now. My boss is missing on the eve of our new product launch and I'm needed back at the office. I want him found and I want him found as soon as possible. I will fully cooperate with any reasonable requests you may make, but this dithering around is getting you nowhere."

"If it makes you feel any better, our dithering around currently involves nearly two hundred agents. We're not exactly holding up the investigation by asking you these questions. We want him found as much as you do."

Cassie sighed, more for effect than anything else. She glanced at her watch, "Okay, I apologize for my comments. It's just that I'm getting really worried. Ask your questions and I'll try to answer them as best I can."

"What about his life insurance policy?" continued Treadway, as if nothing had interrupted them.

"There's a key-man policy on Allen that goes to the board members on his death. I believe that each gets five million dollars." She looked at Vivian, "Doesn't that provide a motive for someone else besides me?"

"Yes, it does, but there's also the question of his personal policy."

"I didn't know that he had one."

"Well, he does. It's for fifty million dollars and you're named as the sole beneficiary."

"What!?" Cassie exclaimed. It was apparent to the agents that this was clearly news to her. "What are you talking about?"

Vivian replied, "A little over a year ago, he took out a personal life insurance policy and named you as the beneficiary. Are you sure there's nothing more to your relationship? Anything you might care to tell us?"

Cassie was stunned. She was prepared for almost anything, but this was from so far out in left field that she didn't know what to say. She just sat there and stared at the two FBI agents with her mouth hanging open. Finally, she regained enough of her composure to squeak out, "There must be some mistake!"

"No, no mistake. We're also still more than a little curious about how you came to be in this position. Your only job experience before working for BHC seems to have been part-time work for various educational institutions." Vivian glanced down at the file in front of her and turned a page. "You've never had a driver's license and you didn't get a Social Security number until you were sixteen. We can't locate a birth certificate anywhere and no one seems to know anything about you, other than your stellar track record at various schools, of course."

Cassie was really feeling lost. She was rapidly losing her composure and realized that this woman had her more rattled than she could ever recall. She belatedly realized that this was all according to plan. The FBI were experts in getting people to feel this way. She was right all along when she felt like she was in an interrogation room and not an interview room. She took a deep breath and recited her mantra. She was glad that Allen couldn't see how unnerved she was. She pulled herself together at the thought. "I still think you're wasting your time, but I'll try to fill you in on what I know about myself." She took a sip of water from the glass in front of her before continuing, "I don't know where I was born or what my real name is. My earliest memories are of The Sisters of Mercy orphanage in L.A. around age four or five. They said that I was left on the doorstep in the middle of the night with a note that said 'Take care of Cassandra for me.' I still have the note, if you'd like to see it, but it's back at my condo."

Vivian made a note of this, "Yes, if you wouldn't mind. Please continue."

"By the time I was twelve, I was getting a little too old to interest anyone in adopting me. Everyone wanted a cuddly little cutie and not some headstrong adolescent. By the time I was sixteen, I had graduated from the Catholic high school and qualified for a full scholarship to the University of California, at Berkley. At nineteen, I had earned a BS degree in Computer Science and had been given a scholarship to attend Harvard where I obtained my MBA at age twenty-one. Two years later, I received my Doctorate of Economics from the International School of Business in Phoenix. As you've noted, I worked part-time for the schools while I completed my classes, but when I finished my Ph.D., I decided that I needed a real job. Something that would challenge me. And here I am. Being interrogated by the FBI while my boss goes missing."

Vivian ignored the sarcasm, "According to this, you were the first in your class. Not only in high school, but at Harvard and ISB as well. That's pretty impressive, if you ask me."

"Well, thank you."

"If it's really true," interjected Agent Treadway.

"Ask the schools, why don't you. You're the friggin' FBI, for God's sake."

"We're working on it," said Vivian. She pulled a form from the folder and slid it over to Cassie and placed her pen on top. "Thanks to FERPA, even the FBI needs your permission to get your school records. If you wouldn't mind signing this release form, we can check your story."

Cassie picked up the form and read it. It was limited only to obtaining her school records as Vivian had indicated. She picked up the pen, signed and dated it, and passed it back to Vivian. "Do you need me to sign any other forms while we're at it? We might as well get it out of the way. I have nothing to hide but my impatience and frustration with this entire process."

Vivian was apparently unfazed, "No, I think that's the only release we need, for now."

Cassie slid the pen back across the table and glanced at her watch, "How about we take that break you were talking about now. You can start checking my curriculum vitae after dropping me back at the office. As CEO pro tem, I have some things I need to get done before the day is out. After that, I'll be more than happy to meet with you again."

"Does that mean that there will be a lawyer involved now?"

"Not unless you feel like you really need one. I give you my word that I'm not going to sue the FBI. At least not if you find Allen." She stood up. "I'm done now. Please take me back to the Brookstone Building or let me go downstairs and call a cab."

Vivian stood up and walked to the door and opened it, holding it as Cassie walked through. She glanced back at Treadway and mouthed, "I told you so," before following her out.

Agent Treadway sat for a few moments without moving. Finally, he looked up at the camera and said "Cut!" Then he, too, stood up and left the room, his brow deeply furrowed in thought.

Six Months Ago - Mount Ararat, Turkey

Hazeltine opened the door at the other end of the short hallway connected to Allen's ersatz bedroom and office. The room they were entering was circular, about twenty feet in diameter. In the center was a round table that appeared to be covered in a glass-like material with four chairs evenly spaced around the perimeter. Hazeltine gestured for Allen to take a seat as he himself sat down in the chair closest to the entrance.

"This is the remote admin console that is interfaced directly to our Chaos Machine." Hazeltine laid his hand on the surface of the table and it came alive with numerous displays and virtual buttons. He tapped one of them and a model of the Earth appeared in the center of the table. It was about a foot in diameter and appeared to be floating at eye level above the table top. He pointed to one of the readouts, "This gives you the current global locus and orientation. You can slide your finger along this control here to rotate the model along each of the primary axes or combinations of them." He pointed to another control, "Sliding your finger along this one changes the locus and the local orientation. This readout," he indicated one of the displays, "gives the current time and date of the model. You can slide your finger back and forth to move forward or backward in time. Or you can enter the desired target directly by using the keyboard here," he pointed to the appropriate control. He glanced up at Allen, "For example, I want to show you what will happen in a little over a year from now." He expertly tapped the keyboard and the model shifted slightly. It still looked much the same, but the cloud cover was different and the night-day terminus had noticeably moved.

"What am I supposed to be looking for?" asked Allen.

"Just keep watching," replied Hazeltine. Even as he spoke, Allen could see a small bright pinpoint of light that slowly blossomed outwards from its origin near the north-eastern coast of the Arabian Peninsula. As it grew in size, a small depression appeared underneath it that also began to grow. As its boundary reached the nearby Alps, the entire area began to undergo a transition. With a start, Allen realized that the event was occurring over an area several hundred miles across. He watched in fascination as the entire region was swallowed up and the sea began to flow inland. The model appeared to be shuddering slightly as what looked like several small cracks began radiating outwards from the origin. In only a few moments, the cracks widened, revealing a dull orange glow from the magma below. Allen wasn't entirely sure, but it looked like the fissures were developing along the major fault lines in the area as they continued to spread. In another few seconds, the cracks suddenly appeared as a fiery network encircling the globe and then the whole thing exploded in a burst of pure white light that literally hurt his eyes. As his vision readjusted to the darkened room, he realized that he was looking at a cloud of vapor and that nothing at all remained of the model of the Earth.

"You have just witnessed the end of the world," solemnly intoned Hazeltine. "This is what the future holds for us and it doesn't look like we can do anything to prevent it, this time."

"What do you mean, 'this time'?"

"We do not like to interfere unless it's absolutely necessary, and then only when we are sure that the change will produce a better prognosis." Hazeltine paused, "If we could do anything to stop this or change the outcome, we would have already done so. Or be preparing to do so. As it is, all of the other scenarios we have projected will not change the sequence of events."

Allen stared at Hazeltine. The man was obviously mad. Up until now he had been gradually building up a trust in Hazel that was now instantly shattered. "Do you really expect me to believe that the end of the world is nigh and that you can't do anything to stop it? All based upon some elaborate computer model you've developed? No offense, Hazel, but I think that you're clinically insane."

"Then prove me wrong, Allen. That's why we've brought you here. Our Chaos Machine not only projects what will happen, but also allows us to run simulations of alternate outcomes depending on the changes we make. The key is in finding the smallest change possible that will produce the best possible outcome."

"The Butterfly Effect."

"Exactly. We have spent a long time looking for alternatives and have finally concluded that there aren't any. Our only hope at this point is that there is some fundamental flaw in our systems. Personally, I believe that they are infallible, as do all of our best technicians. We are hoping that an outsider might see something obvious that we are overlooking." Hazeltine looked earnestly at Allen, "Find the flaw, Allen. Prove that this is not our future. Prove to me that we're wrong." He smiled wryly, "Help us Obi-Wan Kenobe, you're our only hope!"

December 7, 1947 - Murray Hill, New Jersey

William peered through the stereo microscope at the apparatus he was working on. He was beginning to feel like they were trying to drive finishing nails with a sledge hammer. He knew that they were on the right track, but they were still unable to duplicate the artifact's construction. In test after test, they would get some of it right, but the rest would be buggered. Although it was simply a matter of trial and error before they got just the right result, there was no real guarantee that they would ever be successful. He could see that if they ever hoped to make this process repeatable, they were going to have to build some very specialized equipment to make it happen. As he sharpened the focus, he could see that they had almost succeeded this time. The substrate was clean, the junctions perfect, but one of the whiskers had failed to bond. He cursed under his breath and almost angrily ripped the crude assembly from the microscope's stage. He stood and stretched and decided it was time for a break. He left the lab and wandered down the corridors to the cafeteria, deep in thought. A calendar on the wall caught his attention and he suddenly remembered that it was Pearl Harbor Day. Six years had passed since they had been dragged into the War. Nearly four years had passed since he had been tapped by the military to work on a replacement for the vacuum tube. The electronic heart of the radar that had helped to alter the balance of the War was too slow to be pushed any further. If a better system was to be developed, it would have to use something to amplify the signal that had a much faster response time. He randomly picked some food from the buffet and carried it over to his usual table near the back of the room. He liked eating alone and usually used the time to think through things without the distraction of having the tools at hand to immediately act upon his ideas. As he sat and absentmindedly picked at his food, he reflected on the years of blind effort to discover some new materials that would achieve the desired effect. They were getting nowhere until a few months ago when they were given the artifact to study. While no one would say where it came from, it was clearly fabricated by a technology more advanced than anything he was familiar with. And the damned thing worked. A voltage of minimal current applied to the input could be controlled by varying the current to the base. The output yielded a signal gain of over 10,000 relative to the input. It was a lot like Tantalus's Cup. They were handed the solution on a silver platter and still couldn't make one on their own. He had asked if they could get another one to study and was stonewalled at even the highest levels. The current scuttlebutt was that it had been found in the wreckage of a weather balloon that had crashed in New Mexico, but he was unable to independently confirm this or any of the other wild speculations that had been discussed regarding its origins. He ate the last of his pie and then sat for a few minutes idly stabbing his fork into his uneaten gelatin dessert. He stared at the holes left by the tines as an idea began to form in his mind. He kept thinking, it's already been done and we know what it's made of. A slight spring entered his step as he jumped up and deposited his tray in the receptacle. As he made his way back to the lab, the idea began to fully take shape. Maybe if they immersed the assembly in a gelatin of some sort to keep everything in place until they were done processing. Then they could remove the gelatin and, voilà! Perhaps some of the glycol borate they had might do the trick. He hurried on back to the lab, eager to pursue this line of thought.

5342 BC - NW Persian Gulf Sea Floor

Mirta entered the navigation room and sat down at the main console. She had planned on poking through the logs, but was distracted by the unusual looking headset that was lying there. She had never seen it before and wondered where it might have come from. As she idly speculated on its origin and purpose, she placed it on her head. Immediately there was a flash of white-hot pain that shot through her mind and suddenly she was the ship. She perceived that she could sense everything directly. Her cardio-vascular system became the ship's life support system, her body became the decks and passageways, and her brain became the navigation system. As she marveled at the experience, she suddenly realized that they were going to jump in only a few seconds. As the last second expired, her brain slowed down. It seemed like an eternity had passed until the point when they actually jumped. For a long drawn out moment, she could sense the entire universe. Her mind simultaneously knew everything around her as well as almost everything at the far fringes of the universal expansion. Her mind had stretched and stretched to encompass it all, but it could only handle so much. There were gaps in the fabric like a loose-weave material that had been pulled taut. She could sense the whole, but not all of the details. And then the next instant clicked by and suddenly she was on an unknown planet and her mind had shrunk to surround it. Now she could see everything, every detail, every singularity in its exquisite glory. There were no gaps in the fabric anymore. She ripped off the headset and found herself sitting up in her bed. She looked around her cabin and realized that she had been dreaming. The overpowering feeling of sensing everything slowly faded as she became fully awake, but it left behind the seed of an idea. She stepped out of bed, pulled on her robe, and went over to her desk. She sat down and began looking up information on the navigation system and its basic theory of operation. She vaguely recalled reading somewhere that this had been done before, but she couldn't remember the details or whether or not they would even have the equipment on board to make it work. Humming softly to herself, she became quickly enmeshed in researching her brainstorm.

+ + +

Ferta was finishing her daily update on Mardu. Nearly a month had passed since she had first spoken to him and they had made it rain twice more to insure adequate water for the crops. During this time, she had gotten in the habit of providing a daily summary of events and things that she had learned about Mardu's people during the dinner hour. While each of the crew members could easily fix their own meals any time they wanted, ship's protocol required that they eat dinner together every evening at the same time. This served the dual functions of allowing them to exchange information in an informal environment as well as providing stability to their on-board routines. Since she had started giving the updates, the rest of the crew had begun looking forward to them as a welcome break to the boring sameness that now permeated their days.

"So when will they be leaving?" asked Rolli.

"Not for another six weeks or so. Mardu says that this year's harvest has been one of the best anyone can remember."

"All thanks to us, of course," smiled Lonni.

"Yes, thanks to us and your creative use of the microwave array to vaporize the sea-water. When I think of the alternative, of their entire tribe starving to death, I can only conclude that we did the right thing. I can't wait until we deploy the probes so that we can gather more information about this world." She turned to Altair, "We have thirty-seven more days until the hundred days is up. If we can get them on station at that time, we can follow Mardu and his tribe as they migrate north for the winter."

"We might not have to use the probes, after all," said Mirta.

They all turned to look at her. "What do you mean?" asked Altair.

"I spent most of the day figuring out how we can re-purpose the backup navigation system to give us everything we need, without using them."

Altair frowned, "I don't understand."

"Well, as you know, the heart of the nav system is the quadro-trilithium crystal that is tuned to singularities distributed throughout the universe. Normally, this is formed under controlled conditions on Braxor Beta II so that all ship's systems have a common reference point. Combined with its mate in the dilator valve, it provides the resonant field necessary to not only make the jumps, but to also insure that we arrive at our desired destination."

"But the crystal in the dilator valve is shot, Mirta, or have you forgotten that already?" interjected Lonni.

"No, I haven't forgotten, but keep in mind that the nav system doesn't need it to function. It's only needed if we're actually planning on going somewhere. Since we don't know where we are, it's pretty useless right now because it has no frame of reference. However, if we anneal it properly, it will re-create the lattice to resonate instead with only the nearest singularities. In short, it will be attuned to the singularities making up this system." She waited to see if anyone would pick up on the implications of this.

Lonni looked puzzled, "But if you do that, we won't be able to see anything beyond this region of space."

"But we'll be able to see the whole planet in detail, won't we?" asked Sparta excitedly.

"Exactly," said Mirta. "Instead of showing us the universe, it will show us this world instead." She paused to let this sink in.

"I get it," said Altair. "We will actually get a better look at things through the navigation system than we could ever hope to get using the probes." He looked at Mirta appreciatively, "Great idea! Will it work?"

"I'm pretty sure that it will. It turns out that this is nothing new although quadro-trilithium hasn't been used in this fashion for several million years. Other systems are much better suited for planetary use, but we didn't happen to bring any of them along with us. By using the backup system, we will still be preserving the ship's logs and all of our historical data in the primary."

Altair looked around the table at everyone, "If anyone can think of a reason not to try this, please speak up now." He waited until each of them slowly shook their heads. "Okay, Mirta, it's unanimous. Any idea how long this might take?"

"If Lonni's willing to help me, I think that we can have a first look sometime tomorrow."

"Count me in," replied Lonni, "I can't wait to take the grand tour of this place!"

Everyone looked a lot cheerier as they each got up and dumped their leftovers into the converter. While it went unsaid, they were all very much relieved at the thought that they might not have to open any of the cargo after all.

Five Months Ago - Mount Ararat, Turkey

Allen entered the Jack in the Box and walked up to the counter. The young kid on duty turned to him and said "Be with you in a sec!" He finished what he was doing and came over to wait on Allen. "Good afternoon, sir. What can I do for you?"

"I'd like a bacon-ultimate cheeseburger and a small order of curly fries."

"Do you want a drink with that?"

"Yes, I'll take a Coke, please."

"If you order the combo meal, you'll get the large drink and save a few cents as well."

Allen smiled at the suggestion since there was no money changing hands in the first place, "Okay, sounds good to me."

"Will that be for here or to go?"

"Here, please."

"Okay. Here's your number. Your order will be ready in just a couple of minutes."

Allen took the receipt and glanced at it. He was expecting to see the number "001" printed on it as usual, but this time it said "002" instead. That's odd, he thought. He glanced around the room and saw Wyatt seated at a table in the corner. He was surprised to see anyone else here. In the last month or so eating here, he had always been the only customer. He called out, "Hi, Wyatt! What's happening?"

"Not much, Allen."

"I haven't seen you in here before. I didn't think anyone else ate here but me."

"I've never eaten at a Jack in the Box before Hazel opened this one up. Since then, I've been trying different things from their menu. I can see why you like this place!"

Allen's order was ready, "Number 2!" called out the clerk. Allen went over to the counter and picked up the tray with his order. He went to the drink dispenser and added ice and soda to the large cup that had been provided. He looked over at Wyatt, "Mind if I join you?"

"Not at all," answered Wyatt, "Come have a seat and fill me in on how it's going."

Allen crossed the room and sat down across from Wyatt. He wasn't really sure what to talk about, so he focused on unwrapping his cheeseburger. He looked up at Wyatt who was watching him expectantly. "I've been meaning to ask you about your name," he said. "That is, if you don't mind me asking," he added somewhat apologetically.

"Don't mind at all. My name is Wyatt because that's what my momma named me." He smiled.

"Was she a fan of Wyatt Earp, or something?"

"You mean the famous lawman?"

"Yes."

Wyatt smiled again, "I can see that Hazel didn't bother to fill you in." He laughed. "I'm not named after the famous lawman, because I *am* the famous lawman." He seemed amused by the expression on Allen's face. "Of course, I'm not so famous any more since I've had to keep a rather low profile for the last eighty years or so."

"I'm sorry, I don't understand."

"I was sort of drafted by the organization. They took me from my death bed and rejuvenated me. Since then, I've done odd jobs and assignments as needed."

"What do you mean, rejuvenated you?"

"Famous or not, I didn't lead a very nice life. I drank and smoked and did things I'm too ashamed to admit. But that was how it was, back then. I lived hard but didn't die young. By the time they came for me, I couldn't even sit up in bed without gasping for breath. My liver and lungs were shot and I couldn't wait to die." He paused for a moment before going on, "They changed me, Allen, they took my old body and made me young again. But it also changed my outlook on life. They gave me a new start and I've done everything I can to live right this time around."

"You sound happy."

"I am. These are good people, Allen. I spent my first life dealing with the scum of the earth. I got to know people too well and see inside them and had eventually given up on humanity." He looked around the room and then leaned closer to Allen, almost conspiratorially, "It's weird, Allen, the people here have no dark side. It's not like they're perfect little goody two-shoes or anything, but it's like there's only the good stuff and all the bad stuff got left out."

"I think I know what you mean. They've effectively kidnapped me, but I don't feel really threatened. Not even when you first surprised me in the bathroom." He suddenly remembered, "Hey, I've been meaning to you ask about that. I've been so caught up in learning their systems that

I never quite got an answer from anyone. What exactly happened? How did you do it?"

Wyatt blushed slightly, "I'm really sorry about that, Allen. I trust these people and I do what they tell me."

"Don't worry about it, Wyatt, I'm having more fun than I've had in nearly twenty years. But I'm really curious. How did you do it?"

"I'll try to explain." He looked thoughtful for a moment, "When you went down your hallway and came out of that doorway over there, you crossed a teleportal that links the two."

"So you just teleported in and out?"

"Yes, but it was a little more complicated than that. In order to connect one place to the other, you need a unit on each end. We mailed a sample cleaning agent to your office with a locator beacon inside. Once it was stored with the cleaning supplies, I teleported there and added a bar of soap to the stack of soap boxes."

"The bar of soap had another beacon in it, I suppose?"

"Yes. I was told exactly where in the stack to place it so that it would eventually wind up in your bathroom. Then I took the cleaning agent with me and teleported back here."

"The FBI wondered what happened to the soap. You took it with you when we teleported to here."

Wyatt's face reddened, "I screwed up. I had brought another bar of soap with me and I was supposed to leave it in the dish. Once we left, I couldn't go back, of course. If Hazel were normal, he would've reamed me a new one, you know what I mean?"

"I know what you mean by not normal. I also know what you mean about there being no dark side. Everyone here is ... is ..." Allen was clearly fumbling for the appropriate words, "Well, you know what I mean," he finished lamely.

"Yes," said Wyatt, "I really do." He sat back in his chair, "So what have you been up to? I understand that you can leave at any time, but that you've chosen to stay?"

"I can't pass up the opportunity. Hazel's made it clear that I can leave, but I might not be allowed to come back. Every day here has been one incredible revelation after another. My company's just unveiled our new distributed data integration model, and Hazel's showing me this repository that apparently can hold pretty much everything in a tiny crystal." He shook his head, "How can I turn my back on this?"

"Speaking of your company, aren't they going to miss you?"

"Not really. I think that the only one who would even care is Cassie."

"Who is Cassie?"

Allen smiled, "She's the best thing that ever happened to me."

"Ah, a woman enters the picture." Wyatt smiled, "I happen to know a lot about women."

"It's not like that. I was overwhelmed with the day-to-day operations of BHC and was no longer able to be creative. I hired her, ostensibly as my personal assistant, but for the last five years, she's been running the whole she-bang. I wish that I could let her know that I'm okay, but she's got the right stuff. She'll muddle through. She'll take care of things until I get back."

"Have you mentioned this to Hazel?" asked Wyatt. "I'm sure that he would allow you to get a message to her, somehow; something to let her know that you're okay. Why don't you ask him?"

Allen looked thoughtful, "I think I will. I would feel a lot better if I knew that she's no longer worried sick about me."

"Do you have any idea how long you will be away?"

"I don't know. I gave my word to Hazel that I'd try to find out what's wrong with their systems. So far, however, I'm only on page 2,000 of this 100,000 page instruction manual. I thought I knew a lot about technology, but now I find myself back in first grade again."

"Hang in there," said Wyatt. He stood up to leave, "I know that you'll find the answer that Hazel's looking for."

5342 BC - NW Persian Gulf Sea Floor

The next afternoon, they all eagerly gathered in the navigation room. Normally intended for only one person, they clustered tightly around Mirta who was seated in the reclining chair located in the center of the small cabin.

"Is everyone holding on to something?" asked Mirta. "This is a bit unsettling at first if you're not in the driver's seat."

"On with the show!" ordered Altair, cheerfully.

"Aye, aye, Cap'n," she replied as she moved her hand over the arm of the chair. The room faded from view and they found themselves standing on a flat plain that stretched off into the distance in every direction. As they looked around themselves, Lonni started laughing.

"What's so funny?" asked Tommi.

"I feel really silly crammed in here like bandas when I'm clearly standing out in the middle of nowhere." He laughed again, "This is really amazing, Mirta. It's just like really being there."

Ferta spoke up, "Where are all the people? Where is Mardu?"

"Somehow I just *knew* that you'd ask about Mardu," smiled Mirta, although she was no more visible to the others than they were to her. "I thought I'd start us out a hundred kilometers away to give you a feel for what this part of the planet normally looks like."

"It looks pretty barren, if you ask me," said Sparta. "I can't imagine trying to grow anything here, even if I *could* make it rain whenever I wanted it to."

"Hang onto to something and we'll go look for Mardu now," warned Mirta. A moment later they appeared to rise up from the ground a few hundred meters and then streaked eastward so quickly that the ground below them was literally a blur. There was a collective gasp from everyone but Mirta as they clutched her chair and each other. Before they could even catch their breath, they slowed to a stop, still several hundred meters up. Below and around them, they could see several square kilometers of farmland that was a haphazardly broken into individual areas. They began to move slowly toward one area in particular while angling downward.

As they neared their destination, Ferta exclaimed, "That's Mardu's tent! And there's Mardu!"

For the first time, they were afforded a view of Mardu and his surroundings that had not previously been possible from the vid-feed alone. Mirta manipulated the controls to apparently set them down on the ground near Mardu while they watched him hack the upper stalks of wheat free with his bone knife. As he cut the wheat, he placed it carefully on the ground until is was a sizable bundle, and then he wrapped a strip of animal hide around it and carried it back to his tent where he added it to the much larger pile that was accumulating. As he made his way back for the next batch, he saw Itok carrying a similar load on his way to the tent. He smiled and waved.

"That looks like an awful lot of work," commented Rolli.

"Not only that, but they're spending most of their time walking back and forth. If they worked together, they could rig a litter between them and easily carry five times as much each trip," pointed out Lonni.

"Well, they seem pretty happy to me," said Ferta. "I guess the other choice would have been no crops to harvest at all." She solemnly intoned, "Nammu has provided for them."

"Maybe Nammu should tell them how to lash some reeds together to carry more wheat each trip?" joked Lonni.

Ferta looked thoughtful, "That's not a bad idea." She smiled a Cheshire smile that no one else could see, "That's not a bad idea at all!"

"Is there any way that we can pipe this down to the entertainment room?" asked Altair. "I'm already getting a crick in my neck trying to see everything."

Mirta thought for a moment, "Routing the feed through the entertainment system isn't a problem, but I'm not so sure about the control interface. Why don't we take a quick break while I set that up. I'll stay here and drive while the rest of you make yourselves comfortable in the theater. I'll leave the comm channel open so that we can talk."

"Sounds good to me," said Ferta.

"Let's do it," said Altair. As the scene around them faded from view and the nav room re-appeared, they began leaving through the narrow doorway. "Let us know when we're ready to start."

"Will do, Cap'n."

+ + +

A short while later they were all sitting in the viewing chairs arranged in a circle in the center of the entertainment room. "This is more like it!" said Sparta as she settled into her favorite lounge chair.

Mirta's voice came over the sound system, "Is everyone all comfy now?"

"Any time you're ready," replied Altair.

The room slowly faded and they once again found themselves in the middle of the barren plain. "I thought that we'd start with a quick tour of the planet," said Mirta. As she spoke, the ground dropped rapidly out from under them. They appeared to rise quickly and the flat horizon around them slowly became a curve that grew more pronounced as they ascended. In only a few moments, they were able to see the entire planet beneath them.

"I had forgotten how big a planet really is!" commented Ferta.

"Me, too," chimed in Lonni.

Mirta's voice assumed a decidedly tour-guide tone, "Directly below us you can see the waterway where we splashed down." As they looked, a bright red dot appeared. "That's our current location. We are at the northernmost end of a narrow sea formed by the continental plates. As with most water planets, this one apparently started out as one big super-continent that broke apart and drifted to form the individual land masses." As she spoke, the planet began to slowly rotate beneath them. "As we move eastwards, you can see that the bulk of what's left of the super-continent is mostly in the northern hemisphere while a sizeable chunk of it drifted well to the south." They watched as the rotating planet below them traversed a large body of water and then more land came into view. "The next largest land group are two large continents that span almost the whole globe from north to south. It appears that these drifted westward until coming up against the eastward expansion of the super-continent." They continued to watch in fascination as they crossed another large body of water and then once again saw the area of the planet with their location indicated by the glowing red marker. "At the polar extremes, we have a large land mass at the southern pole and frozen sea-ice at the northern pole." The planet below them rotated quickly northward so that they could clearly see the white frozen wastes of the southern continent.

"I assume that's snow down there?" asked Tommi.

"Yes, similar to Shoomar, the normal temperature variation of this planet allows for all three phases of water vapor. The clouds, oceans and lakes, ice and snow are pretty much the same as on Shoomar. So are the land masses. Although totally different in distribution and appearance, they are otherwise remarkably similar to Shoomar with one notable exception."

"Which is?" prompted Sparta.

"This planet's axial tilt is nearly twenty degrees more than Shoomar's. This means that the temperature variation is more extreme than what we would normally experience. This results in severe summers and winters in some regions of the planet as well as violent weather formations caused by the large temperature differentials."

"How violent?" asked Altair, somewhat concerned.

"Let me show you," replied Mirta as the planet revolved rapidly toward the east. As they came to a stop over the western ocean, they appeared to drop down lower until they spotted the large swirl of clouds directly beneath them. "This is a storm that's several hundred kilometers across. It's so large that the sea-warmed air rising up is causing the winds to circle due to the coriolis effect. This circular impetus feeds on itself and the storm grows in strength." They appeared to descend lower into the very storm itself. All around them, they could see and hear the water blowing sideways with a roar as loud as that of one of the attitude thrusters. As they neared a small land mass, they could see the tall slender trees bent over in protest. Mirta raised her voice to be heard over the storm, "The effective wind velocity at this point is about 180 kilometers per hour at the outer edge of the storm. Toward the middle, of course, it drops off until the dead zone at the center of the formation." The noise quieted to almost nothing as they moved into the storm's eye.

"That's pretty incredible," commented Rolli.

"Isn't that like the storms they get on Quantus and Serebrus?" asked Lonni.

"Exactly like them," replied Mirta. "As a matter of fact, the history lesson of the planet I've been giving you is a composite of several planets with similar axial tilts and solar exposure. Quantus and Serebrus are two of the seventeen that have been linked to the simulator. Since we only just arrived, I obviously can't claim to know the exact history of this planet, but the nav system indicates that the composite is 99.7% accurate."

Sparta interrupted, "So what about the people? Mardu's tribe isn't the only one, is it?"

"No, it's not the only one, although they are biologically typical of the bi-pedal species that is spread around the planet. As we already knew from our initial scans while still in orbit, they have clustered in small groups around various sources of water and, depending on their location, have developed limited tools from the various natural resources at their disposal. They are about as primitive as a species can get and still be considered intelligent on the Tantry Scale. Mardu's tribe, for example, uses mostly animal bone for their knives, animal skins for their clothing, tents, and thongs, and woven reeds for their baskets and sandals." As she spoke, they appeared to rise up from the storm cloud and move to the north-west where they slowly descended toward the mouth of a large river. "Here we have tribes that use stone for their utensils and knives, animal skins and wood for almost everything else, and woven plaits of grassy plants to make rope." The scene changed again as they rose up and quickly traversed the continent to the south-west. "Given the abundance of stone here, it's no surprise that the tribes use it for their dwellings along with their utensils. Without the splintery rock available to the last tribe, however, these use bone knives much as Mardu's tribe." Mirta's voice shifted from tour guide to her own for a moment, "All of these parallel the current development of other species on thousands of other planets as well what we ourselves were once like on Shoomar tens of millions of years ago."

"When we first landed, didn't you indicate that it'll be forty thousand more years or so before these people get their act together?" asked Altair.

"Yes, but that was based on the limited information that we had at the time." Mirta paused before somberly continuing, "I hate to be the bearer of bad news, especially since we've grown so attached to Mardu and his tribe, but I've run the simulations several times and it's not good."

"Define 'not good'," said Altair.

"According to the nav system's projections, they'll all be gone in less than a thousand years." She tried unsuccessfully to keep her voice from quavering slightly, "Every last one of them."

Five Months Ago - Mount Ararat, Turkey

Allen shook his head, "Why doesn't it ever fill up?"

He was sitting in the console room with Minerva who was trying to explain how the information was stored in the Chaos Machine. Allen had mastered the basic interface and had satisfied himself that he understood how most of it worked. But now he was trying to understand the mechanics behind the system and had wandered into a wholly different world. In front of them, about a half-meter above the console, floated a dully glinting sphere. It was clearly opaque, but had a shimmering luster about it that made it appear vaguely out-of-focus. Although they were only looking at a projection, Allen was assured that the real quadro-trilithium crystal at the heart of the machine looked no different.

"You indicated that you understood the nature of the synchronized singularities when we initially studied this," said Minerva.

"Yes, I did. I understand that the singularities in the crystal are attuned somehow to the ones making up the Earth and everything on it. I also understand how the singularities in the crystal can be read-out real-time to display the virtual mirrors of what the Earth singularities are doing. But there's a finite number of singularities in the crystal, right?"

"Well, yes," agreed Minerva, "but only in a volumetric sense. Remember that there's only one singularity to begin with."

"That's the part I'm struggling with, I guess. How can there only be one of them and yet they make up the crystal?"

"I think I see where you're going off track. I don't think that I explained that the entire universe is made up of just the one singularity. It is everywhere in everything, including the crystal, because it literally *is* everything. All matter, as we know it, is the result of the composite interactions of the nodal manifestations of the singularity." She paused a moment before continuing, "We live a very sheltered life here. I sometimes forget how primitive the state of knowledge is in the outside world. I skimmed through some of the current physics papers to get a feel for how little you know about matter in general." She looked at Allen with sincerity, "You're just going to have to trust me on this."

"I'm no physicist, but it was my minor in college and I was able to work through the math in quantum physics. Of course, the books I learned from have mostly been proven wrong or misguided, but I think I can understand it if I keep at it. You're so patient with me, Minerva!"

Allen smiled and leaned back in the chair, clasping his hands behind his neck, "Fire away."

"If I didn't think you could understand it, I wouldn't waste your time." Minerva smiled back at Allen, "Hazel wants to make sure that all your questions are answered completely. He said to hold nothing back." She touched the controls on the console and brought up one of the simulacrums from the manual, "What we loosely call a singularity is conceptually what you might think of as a point or locus in space. It has no length, width, or depth. No dimensionality whatever."

"Check."

"So how many singularities can fit in a small volume, a pea perhaps?"

"How many angels can dance on the head of a pin?"

Minerva frowned, "I don't think I understand your question."

"Never mind," replied Allen. "An infinite number can fit in a pea."

"And how many can fit in something much smaller, like a grain of salt?"

"Still an infinite number." Allen grinned impishly, "But they're much closer together."

Minerva ignored him and continued, "So how many would fit in a singularity?"

Allen thought for a moment. For a brief instant he felt he could see what she was driving at and then the thought eluded him. "While the singularity has no volume, it can still contain an infinite number of singularities within itself."

"Exactly, only now they are crowded in so close together that they are indistinguishable from only one singularity."

"But if there's no volume, then they're not really contained, are they?" Allen frowned and rubbed his temples, "On the other hand, if they have no dimensionality, no volume is required." He looked at Minerva, "And if they have no volume they have no mass, either."

"Now you're getting it. If you can conceive of an infinite number of singularities contained in a single singularity, it becomes a little easier to understand the next part. While our math works out for an infinite number, it also holds true for a finite number. This suits our needs very well because there is a finite number of singularities comprising all of space-time and the equations are readily solvable for finite values."

"Okay, I think I'm with you so far, but I'm not sure where this is going."

"Consider what is commonly called The Big Bang. Just prior to that first moment, all the singularities in the universe were contained within themselves. Itself. And then something happened. They were suddenly allowed to spread outwards from the central locus. This spreading out, if you will, is what we perceive as matter. The movement of the singularities in relation to all the other singularities determines our perception of them. Some of them are neutrons, protons, and electrons making up atoms while others are photons, quarks, and dark matter and such. The singularities themselves have no size or mass, but their interactions produce a unified field that changes in quantum steps."

"I'm assuming this is not the same quantum theory I learned?" Allen asked.

"No, but it's similar in the sense that a singularity has one state at one moment and a different state in the next moment." She anticipated Allen's question, "A moment is defined as a very short period of time. Very, *very* short in this case." She continued, "So, moment by moment, the singularities throughout the universe change state in lock-step with each other. They are able to do this because they are simply different states of one singularity and merely appear as many."

"So the state of a particular singularity, or the apparent manifestation of one, determines what it is?"

"In a nutshell, yes. The real key is in understanding the relationships and how to manipulate them between moments. The food processor, for example. You take a fresh cheeseburger and store the states of its singularities in a template. Then you take a source volume of necessary atoms and rearrange their states to match those of the template. Swapping states between source and destination requires no energy. Moving them a short distance requires only a little bit. However, changing their state from one to another may require enormous amounts of energy or supply it in return. State-wise, everything balances everywhere throughout the universe."

"I think I follow you, so far. But I'm not sure what you meant by manipulating them between moments."

Minerva replied, "When the singularity changes states, there is an instant where it's in no state at all. Without outside influence, it will normally become the same state again the next moment. It is during this instant that you can influence the state it next assumes. Changing the state of the singularities in an aluminum atom so that it becomes a gold atom is possible, but this requires an immense amount of energy plus the addition of a lot more singularities. Changing the states of gold to aluminum, however, yields up energy and provides a source of singularities."

"So you make food and energy from raw materials. And, if I understand you correctly, as long as your state conversions run downhill, the energy output can be used to push some of them uphill where necessary."

"If by uphill and downhill you are referring to net energy input and output, then you are exactly correct."

"And the singularities in the quadro-trilithium crystal are in lock-step with all the singularities in the Earth?"

"Yes," replied Minerva, "and don't forget that the spherical boundary extends somewhat beyond the asteroid belt as well."

"But there's more singularities in our solar system than could possibly be in that crystal!"

"They are the same in number, but as you pointed out earlier, they are packed much closer together. After all, they have no volume."

"Then why doesn't the crystal weigh as much?"

"Due to the unique properties of the crystal lattice, they interact in such a way as to cancel each other out. The crystal has volume, but no mass, as we know it. It sits suspended in a force field to keep it stabilized."

"But there's still a finite number of singularities, yes?"

"Yes."

Allen shook his head, "Then, why doesn't it ever fill up?"

Five Months Ago - San Francisco, California

Cassie slowly stirred in her bed. Her head felt like it was twice as big as normal and it hurt like hell. She tried to go back to sleep, but her guilty conscience was nagging at her to get up. She sat up slowly and waited for the bright flashes to settle down a little before she got out of bed and staggered into the bathroom. She opened the medicine cabinet and fumbled at the bottle of ibuprofen. She squinted at the alignment marks on the container as she cursed the makers of child-proof caps. She finally managed to get the cap off and gulped down two of the pills. After finishing her mental tirade of the pharmaceutical companies, she next started in on herself. It was Saturday, but she had things that needed to be done. She had only meant to have one glass of wine before going to sleep, but she had somehow managed to polish off the whole bottle before staggering up the stairs and collapsing in her bed. She rarely drank alcohol and then only a glass of wine or champagne when socially required. She didn't like the feeling of losing control of herself and had only been truly drunk one other time in her life. She shook her head and grimaced with pain. Damn him, she thought. Where is he and what's happened to him? She had filled a small glass of wine in a toast to Allen in celebration of the new product launch. Orders were already coming in faster than they could ramp up to meet them. However, as she raised her glass to Allen, wherever he was, she thought back over the past five years and all the fun they'd had together. Well, reflected Cassie, at least it was fun from her perspective. She had downed the glass and refilled it as she started crying, finally letting go of the pent up feelings that had been steadily building for the past month. It wasn't like she was actually in love with Allen, but it was as if they were two halves of a whole. A whole that had functioned as a single entity with regards to the company and its corporate expansion. A melding of two minds that each complemented the other by filling in the deficiencies of the other half. Where Allen procrastinated, Cassie pushed forward. Where Cassie wavered, Allen's logic persevered. And then suddenly, Allen was gone. It didn't help much that the FBI had formally suspended the investigation into Allen's disappearance. Cassie didn't blame them for that. When she had reviewed the security tapes immediately following Allen's sudden vanishing act, she had already concluded that he wouldn't easily be found. But what were the possible explanations? Alien abduction? Spontaneous combustion? A portal to another dimension? Wherever he went, Cassie hoped fervently that he was okay. As long as she believed that he was still alive, she could continue to nurse the hope that she would one day see him again. She shook her head gingerly as she admonished herself for being so maudlin. She didn't have time for this. She swore that never again would she have more than a token glass of wine when necessary. She turned on the shower and waited until the water was good and hot. Stripping off her pajamas, she stepped into the spray and simply stood there for a good five minutes until her head and body felt marginally better. By the time she had finished washing herself and shampooing her hair, the ibuprofen had kicked in and she was feeling more like herself again. As she turned off the water and stepped from the shower, she was already planning the day she had ahead of her.

+ + +

Two hours later, she was finishing up her weekly status report for the Board. The second production line would be ready in another two weeks and they were running three shifts on the current one. While they were experiencing a two-month backlog in filling orders, the second line would allow them to be completely caught up by the end of its first week of operation. Having more orders than they could fill was a problem Cassie relished solving. She put her computer to sleep and went into the kitchen to refill her coffee mug. She filled her cup and set it down on the table as she went outside to see if the mail had arrived. She returned to the kitchen and sat down at the table to go through the rather large stack of bills and catalogs. She must be on every mailing list in the world, she mused wryly. Why she continued to get enough catalogs to decimate a small forest was beyond her. She did almost everything on-line and idly wondered how much energy could be saved if everyone quit sending junk mail printed on paper. Of course, if they actually did that, they would have to shut down entire armies of people in the layout, type-setting, and printing business as well as lay off maybe half of the Postal Service, and then where would we be? As she was sorting through the envelopes and setting aside those that actually warranted attention, she was startled to see one that bore only her name on the front written in what looked like's Allen's illegible scrawl. She turned it over and back several times as her mind raced through the possibilities. Lacking a postage stamp and address, it had obviously been placed in her mailbox by someone, maybe even by Allen himself. She stared at her name analytically and concluded that if it wasn't Allen's handwriting, it was written by someone who could successfully imitate it. She paused for a moment considering whether or not she should open it herself or turn it over to the FBI untouched. By opening it, she may be destroying any forensic evidence that might help to find Allen. On the other hand, if it really was from Allen, he was probably counting on her to open it herself. It took less than five seconds from the moment she first saw the envelope to arrive at her decision. She grabbed the letter opener from its holder in the center of the table and carefully slit open the flap. Inside, she found a single sheet of paper folded neatly in thirds. She held her breath as she unfolded it to reveal several paragraphs in what could only be Allen's handwriting. He's alive! she thought excitedly. She was no expert, but she could tell at a glance that this was no different than any of the hundreds of handwritten memos Allen had left on her desk over the years. She realized she was still holding her breath and let it out slowly as she smoothed the page down flat on the table and began deciphering it.

Hi Sunshine!

I've finally been allowed to break radio silence long enough to let you know that I'm alive and well. You must tell no one that you received this and destroy it when you are done wading through my chicken scratch. The short version is that I've been called away on a secret mission and will be gone until I finish my assignment.

I wish I could fill you in on more of what's happening, but the folks here have one heck of a non-disclosure agreement. I know this sounds a little melodramatic and all, but when I'm done, I'll be able to fill you in on all the gory details, including my new magic trick of being able to disappear into thin air.

I'm counting on you to keep running the ship until I get back. I've been eagerly following the new product launch and you're doing a fantastic job (as usual).

Keep up the good work!

PS: Burn this letter when you're done ... and don't forget to stir the ashes!

Cassie read the letter through several times until she had it committed to memory. It could be from no one else but Allen. She got up and walked over to the sink where she lit the envelope and letter with one of the large kitchen matches and watched as it slowly curled up and turned black. She turned on the exhaust fan and then waited until every little scrap was consumed, poking at it occasionally with the letter opener until there was only ash. She rinsed the remains down the drain and went back to the table where she sat back down and picked up her coffee mug. He's alive! she thought again. As she took a sip of the hot brew, she smiled and stared off into space, wondering where he was and what he was doing. Secret mission, radio silence, and his new "magic trick." Allen was fond of saying that sufficiently advanced technology was indistinguishable from magic and she knew that this was his way of telling her there was a logical explanation for his disappearance. Maybe "alien abduction" wasn't as wild of a guess as she had thought. She smiled to herself as she finished her coffee. Wherever he was, she hoped that Allen was having fun.

Four-and-One-Half Months Ago - Mount Ararat, Turkey

Allen sat nervously in the Council Room. Up until this point, he had dealt directly with Hazel and had never met the other Council members. Now he had been asked to present a progress report to the full Council and he was trying to ignore the queasy feeling in his stomach. Relax, he told himself. It won't be so bad. After all, he had given a preliminary report to Hazel the day before and it had been well received. As he went down the several items listed on the tablet in front of him, he thought back over what he had learned in the past six weeks.

It had only taken him two weeks to become proficient at operating the Chaos Machine in view-only mode. He could jump to any point on the planet and orient himself to any position with a few deft manipulations of the console. As he had experimented with the viewer, however, he had found himself irresistibly drawn into a frame of mind that bordered on pure voyeurism. At first he merely went to various places around the globe that he had always wanted to visit, but had never had the chance to do so. He "strolled" through Moscow Square and "lounged" on the beach in Tahiti. He "snorkeled" the Great Reef and "sky dived" from a thousand miles up into Mauna Loa's active volcano. He had been to the center of the Earth and ventured out beyond Mars and "swam" among the asteroids. He "sun-dived" into the Sun itself and back out the other side nearly a million miles away. He "attended" intelligence briefings in the Oval Office as well as the Kremlin and the Zong Tong Fu. Allen was simultaneously overwhelmed with the veritable tsunami of new information and yet could comprehend almost none of it because of its vast scope. When (or if) he had the proper time, he promised himself he would come back and systematically explore the solar system with this incredible tool. Not that he could ever share the results with anyone. Nor would it matter if he couldn't figure out how to avert the alleged End of the World.

By the time the novelty had worn off, he was quite proficient with the controls and turned in idle curiosity to what his competition was doing. He "sat in" on the board meetings of several of them and gloated as he heard them scrambling to come up with something to either latch onto his product or pre-empt it with something better. It was at one of these meetings that he became intrigued with an incredibly sexy vice-president. When she got up to leave at the end of the meeting, he touched the controls without even thinking. Before he knew what was happening, he had "followed" her to a local bar while she had a quick drink with some of her co-workers. When she left the bar, he had "followed" her home and watched in fascination as she undressed and took a long shower and then donned a pair of lacy panties and a baby-doll top. It wasn't until she had climbed into bed and turned off the light that he had finally come to his senses. He had never done anything like this before and he was horribly ashamed of his behavior. With a start, he realized that this was only the culmination of nearly a week of doing nothing but looking at things. Since he had started experimenting with the console in this fashion, he had done absolutely nothing else productive. Whatever he hoped to accomplish had been thoroughly sidetracked by the overpowering experience. How would Cassie feel if she knew what he was doing? She had always understood the need for testing the equipment, but she would eventually chastise him when he took longer than necessary. The thought suddenly put everything into focus with his usual clarity of mind. He began to understand why Hazel and company didn't want to share some of this technology with the rest of the world. They were already living in a goldfish bowl, but an individual's right to privacy should somehow be safe-guarded. By recognizing the drug-like pull of this ultimate voyeuristic device, he had since been able to resist it and had once again been able to focus on the task at hand.

He had next experimented with the forecast-mode and had spent a week projecting the next few day's events and then following up on them with the many news feeds that Hazel had available. Still curious about the predicted cataclysm one year hence, Allen advanced the timeline to that point and then paused everything at a point the day before the Earth exploded. He wanted to see what caused such a massive upheaval. However, when he "drilled" down into the ground near the origin of the explosion, he encountered a spherical void that began about 150 feet below the surface. By experimentally crisscrossing the featureless volume, he determined that it was roughly 2,000 feet in diameter. By carefully advancing along the timeline, he watched as the void shrank to a point and then swelled again until the entire planet was engulfed and vaporized. Resetting the timeline back to the present showed that the same void existed now, but still shed no enlightenment as to what it might be. Some kind of doomsday device, apparently, but placed there by whom? And when? Allen became even more curious when he encountered a second void. He discovered that another one also surrounded the region underneath Mt. Ararat itself when he went looking to find himself. It was far smaller, but contained the same empty noneness that the other void offered. He made a mental note to ask Hazeltine about this as well as some of the other things he had queueing up on an FAQ list in his mind. Such as why he himself never showed up anywhere in the future timeline (except in a documentary that aired on the anniversary of his disappearance). When the world ended, Cassie was holding a press conference about BHC's latest product.

He was still struggling with the technical explanation of the system itself and had been assigned a technician to answer his questions. Her name was Minerva and she had been very patient with him. She had explained the basic concept of the singularity synchronization over and over in many different ways until Allen had finally grasped the concept. He first had to learn some new physics, however, before it finally made sense. He was continually amazed at the sophistication of Hazel's organization and the peculiar way that everyone behaved. While they never seemed to hurry or rush for any reason, they never appeared to stop working either. It was like they were part of some vast machine and everyone cheerfully focused on their work. Hazel explained that it was due to everyone not lacking for anything and their knack of finding the right job for the right person. Everywhere he went, Allen was greeted with a smile as people passed by. If he stopped someone to ask a question, they would patiently answer him or take him to someone who could. He couldn't quite put his finger on it, but it was like he was living with a group of children who were wise beyond their years.

He was slowly working his way through the instruction manual for the Chaos Machine. He still hadn't quite mastered the art of making minor changes to the input and analyzing the extrapolated effect of the changes, but he understood the process enough to move on to the history-view mode. It was here that he encountered his first true roadblock. No matter what he did, he couldn't get any of the functions to work. When he had finally given up and asked for help, Minerva had explained that his access was limited to only the present forward. He had asked Hazel how he was supposed to analyze their system if he couldn't use all of the functionality and was told that he would have to have the permission of the full Council to do so. It was at that point that Hazel set up the meeting that would occur in just a few moments.

Allen's reverie was interrupted as the door to the Council Chambers opened. He stood up as Hazeltine walked in followed by six others that Allen had never seen before. Three of them were women and the other three were men. They walked to the semi-circular dais that faced Allen and took their seats. Allen couldn't help but notice that the three women were quite pretty and they all shared the same similar fair-skinned bodies and blond hair. The three men shared the same hair and body coloration, but each of them sported a short beard as well. He guessed their ages to be from thirty to forty-five years old. Allen sat down as Hazeltine called the meeting to order. Skipping any introductions, he asked Allen to present what he had accomplished in the last six weeks. Allen faltered a little as he began, but he quickly recovered and presented his progress report beginning with his initial contact with the Chaos Machine and ending with his request to be allowed access to the history-view mode. He sat back and waited as a quiet discussion ensued among the seven Council members. Although he could barely hear their words, he couldn't quite make out what they were saying. The few snatches he could hear didn't make any sense and he belatedly concluded that they were speaking in some language that he didn't understand. After only a few minutes, Hazel turned to address Allen again.

"The Council has agreed to give you access to the last five hundred years so that you can see first-hand what changes had been made during that time."

"I don't think I understand," said Allen.

"Once you start exploring the past and follow some of the bookmarks, it will become self-evident. If you need assistance, Minerva will be able to answer any questions you might have." Hazel paused a moment before continuing, "Is there anything else you require of the Council?"

Allen looked from one member of the Council to the next before replying, "Actually, sir, there is." Allen glanced down at his notes and then raised his gaze back to Hazel. "Five hundred years is not enough. Your Chaos Machine has a specific beginning when it first began enfolding data into the repository. I want full access all the way back to the start of the epoch. Without that access, I'm afraid I can't help you." Allen held eye contact with Hazel and said, "But you already know this."

Hazeltine allowed a brief smile to form before turning it into a pained grimace, "Yes, I do. But I can't convince the Council. Either we all agree or nothing happens."

"Well, then, maybe you should try a little harder to convince them." Allen sat back in his chair and folded his arms across his chest. "Take your time, Hazel."

The elderly man sighed and spoke quietly to the other members of the Council. As before, Allen caught snatches of the conversation, but understood none of what he heard. A lot of it involved someone pointing at him and going on at length. Then someone else would point at him and apparently answer back. Finally, one of the women held up her hands until everyone was quiet. She looked at Allen and then turned to the others and said something at length. By the time she was done, everyone was nodding their heads at her words. When she finally stopped, Hazel turned to Allen and said, "The access you request will be granted. With it comes our request that you understand it is only because Ferta here has taken a liking to you. She has convinced everyone that you have shown yourself to be a trustworthy person and we might as well go all-in. Please don't let her down," Hazel beseeched him, "She doesn't take rejection well."

"I understand and I give you my word that I am only trying to solve your problem," Allen replied. "And save the planet as well, of course."

Hazel beamed, "Of course! We are pleased at how quickly you have ramped up to speed and we are all in agreement that bringing you on board has been the right thing to do." Hazel looked around the room before facing Allen again, "Thank you for your time here today, Allen."

It was clear that Allen was being dismissed and so he stood up, gathered his tablet and notes together, and left the room. After the door had closed behind him, Hazel addressed the rest of the Council, "I know that he's an outsider, but I don't think we have any choice but to let him proceed." There were nods of agreement from the other six members. "We can only hope that he can find the error in our ways."

"If there is one," replied the woman closest to Hazel.

"Yes, Ferta, if there is one," said Hazeltine solemnly. "Meeting adjourned."

5342 BC - NW Persian Gulf Delta

"Mardu, wake up."

Mardu woke up quickly at the sound of Nammu's voice. He had grown accustomed to her visits in the night when only he could hear her. "Yes, Nammu, how can I serve you?"

"I want you and Itok to remain here for the summer. I have much for you to do."

Mardu and his brother had packed up everything they owned except for the tent itself. Tomorrow, they would fasten the bundles to the oxen and goats and begin their annual trek north for the summer. "But we will die from the heat, Nammu! No one survives the summer here!"

"Do you not trust me, Mardu?"

Mardu was silent for a moment. Then he said slowly, "I have pledged myself to your service and agreed to obey your commands. I will gladly stay behind, but I cannot speak for Itok."

"Have you told Itok that I speak to you?"

"No, Nammu, you told me to tell no one and I have obeyed."

"Go and wake him now. Tell him Nammu wants to speak with him."

Mardu hesitated and then went over to Itok's sleeping form. "Itok, wake up!" he said as he shook him gently.

"What is it, Mardu? What do you want?"

"Nammu wants to speak to you."

"What? What are you talking about?"

"Nammu wants to speak to you," he said again as he held the meme out to Itok.

"Hello, Itok," emanated the voice from the small cube. "It is I, Nammu. Up to now, I have only revealed myself to Mardu until I knew that I could have your trust as well."

Itok sat up and stared at the meme in Mardu's hand. "Nammu," he stammered out, "Is it really you?"

"Yes, Itok. I who came from the sea and brought you the rain. Mardu has proven himself worthy of my attention. Are you willing to be my servant and obey my commands as well?"

Itok was stunned. He didn't know what to say. He hadn't really believed that Mardu was getting his visions directly from Nammu. "If you are my goddess, how can I refuse such a request?"

"I want you and Mardu to remain behind this summer. I need your assistance with many things that need to be done."

"But we will surely die!" said Itok, reflecting his brother's earlier reaction. Everyone knew that the summer brought great heat and no rain and that was why they made the trek north each year where is was cooler and plentiful rain provided for the summer crops.

"You must trust me," came the reply. "I will provide for you and you will not die. But you must be willing to work hard and do as I say."

Itok looked at Mardu who simply shrugged. He wanted to say no to Nammu's request, but was she not, in fact, a goddess? How could he deny her request after she had clearly brought the rain and given them the best bounty ever. "I will stay with Mardu. We will do whatever you ask of us."

"I am pleased. You must not tell anyone that I have ordered this, but you may tell them that you will see them again when they return. Collect any belongings that they may be leaving behind and tell them you will keep them safe while they're gone."

"Yes, Nammu!" said Mardu and Itok in unison.

+ + +

Later that morning, Mardu and Itok bid their friends farewell. They assured the others that they would be okay, but they were met with skeptical looks. None of them appeared to believe that they would ever see them again. Naim had almost cheerfully assured them that he would see to it that they would get a decent burial ceremony when they returned. On that note, the nomadic tribes-people began their weeks-long walk to their northern home in the mountains. Itok and Mardu watched for a long time until even the dust cloud they were raising had disappeared.

"So what now, Mardu?"

"I don't know. I guess we wait for Nammu to tell us what to do."

"I'll fix us some lunch while we wait."

Mardu didn't reply. He was thinking about Nammu and hoped that she knew what she was doing. He shook his head slowly and went to help Itok with the fire.

+ + +

"What do you think?" asked Ferta. She was wearing a loose robe made from one of the bed sheets that she had wrapped around her such that it swirled when she moved. Underneath, on a belt strapped around her waist, she wore a force field generator that Lonni had removed from one of the EV suits. He had modified it so that it cast a shimmering blue aura around her. "Do I look like a goddess should look?" She was facing the rest of the crew as she pranced back and forth in front of them.

"Looks good to me," said Altair. "I'm still against having physical contact with these people, but if you insist on meeting them, I have to admit that you certainly look the part."

"I agree," said Mirta. "I think that her light-colored skin and fair hair will help accentuate the fact that we're not like them."

"So Ferta's going to be Nammu and Lonni's going to be Enki," said Rolli, "I keep forgetting who I'm supposed to be."

Ferta sighed, "You're supposed to be Enkimdu, the god of irrigation."

"I knew that," smiled Rolli.

"Now all we have to do is get you guys in costume and we're ready to go meet our people." Ferta looked at Lonni and Rolli anxiously, "Are you sure you know your lines?"

"Yes, Ferta. Relax. This is going to fun," said Rolli. They both grinned at her.

The week before, Lonni had made another night-time trip to the shore after Mirta made sure in advance that no one was around. He had added some repo-putty to one of the spare transporter beacons and shaped it until it looked like one of the native rocks. He had then used the molecular spray to give it the appearance of stone. He had left the beacon in an outcropping of rock that obscured the view from all sides but that which faced the water. Since he had not been transported there in the first place, he had to make the swim back to the ship for what he hoped was the last time. Once he was back on board, Altair himself had teleported to the shore and back to test the setup. Since then, everyone had been allowed to have an hour's excursion along the banks, but only at night and always well away from the settlement. Mirta, of course, kept a lookout using the modified nav system and was prepared to alert them at the first hint that anyone might be headed their way. They all agreed that the fresh sea air was quite invigorating after spending nearly a year breathing re-circ. After much debate, they had finally decided that they needed to teach Mardu and his people how to do things more efficiently. The projections Mirta kept running all concluded with a gradually dwindling food supply and the eventual dying out of Mardu's species. If these people had any hope of surviving, they had to alter their way of life before it was too late.

Along these lines, Mirta had pulled up several parallel planets and compared their development with this one. She had identified at least eight types of plants that were likely useful in many different ways as well as best practices of animal husbandry and breeding. If they could teach them how to better utilize what they had, they would be more likely to sustain their population. They were all appalled at how little these people knew about even the most basic mechanical processes.

The two men donned their make-shift garb and field generators. After promising Altair that they would stick to the script he had approved, they entered the lift together. "Shore!" spoke Ferta and they blinked their eyes in the bright sunlight as they suddenly appeared on the rocky shore two meters from the beacon.

"Rolli," chastised Ferta, "You forgot to turn on your aura!"

"Oops, sorry about that." He fumbled at the switch through his robe, "There, does that look any better?"

"Much." Ferta started off toward Mardu's tent, "Walk slowly, with dignity. Remember that we're gods and these are our people. We want them to see us coming from the distance." She tapped her comlink, "Mirta? Can you patch me through to Mardu now?"

"Sure," came the reply. "You're live in three ... two ... one ...."

+ + +

"Mardu!"

Mardu jumped at the sound of Nammu's voice. He picked up the meme and held it out so that Itok could hear as well. "I am coming to meet you and Itok. I am bringing my two sons with me as well. Be not afraid."

"I am not afraid," said Mardu bravely.

"I am not afraid, either," allowed Itok.

"Look toward the sea and you will see us approaching. Wait there for us and we will join you."

Both Mardu and Itok ran from their tent and looked toward the sea. They saw three glowing figures walking slowly towards them. As they gradually drew nearer, Mardu and his brother could make them out more clearly. They were clothed in white to the ground and looked as if they may be floating, so smooth was their movement toward them. Their faces were almost as white as their clothing and their hair was the color of the sun. Itok bent down and bowed his head with his arms outstretched while

Mardu continued to stare. The three shimmering figures stopped only a few steps away.

"Hello, Mardu" came Nammu's voice from the cube, but the words that came from Nammu had a different sound. "I speak the language of the gods and my meme speaks to you so that you will understand." She pointed to Lonni standing on her left, "This is my son, Enki." She turned and pointed to Rolli, "And this is my other son, Enkimdu."

Mardu threw himself fully prostrate along-side his brother. He had grown comfortable talking to Nammu, but here was Enki! And his brother as well!

"Rise up, Mardu and Itok!" Mardu and Itok slowly did so, although it was obvious that they were somewhat afraid.

"What is it you wish, oh great Nammu?" asked Mardu.

"We are going to build a city surrounded by farmlands and irrigation systems and we need your help. Enki will help to build the main temple that will be at the heart of the city and Enkimdu will help dig the canals and ditches to bring the river to your crops. Around the city we will build a wall to keep the river away when it floods." Nammu smiled at the two brothers, "This is why I have asked you to stay behind. When the rest of your people return, you will have a place for them to live and a means to grow crops all year 'round. No more traveling to the north and back. You will have a permanent home that will provide everything you need and more."

Itok's mouth fell open while Mardu collapsed at his side.

"Oh, dear," said Ferta.

"I don't think that you're quite getting through to them," giggled Mirta's voice in her ear.

Four Months Ago - San Francisco, California

Special Agent Vivian Williams was seated behind her desk in her office. Sitting in the two chairs facing her from across the glass surface were field agents Sam Peterson and Terrye Sanders. They were concluding the weekly status report on their on-going sting operation.

"So you really think this is it? By the week's end you'll close the net?" asked Vivian.

"I know that's what we said last week, but as you already know, the delivery guy called in sick and so we simply shifted the op to this week," replied Agent Peterson.

Agent Sanders chimed in, "And we've already confirmed that he's feeling better and plans to be on the job Thursday."

"Very good," smiled Vivian. "Call me if anything changes."

"Yes, ma'am," uttered the two agents as they stood up and quickly left the room.

Vivian smiled at them as they left. They were good agents, but a little optimistic at times. She sighed as she thought of how each time they had tried to conclude the affair, one little random thing would trip them up. It's chaos, she thought, just a random pattern in a broader pattern within a broader pattern, ad infinitem. She shook her head and made a final note in the file in front of her. She then closed it and moved it to the top of the larger of two stacks of folders on her otherwise sparsely covered desktop. The other stack now consisted of only one file and she wearily dragged it in front of her and opened it. She scanned the front sheet for the thousandth time, frowning as she did so.

"Where are you, Allen Brookstone?" she asked out loud. Since day one, more than ten thousand man-hours had been spent looking for additional clues to his disappearance and whereabouts, but not one useful item had turned up. Nothing. Nada. Zip. He simply walked into his bathroom and disappeared off the face of the planet.

The phone buzzed and startled her from her musings. She glanced at the incoming ID and groaned. After two more buzzes she picked it up and spoke in her best secretarial voice, "FBI Regional Headquarters, San Francisco, how may I direct your call?"

"Very funny," came the reply.

"I'm sorry, sir, we don't have anyone or any department by that name. Can you be more specific?"

The voice on the other end gave a quick chuckle, "Okay, okay, you don't want to talk to me because you don't have any news about Allen Brookstone."

"You're very perceptive, sir," answered Vivian. "And your timing is flawless as well. I am reviewing the case even as we speak."

"I was actually calling for two reasons. You're the best person I know for this job and if you aren't making any progress, then there isn't any to be made."

"But ....," Vivian let her voice trail off.

"But, I thought that maybe some fresh insight might help. Two weeks ago, I authorized the release of a copy of the video files taken from BHC's security system to the NSA. They, in turn, passed along a copy to the folks at Area 51, who are very much interested in your case."

Vivian was furious to learn that he had gone behind her back without even a courtesy call, but she calmly replied with feigned relief in her voice, "So I can turn this cold case over to them now and get on with my life?"

"Not exactly," came the reply. "I, myself, don't know exactly who's been brought in on this. The Chief himself wants answers and things are happening in other channels outside the FBI. The consensus is that you did everything perfectly by the book and whatever's been done or worked on outside your office has produced nothing of value."

"So basically, you called to tell me that your lack of faith in my abilities resulted in parallel inquiries that resulted in restoring your faith in my abilities?" Vivian laughed sincerely, "That's why I never married you, you old codger. You could never really trust me and that is the only thing I require in a man."

"'Trust No One', that's my motto alright," he said, somewhat ruefully. "Okay, maybe I deserved that, but my hands were tied. I was specifically instructed to keep you in the dark by my boss. I told you he wants answers." He cleared his throat before going on, "I called to set up a meeting between you and some Air Force Colonel from Area 51 who's very anxious to meet with you and Cassie Stevens."

"Are you serious?" asked Vivian, but she was already bringing up her calendar on the monitor to her left. "If they leave early in the morning, they can easily be here by tomorrow afternoon. How about 3:00 PM?"

"Maybe I should check my Faith-O-Meter again. The Air Force does not drive to San Francisco, Vivian. Less than an hour ago, Cassie Stevens granted them permission to land one of their VTOLs on the roof of the Brookstone Building at 2:00 PM. She's hoping that you can attend as well. I confirmed your appointment with Miss Stevens for 1:30 PM since your calendar seems free this afternoon."

Vivian was really steamed, but she slowly counted to three and replied evenly, "Sounds good to me sir, I'll be there. To be perfectly honest, I don't have any more leads or avenues to explore. If this Colonel can possibly help turn up anything, I am truly appreciative."

"I know you are, Vivian, I told the Chief as much. He just wants the thing to go away before the media storm that's about to ensue."

"I'm surprised that it hasn't erupted yet. Rumors have been spreading like wildfire. It's impossible to prevent leaks when you have so many people working such a high-profile case. Someone tells their wife who tells her mom who tells her friends about the case her son-in-law's working. It's human nature, I guess."

"Well, the media has been cooperating only to the extent that they're not going to saturate the airwaves with anything until they have something more than un-substantiated rumors to go on. Which segues into the second reason I called. About a half hour ago, Cassie Stevens called the major broadcast and cable networks and announced a press conference to be held at 3:00 PM at the Brookstone Building."

"Our Cassie's been a busy little girl, it seems. Any idea what's up?"

"Not a clue. I'm hoping that you can find out more before the press conference in case we need a heads up. Which is why I took the liberty of confirming your appointment with her before talking to you. Miss Stevens is a very forceful woman and I found it difficult to say no."

"She called you?" asked Vivian, somewhat incredulously.

"My own private line, no less. We're still looking into how she obtained the number. The call itself was placed from her office."

Vivian smiled at the thought, "I'll give her your regards when I see her, sir." She slowly hung up the phone and looked thoughtful. "The game is once again afoot!" she said to no one in particular.

+ + +

Cassie fidgeted impatiently in front of the glass expanse in the lobby facing the parking lot. It was only 1:25 PM, but she was more than a little anxious to speak with her. She really liked Vivian on a personal level and felt guilty about yanking the rug out from under her. She wanted a chance to try and explain her actions in the hope that Vivian would understand and not hold it against her. She straightened up slightly and went into business mode again as she saw the Special Agent's black SUV pull into a parking slot. Vivian stepped out of the vehicle and then leaned back in to retrieve her briefcase. She closed the door and walked the short distance to the front door where Cassie was waiting to hold it open for her.

"Good afternoon, Miss Stevens, it's good to see you again," said Vivian, smiling and extending her hand.

Cassie shook the proffered hand firmly and said, "It's good to see you, too, Vivian. And please, call me Cassie." The door swished softly closed behind them as they crossed the lobby and strode toward the elevator bank.

"Very well, Cassie. I'm led to believe that I have you to thank for filling in my afternoon schedule for me?" Vivian smiled again, "I had hoped to swing by the cleaners and pick up my laundry. This is my last clean suit, you see."

Cassie wasn't quite sure what to make of this. The door to the elevator in front of them opened and two people exited. Cassie stepped in, and pushed the button for the second floor. She turned to Vivian as she entered and said, "I owe you an explanation and I wanted a chance to tell you in person before the Marines landed."

"The Air Force, actually. And I must admit that it would be nice to know what the hell is going on."

The elevator stopped and the doors opened into the cafeteria. Cassie waited for Vivian to exit first and then headed for the coffee bar. "C'mon, Vivian, let me treat you the best latte this side of Seattle."

As they placed their orders, Cassie remarked, "I don't remember if it was the Air Force or the Marines or the Army. I was never a war-monger and focused on the private corporate world. All I know is that we're meeting with Dr. Alex Montana, who's some sort of government physicist, and he's being flown here from parts unknown."

Vivian frowned, "That's interesting. I was told that we're meeting with Air Force Colonel Alex Montana. One of their brass."

They took their drinks to an isolated area of the cafeteria and sat at a small table facing each other. Vivian looked around at the handful of others in the room and commented, "I guess lunch hour's over, from the looks of it."

Cassie explained, "We don't really have hours here. We provide free food and drink to the employees any time of the day or night. The complete buffet menu rotates, but it always has an amazing selection of what is generally regarded as some of the best food in town."

"So I've heard," replied Vivian. She sat there and took her second sip of the latte and reflected that it was better than any she could remember. "I'm sorry, Cassie, but I came out here very angry with you and I hate to admit it, but this latte alone was worth the trip."

"I know you're angry. If I were in your place, I would be furious. And I'm afraid what's going to happen next would only make you angrier unless I have a chance to explain my recent actions."

"Go on, I'm listening and I'm setting aside my current prejudice to hear you out. But it better be good."

Cassie paused for a moment before speaking, "I've rehearsed this in my mind for some time now, but I'm still not sure where to start." She cleared her throat. "About a month ago, I received a letter from Allen telling me that he was okay and that I was not to tell anyone else, especially the FBI."

"Where's the letter?" asked Vivian.

"I burned it." Cassie raised her hands, "I know, I know, destruction of evidence in an open investigation. But if someone disappears of their own free will and lets the concerned parties know that they're okay, then why is the FBI involved? Where's your jurisdiction?"

Vivian stared at Cassie before smiling and then finally starting to laugh.

"What's so funny, Vivian?"

"You, Cassie, you are. I give up. I really do. In nearly thirty years of work for the FBI, you are singularly the most remarkable person I have ever encountered." She was trying to calm down, but this had been building ever since day one of this case. "And I can't even stay mad at you no matter what's going down at work. When I began my rather exhaustive check into your background, I kept comparing you to all the other executives, CEOs, and CFOs I've checked out before. And then I started reading about BHC and their financial track record before and after you came on board and was finally convinced to do something that is so out of character, it's not even funny."

"What's that, Vivian?"

"I've never owned any stock. I don't believe in the slot-market, as I call it. But I took everything I could out of my life savings, even the ones where I had to pay a pretty hefty fee to get it. I sold my T-bills, my CDs, and emptied my 401-K account." She smiled at Cassie, "All because I believed in you."

It was Cassie's turn to look perplexed, "I don't understand."

"I already told you how singular an individual I think you are, please don't make me say it again. As you know, the investors were speculating that the product demo was going to be a big flop since Allen himself wasn't preening daily for the cameras. The day before the demo, I bought nearly $730,000 worth of BHC stock, because I knew that Allen had nothing to do with its success. You did. I invested my life savings on a hunch."

Cassie smiled as she realized where this was going. "If I understand what you're telling me, you bought our stock at roughly eight dollars a share and now, only six or seven weeks later, you've discovered that you're worth nearly fifteen million dollars. Kind of makes you feel giddy, doesn't it?"

"I am a logical person who has performed an illogical act and have been rewarded with illicit gain. I feel giddy and guilty at the same time. Giddy because of the money and guilty because I betrayed myself." She took another sip of her latte, "Of course, I keep reminding myself that I am not a rational animal at all, but merely an animal that can rationalize." She held up her wrist and displayed her watch, "My new Rolex is part of my rationalization and it says that the Air Force is due in fifteen minutes. Are you still going to fill me in on what the hell is going on?"

Cassie laughed, "Sorry, I guess we got a little side-tracked from the agenda. Where were we?" She paused a moment to collect her thoughts, "As I started to say before I was so rudely interrupted, I received a letter from Allen. I found it in my mailbox along with the regular delivery. It had nothing on it but my name in Allen's handwriting. I knew that I should have called you and turned it over for forensic examination, but my loyalty lies with my boss. Inside was a note from Allen that correctly used the code phrases to let me know he was okay, but simply AWOL."

"Sorry to interrupt, but what code phrases?"

"Due to the potential of Allen being kidnapped or otherwise forced to communicate under threat of bodily harm or drugs, we had worked out a system of phrases that he would use to let me know if he was under some kind of duress or not. The presence of the code phrases indicates he's controlling the content of the message while the lack of them would signify someone else wrote the text. I can guarantee that there's no way anyone but Allen could have written that message, even if they were perfect forgers of his handwriting. His message told me clearly that he was in no danger, but that he was unable to communicate with me freely. He also indicated for me to hold down the fort until he got back which indicated that he was doing this of his own free will. And finally, he alluded to the fact that he had been whisked away by aliens. Or something."

"Aliens?"

"Well, I keep thinking of it as an alien abduction. You know, like when they beam you up to their spaceship?"

Vivian looked thoughtful, "I wonder if that's why Area 51's so interested."

"Area 51?"

"You know, the top secret military installation in Nevada that no one knows about? Where they have the Roswell saucer stashed away in Hanger 19? Where Colonel Montana is stationed?" She glanced at her watch again.

"I know, don't worry. If we're late, they'll just have to wait for us. I'll try to wrap this up as quickly as I can." She picked up where she had left off, "I burned the letter and told no one about it. As a matter of fact, you're the only other person who knows. For some reason I feel that I can trust you. Even if I can't, I feel like I owe it to you."

"And you're telling me this now, because?"

"Because, two days ago, I received a package here at the office from Allen. I opened it and there were very specific instructions from him as to what to do with the smaller package inside."

"What's inside the smaller package?" asked Vivian.

"I don't know. It's only to be opened in the presence of yourself, this Dr. Montana from wherever, and me, of course. The instructions included a number to call and specific information to pass along. When I dialed the number, it was answered by the Attorney General himself and so I gave him Allen's message. After confirming arrangements for this afternoon, I immediately scheduled a press conference an hour after the package is to be opened. Also per the instructions."

"And you have no idea what's in the package?"

"None, and I saw no reason at this point to hide from you my earlier letter from Allen. Which, unless it's really necessary, is something I am personally asking you to keep in confidence. If it gets out that a girl broke silence on her man, it's all over but the whining."

Vivian was non-committal, "We'll see. Meanwhile, maybe we should be getting up to the roof to greet the brass? They're very punctual and if I know my colonels, he won't be used to waiting."

They stood up and carried their cups to the recycle bin. Cassie strode over to the rightmost elevator and passed her badge over the panel. The door opened up and they stepped in. Cassie pressed the button for the roof and the door slid shut.

They exited the elevator into the rooftop enclosure located at the corner of the building. The Osprey was making its final clearance circle and hovered over the landing target for a moment before lightly touching down. The engine whine tapered off as the pilot climbed out of the cockpit and removed his flight helmet. Cassie and Vivian suddenly realized that it was a woman with short raven black hair which she loosely shook out before donning a colonel's flight cap. She leaned back into the cockpit to retrieve her briefcase and then walked smartly toward the corner building. Cassie stepped forward and pushed open the glass door to greet her.

"Dr. Montana, I presume?"

"Yes," she said as she removed her Ray-Bans. "Alexandra Montana, just in case you're wondering. But, please, call me Alex. You must be Cassie and this must be Vivian standing behind you. It's nice to meet the two of you although I would ask that you kindly ignore my hair. It's an occupational hazard. I understand that there's a press conference at three? Allen didn't leave us much time, I'm afraid, so we need to open that package as soon as possible." She looked from Cassie to Vivian and then back to Cassie again. "That is, if it's okay with you?"

"Sounds good to me," said Cassie. She flashed her badge at the elevator panel and the door slid open. "After you," she smiled at Dr. Montana and then threw a quizzical look at Vivian behind her back. Vivian raised her eyebrows slightly in acknowledgement. She followed the other women into the elevator and pressed the button for the next floor. Allen had specifically instructed that the package was to be opened in his office and that its video surveillance be turned off prior to the meeting. Cassie led the others to Allen's office and directed them to the small conference table in the corner. On it lay a small mailer box that was sealed with packing tape.

"May I?" asked Dr. Montana.

"Help yourself," said Cassie, "Allen instructed me to turn this over to you once we were here." They seated themselves around the table.

"Okay, then. First the preliminaries, of course." She placed her briefcase on an empty chair and opened it up. She pulled out three forms and passed one to each of them and kept the third for herself. "NDAs, naturally. For all three of us. Before we can open the package, we all have to sign these."

"Why?" asked Cassie. "I mean, I get the need for non-disclosure, but why do you need to sign one as well?"

"It's the only way I'm allowed to open the package. The NDA is with Allen. Read the fine print."

Cassie and Vivian quickly read through the agreement. It required all three of them to sign in the presence of each other before they could proceed.

"What if we don't sign them and just open the package? What's stopping you?" asked Vivian.

"I gave my word. Look, I'm a Colonel in the Air Force, and I can fly a plane or two, but my main job is to look into the impossible. I head a team of scientists that monitor and filter everything from around the globe that our military intelligence can dig up. Anything and everything. Almost all of it filters out as of no interest to us and we pass it on to those to whom it might be. Occasionally, we look into something and find the explanation that makes it possible. And, once in a blue moon, we find something that can't be readily explained and then it comes to my personal attention. Like when someone goes into that bathroom over there and never comes out again. Someone who is now asking us to open this package and maybe find the answer." She pulled her pen from her briefcase and signed and dated the paper in front of her. "I'm like a little kid at Christmas and I can't wait to see what Santa brought me!"

"What the hey," said Vivian, and signed her copy. Cassie quickly complied as well. They passed them to Alex who placed them in a prepared envelope and sealed it. She next removed a small leather case and laid it on the table. Opening it, she removed some small forceps and a scalpel and carefully slit the packing tape.

She looked up at Cassie and Vivian, "I'm preserving the packaging, not necessarily for possible forensic analysis, but because it goes against my nature to just rip open things. If I'm allowed to keep it, I'll certainly give it a good look, but I don't think it will tell me as much as what's inside." As she said this, she lifted the lid with the scalpel and opened it back so they could see the four digital cassettes inside. Each had a label affixed to its case.

Vivian read them off aloud, "'Master', 'Master Copy', 'Media', and 'Play Me First'. Which one do you think we should we look at first?"

"Play Me First?" suggested Alex and Cassie in unison.

Alex deftly opened the cassette case with the scalpel and removed the cassette with the forceps. "I assume that there's a player here somewhere? Try not to handle the tape if you can avoid it." She handed the forceps to Cassie who stood up and crossed over to the media center and popped it into the digital player. She returned with the remote control and turned on the eighty-five-inch wall monitor. After a moment, it was ready and she pressed play. The image faded in from black and showed Allen sitting at his desk. He smiled at the camera and began speaking:

If you're watching this, I assume that you've each signed the non-disclosure agreements and that there are only the three of you present. If not, well shame on whomever couldn't follow the rules. I have called you here for a meeting, albeit a pretty one-sided one since I'm going to be doing all of the talking. If things have gone according to plan, there should be a press conference scheduled in about forty-five minutes, give or take. So I need to move this along. But first, I want to apologize to Cassie for keeping her in the dark, and to Vivian for causing her a lot of unnecessary work, and to Dr. Montana for making her come all the way to San Francisco to hear this.

"I wouldn't have missed this for the world," said Alex.

I'm not at liberty to disclose where I am or what I'm working on, but I am perfectly safe and having more fun than I've had in years. It turns out I needed a break from reality. However, the rest of the world needs to know that I'm alive and kicking and doing fine. I'm hearing the rumors and they're about to spill over into a real media blitz. To try to silence these, I've prepared four tapes. The one labeled 'Master' was recorded in the camera itself and never rewound. This one goes to Dr. Montana for whatever evidence she needs to confirm whether it's real or a forgery. The one labeled 'Master Copy' was recorded on a slave device, rewound once, and played back to make the third tape labeled 'Media'. The 'Master Copy' goes to Vivian and the 'Media' copy goes to the lucky media outlet of Cassie's choice after it's played live at the press conference. The fourth tape, the one you're watching now, is for your eyes only. It goes with Dr. Montana who will know what to do with it.

And, of course, everything's covered with enough of my fingerprints that even the greenest techie could still identify me. I promised your boss, Dr. Montana, and your boss's boss, Vivian, that if I could have your co-operation with this, all the media attention would evaporate.

Allen looked into the camera,

I know that I can trust Cassie, and the folks I'm working with vouch for Dr. Montana, but I'm counting on you, Vivian, as well. I'll be back eventually, but the financial world needs to have confidence in Brookstone Heuristics Corporation in my continued absence. Make sure that the press conference goes off as planned and the media buzzards will all lose interest overnight.

He paused a moment before continuing, *"Good luck to the three of you!"* and the screen faded to black.

"Well, that was illuminating!" said Alex, obviously enjoying herself.
"What exactly's going on, Alex?" asked Cassie. "You obviously know something about all of this and you collected those NDAs for Allen. What's your angle?"
"I promise I'll fill you in on everything. But first, there's another contract that Allen wants Vivian to sign. That is, if she feels like signing it." She reached into her briefcase and pulled out several sheets of paper and passed them over to Vivian. "You need to read this quickly, but make sure that you take enough time to thoroughly understand the terms. Cassie will need to co-sign, so let her read over your shoulder. I'll answer any questions you might have when you're done. Meanwhile, let's get the 'Media' tape playing on the jukebox." While she was speaking, she deftly opened the labeled cassette box and lifted out the tape with the forceps. She handed them to Cassie who removed the 'Play Me First' tape from the player and then popped in the next one. She came back and stood behind Vivian and leaned down to peer at the contract over the other woman's shoulder. After a couple of minutes, they both looked up at Alex, who smiled. "Looks pretty sweet to me, Vivian. I honestly think that Allen's trying to bribe you."
Vivian turned to look at Cassie who shrugged, "It's plain, it's simple, and it's binding on my signature. How about if we look at the tape first before you make up your mind. I don't think Allen would want you to

feel pressured about a decision like this." She pointed the remote at the DVP and pressed 'play'.

The screen faded in from black and showed Allen once again sitting at his desk. He looked up from his work and smiled at the camera.

Hello, I'm Allen Brookstone and I'm here to talk about the next generation of storage technology that will be coming from Brookstone Heuristics Corporation. For the last two months, I have isolated myself in my private lab so that I could focus 100% of my attention on a revolutionary method of storing data that will literally change how we use our computers. Strategically convenient for BHC, it only connects to our new MicroMesh software and hardware that is now shipping to a record number of companies. Medium size firms with only several hundred users are seeing the immediate benefits of its use while still larger firms realize even more ROI due to our product's extreme scalability. All of them will be ready to utilize our new device with no additional modifications. CIOs take note, this means no additional costs other than purchasing the new hardware. That is, if you've already purchased our latest product.

He paused to look down at his notes and then looked up again into the camera.

This morning I came out of isolation for the first time and discovered that I was missing. You think that getting behind a day's worth of voice-mail is a hassle, you should try eight weeks' worth! Anyway, to paraphrase Mark Twain, 'The reports of my disappearance are greatly exaggerated.' I purposely cut myself off from the world to work on my new brainstorm, but I certainly didn't intend to cause an intensive man-hunt on the part of the FBI and others. My personal apologies to anyone who may have been part of what I now understand has been a very large effort to find me when I had taken such care not to be found. I have taped this announcement and provided copies to the FBI for verification. The media will get a copy today, as well. To provide further information, I will now turn over the press conference to Special Agent Vivian Williams of the FBI.

Allen paused for effect while continuing to look into the camera. He smiled his trademark boyish grin and said:

If you like what you're seeing with MicroMesh, wait until I give you a good look at MicroStash. It'll blow your socks off!

The screen faded slowly to black.

"Holy shit!" exclaimed Vivian, looking stunned.

Alex started laughing, "I'm sorry, Vivian, I know it's not funny, but I have to ask you: which shit? The part where you have about twenty minutes to prepare the most important press speech in your life? Or the fact that the value of your BHC stock is going to double, if not triple by week's end? Or is it the five-million-dollar-a-year job that Allen's offering you as head of security?" She looked at Cassie, "Are the stock options valued at current price?"

"They are if she signs before the press conference. After that lulu of an announcement, it's going to go straight through the roof."

Vivian skimmed the pages one more time, "In for a penny, in for a dollar." She picked up her pen and signed and dated each sheet and then passed them to Cassie. She glanced through them herself, and then signed as well. Alex pulled a small leatherette holster-like case from her briefcase and opened it up. She removed a rubber stamp from the pouch and stamped each page, initialing the stamps as she went along. Next, she pulled an embosser from the pouch and crimped a seal over each stamp and then signed the last page.

"I happen to be a nationally registered notary," she said by way of explanation and passed the forms back to Cassie.

"I need to call my boss and let him know what's going on."

Alex cleared her throat, "Actually, your ex-boss. While we've been looking at things here, he's been notified by his own boss that you are now retired and moving into the private sector. All but two weeks of your unused vacation time has been applied to give you thirty-plus years of service. The last two weeks are granted in lieu of a two-week notice. When I notarized your signature, it all became final." She grinned at Vivian, "Allen Brookstone's your new boss."

"But I'm representing the FBI at the press conference!"

"Technically, your active duty ends today at 5:00 PM. You need to go out there and explain why the FBI was leaving no stone unturned in looking for one of the wealthiest people in the world. 'Trust no one' is your boss's motto, right? In spite of assurances from Cassie and the Board of Directors that Allen was fine, but impossibly out of touch, you continued to exercise due diligence in searching for him. You can end with how glad everyone is to know that he's alive and well and maybe offer to lease his safe-house for your Witness Protection Program."

Vivian glanced at her Rolex and then opened her own briefcase. She removed a yellow legal pad and started an outline. She looked up at Alex, "I like it. I can do that with a clear conscience. The comment at the end is good, too. If I can end on a humorous note, so much the better." She started writing again on the pad in front of her.

Cassie asked Vivian, "Before you disappear into that, who's your boss? I mean your soon to be ex-boss?"

"The U.S. Attorney General. I'm acting SA, but I report directly to him by special arrangement."

Cassie turned to Alex, "And who's your boss?"

"I'm an active colonel, but I report directly to the President. Also by special arrangement."

"President? As in The President of the United States?"

Alex's eyes twinkled, "Yep! That's the one."

+ + +

Three hours later, Cassie and Alex were sitting in the back corner of Lily's Steakhouse occupying the large circular booth located there. An hour earlier, they had seen Vivian off as she left the Brookstone Building and climbed into her SUV. If she had not known the actual circumstances, Cassie would have easily believed that Vivian had been working on her briefing report for hours instead of only minutes. She smiled at the thought of having someone so capable on hand to help out in a pinch. She didn't question Allen's judgment about hiring her, but she was a little surprised in his confidence that she would sign on with them. It was almost as if he already knew what would happen in their meeting. Vivian had promised Cassie that she would be in the next morning as soon as she could wrap things up with the FBI. Alex and Cassie waved to her as she drove off down the winding drive and then went back inside to Allen's office.

"You and I need to go somewhere and have a little chat, Cassie. I know that you're bubbling over with questions and I promised you earlier that I would fill you in, but not right now. I have a rather long story and I think it might be better to tell it over dinner." She looked at Cassie, "I hear that you're a steak and potatoes sort of person? Is that right?"

"Yes, definitely. And you?"

"My name's Montana, but I grew up in Texas. If I could get my flight bag from the Osprey and change into something more suitable, perhaps we could hunt down a cow somewhere? It's been a long day and I haven't eaten since breakfast, so I'm more than a little famished!"

"Sounds good to me."

They had both declined drinks when they were seated and had opted for a pot of coffee instead. As soon as the waitress left, Alex opened her briefcase and removed what looked like a pager and placed it on the table. She pressed a button on the side and a small green indicator lit up on the face. She smiled at Cassie, "The NDA we signed with Allen covers this conversation. This little gadget here insures that we aren't overheard by anyone."

"To be perfectly honest, Alex, I am totally adrift here. How do you know Allen? And how did you get those agreements? And where is he, anyway?"

"All in good time, all in good time." She paused as the waitress brought them their coffee and filled each of their cups. When she had taken their orders and departed, Alex resumed, "Some of what I'm about to tell you is highly classified information. Some of it is personal. Some of it I've never shared before with anyone and you'll be the first. Why I've decided to do so will become clear as I tell you what I know."

"Please go on, Alex. I promise I won't tell!"

Alex grinned, "I'm not sure who you would tell, even if you did." She took a healthy swig of coffee before continuing, "First I need to tell you a little bit about myself. My grandfather was Air Force, my father was Air Force, and so naturally, I was expected to follow in their footsteps as well. As a little girl, I played with G.I. Joe dolls instead of Barbie and Ken. I also played with my chemistry set and my electronics set and read everything I could get my hands on. My mother humored me and was quick to provide a trip to the library whenever I wanted to know more about something. Looking back, she had simply discovered that the way to keep me quiet and busy was to give me a stack of books. Every Christmas, my grandfather would give me some something that was educational, but just a little too advanced for my age. At age five, for example, my father helped me to assemble a real working light bulb from a kit, just like the one that Thomas Edison first made. I didn't quite understand it at the time, but I was able to build the next one on my own before the next Christmas when my grandfather gave me a computer.

Once again, I was in over my head but it kept me occupied for the next couple of years."

Cassie stopped her, "When was this? What year?"

"I was six years old at the time, so it was 1966. Why do you ask?"

Cassie replied, "Grandfathers didn't give their grand-daughters computers for Christmas in 1966. There were only a handful in existence at the time."

"Well, my grandfather did. And yes, it was relatively crude by today's standards. There was no keyboard, only a vast array of toggle switches, and no CRT, only four long rows of octal nixie tubes. But I was too young to know the difference. That Christmas morning, I ran into my playroom and it was sitting in the corner. Roughly the size of two refrigerators and lit up here and there with indicators and glowing numbers. It was the coolest thing I had ever seen." She laughed, "I was also too young to understand that it was twenty-million dollars' worth of military hardware that my grandfather's lab had built. He had claimed that it was easy enough for a child to figure out and I was his proving ground."

"What exactly did your grandfather do, Alex?"

"The same thing I'm doing now. It's sort of a family tradition." She stopped as the waitress approached with their orders and placed them on the table. She waited as the cups were refilled and the waitress had left again. She stared at the slab of beef on the plate in front of her. "Oh my, I think I've died and gone to Heaven." She cut off a piece and ate it hungrily. She took another bite and finished chewing before continuing. "My grandfather enlisted in the Air Force when he was seventeen and went on to OCS where he excelled in physics and math. By the time our involvement in World War II rolled around, he was assigned to security at Los Alamos and placed in charge of policing the scientific community. Nothing went in or out of there without him knowing about it. After the war, the research facility was moved to Nevada and he was put in charge of a new program that was created completely off-the-books. Officially, it was called Project Blue Book, but privately, it functioned independently of the Air Force and my grandfather reported directly to Truman. It was at this facility that he eventually built the computer that became my Christmas gift. When he died in 1969, my father took over his position and carried the ball until his own death in 1989." She sliced off another chunk of beef and placed it in her mouth.

"What was your grandfather's name?"

Alex swallowed her mouthful of steak before replying, "I was kind of hoping you wouldn't ask." She sighed, "His name was Colonel Alex Montana, my father was Colonel Alex Montana, Jr., and it's only by the luck of the draw that I'm not Colonel Alex Montana, III."

"I take it that you took over from your dad when he died?"

"You got it. Which brings me to the next chapter of my little tale. How about we take a few minutes and let me catch up to you on the food?"

"Sure. I need to hit the ladies room to decant some of this coffee." She rose from the booth, "Eat up, I'll be right back."

Alex wasted no time digging into her steak and had managed to polish it off before Cassie's return. She looked somewhat guiltily at Cassie and protested, "I told you that I was hungry!"

"As I recall, you actually said you were 'more than a little famished'," corrected Cassie.

"So I did. You have an incredible memory, from what Allen has told me about you."

"You've talked to him? I mean, directly? Why hasn't he called me? Where is he?"

"I'm coming to that. All of this is leading up to current events. But to properly understand their significance, you'll have to humor me just a little longer." She dipped a fry in some ketchup and bit into it. "When I was little, I would go on long walks with my grandfather. As we walked, he would tell me stories to keep me amused. My favorite was his one about the Others."

"The others?"

"Yes. That's what he called them. They were like little elves or pixies or fairies and they were everywhere. Of course, we couldn't see them because they were magical. He said that they were the ones that hid my slippers from me when I couldn't find them. He said that they watched over me and made sure that I was safe. They lived in a place that only they could enter and that maybe, someday, I might get to see one of them." She picked up another fry and chewed on it thoughtfully. She glanced at Cassie, "My whole life has been spent waiting for that moment and it's never happened." She picked up another french fry.

"You actually believe in these others?"

"Not 'these others', 'the' Others. And, yes, I do. When my grandfather died, I told my dad about our talks and the stories about the Others and he began to take me on long walks as well and tell me more stories. On my sixteenth birthday, he showed me a secret room in the house that I never even dreamed existed. Inside were rows of shelves with various items arranged and labeled neatly along them. He explained that these were gifts from the Others and that I was never to tell another living soul about our family museum that my grandfather had started and he had continued. Later that year, I was sent to Colorado Springs to attend the Air Force Academy and, to make a long story short, eventually became assigned to my father's lab as a young lieutenant. When he died from his heart attack, Ronald Reagan met with me personally and explained that I had been selected to carry the ball."

"The ball?"

"The knowledge that the Others really exist." She ate another fry. "I can't tell you where Allen is, exactly, because I truly don't know. But I *do* know that, wherever it is, he's with the Others and I'm jealous as hell!"

5342 BC - NW Persian Gulf Sea Floor

Lonni was measuring the doorway to the lift again. He shook his head and sighed.

"What's the matter, Lonni?" asked Mirta as she walked down the hallway.

"I've got everything ready for the trencher except for the wheels. The ones I have that will work won't fit into the lift or the waterlock. The ones that do fit are way too small. Everything else has been easy to piece together, but I still don't have any wheels."

"I find that rather hard to believe with all the templates you must have on hand," replied Mirta.

"I have hundreds of small wheels for carts and what not, and hundreds more for almost every surface vehicle imaginable, but nothing suitably large that will fit through a one-by-two-meter doorway into a two-meter diameter lift."

"Would the ones on my sand buggy work?" asked Mirta.

Lonni looked at her for a moment and then smiled, "Why, yes, I think that they just might be about the right size. I had forgotten that you had that old thing. Can we go and take a look?"

"Sure. It's in my locker."

They stepped into the lift and exited onto the main cargo deck. More than ten stories tall, it occupied a central layer of the ship and was crammed to capacity with modular cargo containers of several different sizes. Ringing the central core were six storage lockers, each the size of a small warehouse. Mirta thumbed the lock for number three and waited until the wall had fully retracted before entering. She walked toward the back and unsnapped some tie-downs holding the cargo blanket over one of her most prized possessions.

"Looks pretty good for its age, how old did you say it was when you bought it?"

"It's nearly six hundred and thirty thousand years old. I have a certificate of authenticity from Trammell's. It cost me nearly ten years pay and I've never even taken it for a spin." She looked wistfully at the four-wheeled buggy with its solar powered electrics still fully functional. "They sure don't build them like that anymore."

"That's because no one needs electrics anymore," laughed Lonni. He pulled out his measurer and pointed it at the wheels. "They're perfect,

Mirta!" he said after glancing at the read-out. "Just the right size to roll into the lift and yet sturdy enough to support the matter converter."

"Promise me that you'll be careful with them will you?"

"Of course, Mirta. I only need to remove one of them and make a template from it. I'll be extra careful, though, and when I'm done, you won't even know the difference."

"And that's all you have left to get the trenchers ready?"

"That's it. We can be ready to roll as soon as tomorrow morning."

"Tomorrow morning it is, then. I'll let everyone know that it's a go while you finish up." She walked off toward the entrance, "Don't forget to turn off the lights and lock up when you're done!"

+ + +

After dinner that evening, they all gathered in the entertainment room. Mirta had adapted a remote for the navigation system so that she, too, was able to be with them. "Now that Lonni's got the trencher ready to go, I want to review the layout one more time. It's basically the same as when you last saw it, but I've added a little more detail to the main temple." As she spoke, the room faded out and they appeared to be hovering above the area where the river drained into the sea. Situated on the highest spot nearby, a couple of kilometers from shore, was a large building. It didn't really exist yet, but was a virtual projection of the template in the datastore that they had re-worked. "After the last structural analysis, I've thickened the walls another twenty percent just to be safe. The original design used materials that were substantially stronger than what we have to work with."

"It looks pretty impressive to me," said Sparta.

"I hope that Mardu likes it," added Ferta.

Mirta touched the control on the arm of her chair and a vast network of canals and irrigation ditches sprang into view. "We'll start with the smaller canals first and gradually work our way north and east digging the bigger ones until we reach the river about five kilometers up-stream. Once we connect it to the river, the water will flow evenly throughout the system to the header troughs that will supply each plot." She touched the control again and water burst from the river into the main canal and sluiced down through the channels cut into the earth.

"Looks good to me," said Rolli. "How many linear kilometers are we talking about?"

"About fifty, all told."

"That's not as bad as I thought," mused Rolli. "We should be able to do ten kilometers a day, easily, even while pulling the trencher." He paused before continuing, "I don't suppose Lonni could add a little powertrain to it? It would make things go a lot faster!"

"We're already using the matter converter against all rules of First Contact. We agreed that it's best to limit how much technology we expose to Mardu and Itok."

"I know," replied Rolli wistfully. "It's okay, I can always use the exercise."

Mirta continued with her presentation, "Some of the excavated matter will be used to build the protective wall around the city proper for times when the river floods." She touched the controls and the wall appeared surrounding the temple area. As they watched, the river rose and spread across the flat plain until it covered everything except for the walled in area. "Every spring, the accumulated snowpack to the north melts and causes the river to flood the delta. The wall needs to be at least five meters high to insure against worst case scenarios."

"How long is the wall?" asked Lonni.

"The two long runs are a little over a kilometer each and the two short ones are just under a kilometer. The total is almost exactly four kilometers."

"Ferta, have you briefed Mardu and Itok yet?" asked Altair.

"Not yet," she replied. "I wanted to make sure that everything was ready to go before filling them in on our plans. We will also need another streamer probe for Itok so that he can communicate with us when Mardu is not around."

"I'll take care of that since I'll be working with him," volunteered Lonni.

The virtual display of their plans faded from view and the room appeared around them again. Altair looked at each of his crew members and said, "Let's do it, then!" He raised his drink in a toast, "Here's to our new city of Eridu! May she live long and prosper!"

"To Eridu!" they chorused together.

+ + +

"I want to learn how to speak the language of the gods," said Mardu. Rolli and Mardu were walking slowly along while pulling the trencher behind them. They were being guided by Mirta who was following their progress with the nav system.

"We can already talk using the meme," said Rolli. "We thought it would easier for you."

"It's not the same as talking to you directly. I hear you speak in your tongue and I hear what you say from the meme. If I could understand you, it would be a lot less confusing."

"We'll see," said Rolli. He made a mental note to bring this up at their next briefing. They were all a little surprised at how easily Mardu and Itok accepted their instructions without question. Mardu seemed to regard the matter converter with awe, but had quickly understood the purpose once its use was demonstrated to him. They had been at it for several hours now and had already finished one of the sub-systems in the south-west portion. Lonni had assembled three extension ladders to form a triangular beam. This connected the two replicated wheels from Mirta's sand buggy as a two-meter long axle that could extend to more than ten meters when needed. Mounted in the center of the beam was one of the matter converters that had been removed from the cargo bay. It was fastened to the bottom of the beam with its bell-shaped mouth pointing downwards, its opening about a half-meter above the ground. Connected to each end of the makeshift beam was a high-tensile flex-cable that formed a V-shaped yoke that Rolli and Mardu could use to pull the two-wheeled apparatus from about ten meters away. It was crude, but effective. When Rolli first switched on the converter, a gaping hole had appeared below the trencher as the matter in the converter field was transferred to the containment vessel cradled in a yoke fastened to the top of the beam. Mirta remotely adjusted the field to remove the soil down to a depth of a meter and narrowed it to a meter wide. When Rolli and Mardu picked up the flex-cable and began walking north, it left a meter-wide, meter-deep trench whose sides and bottom were perfectly smooth and glazed with a hard finish. Initially, they had only walked about twenty meters before halting and taking a moment to look back over their handiwork. Mardu had been fascinated by the results and couldn't wait to continue. Since then, Rolli and Mardu had walked steadily while pulling the trencher behind them while Mirta gave them course corrections and modified the trench dimensions according to the design in the datastore.

"Where does the dirt go?" asked Mardu.

"It goes into the bottle I showed you."

"But wouldn't it get very heavy? Look at how much dirt we've dug up!"

"It's the will of the gods," replied Rolli, who had been instructed to use this phrase when asked a technical question. "It will hold a day's worth of digging and not get any heavier. When it's full, we'll give it to Enki and Itok to use to build the temple."

"What are they doing now? While we walk all day long?"

"They're using another trencher to level the ground where the temple will be built. By the time we join them, they should have the whole area prepared."

"Nammu says that Itok and I will live there when it's finished."

"Yes, you will each have your own area and it will keep you cool when the summer's heat arrives." He deliberately didn't elaborate.

They walked along in silence, dragging the trencher behind them as it made ever deeper and wider trenches under Mirta's control.

+ + +

Lonni and Itok surveyed their work so far. They had extended the axle of their own trencher to its maximum and had made multiple overlapping passes over the rectangular area upon which the temple would be built. The first several passes had removed successive layers of soil until the whole area was level to Mirta's satisfaction. The last two passes had fused the soil down to ten meters deep and resulted in a natural ceramic composite that would be able to hold the weight of the temple itself. They still had one more set of finishing passes and they would be done. Itok knelt and felt the glossy surface with his rough and callused hands. He stood up and eyed the large expanse of soil that they had processed.

"Will the temple be as large as all of this?" he asked with wonder in his voice.

"Not quite," smiled Lonni. "The walls will begin a few paces in from the edges. It will leave a nice walkway around the perimeter."

Itok said nothing, although it was obvious that he didn't fully understand everything Lonni had said to him. Lonni had only worked with Itok for a few hours, but he was already growing to like him. He had expected Itok to be ignorant of basic mechanics, but he hadn't been prepared for how quickly he had absorbed new things and set about using them. Once he had seen how the matter converter worked, he had labored the rest of the day without comment until now.

"And Mardu and I will live here?"

"Yes, that is Nammu's wish."

"Ah, yes. The will of the gods," said Itok as he picked up the flex-cable and looked expectantly at Lonni. Lonni picked up his portion of the cable and they proceeded once more to crisscross the building site.

+ + +

Near the end of the day, Mardu and Rolli joined Itok and Lonni at the newly prepared foundation. Mardu and Itok watched intently as Lonni disconnected the bottle from his trencher and, with Rolli's assistance, removed it and set it on the ground. He next unfastened the torq-locks holding the matter converter to the ladder-beam and removed it as well. He carefully set it on the ground next to the bottle that he had removed. He maneuvered Rolli's trencher near his own and pulled down on the bottle thereby rotating the beam about its axle until the matter converter was pointing at the frame of his own trencher. He spoke into his comlink and the trencher vanished. He let go of Rolli's trencher and the bell mouth swung downwards again. He and Rolli removed the containment bottle from Rolli's trencher and replaced it with the one that they had removed from Lonni's. Lonni took note of Mardu and Itok's interest in the process and explained, "The bottle from Mardu's trencher is full of the soil that Itok and I will use tomorrow to begin building the temple. We will no longer need the framework we used to level the site, but will be using a different one instead. Meanwhile, the bottle from Itok's trencher is nearly empty and will be filled up tomorrow when Enkimdu and Mardu dig more irrigation canals. At tomorrow's end, we will swap the bottles and repeat the process again the next day. In five days' time, we will be finished." He held up five fingers to show Mardu and Itok how many he meant. A few minutes later, Lonni and Rolli completed their tasks and Lonni instructed Mardu and Itok not to touch the equipment until they returned. He and Rolli said their good-byes and headed back to their teleport location along the shore, discussing the day's activities as they walked along. Mardu and Itok returned to their tent and started preparing dinner before their own discussions began.

Everyone agreed that it had been a very long, but very productive day.

+ + +

The next morning, Itok and Mardu were waiting expectantly for Enki and Enkimdu to appear at the temple site. When they finally approached from the distant shore, they were pushing a small four-wheeled vehicle in front of them. The small wheels apparently made it difficult to roll across the rough terrain. Mardu and Itok ran to assist them and pushed the cart back to the temple site with some effort.

"Good morning, Itok and Mardu," said Lonni in greeting. "I've brought a new tool that will turn our trencher into a builder." He pushed the cart around by way of demonstration and was pleased to see how smoothly it rolled on the fused foundation. Itok and Mardu smiled, but said nothing.

"Come on, Mardu," said Rolli, picking up the flex-cable for the trencher. "We might as well get started. We have quite a walk ahead of us before we can pick up where we left off yesterday." Mardu picked up his portion of the cable and they started off together. "We'll see you again later this afternoon," Rolli yelled back over his shoulder.

"Have fun," called out Lonni. He walked over to the matter converter and brought it back to the cart. He set it down on the flat surface with its bell pointing horizontally to the side and locked it into place with the torq-locks. He turned to Itok, "I need your help with the storage bottle." They picked it up and carried it to the cart where it was fastened into the cradle underneath the top surface. After connecting the bottle to the converter, Lonni looked at Itok and explained, "Our trencher is now a builder."

"I don't understand," said Itok.

"Help me move it into position and I'll show you." Itok pushed the cart while Lonni steered it into position. Working from Mirta's instructions, they moved it back and forth slightly until Mirta signaled that it was in the right place. "Now watch, Itok. Nammu will make the first block." As he spoke, the air in front of the converter shimmered and became solid. There appeared a large block of stone about three meters high and three meters wide. It was fully two meters thick. In the center was an area that was one-meter square and was clearly transparent, although it was as solid as the surrounding stone. Lonni swept his arm around the site, "One by one, we will place these blocks around the foundation. When we are done, they will make up the outer walls of the first floor of the temple. The clear portion is formed from the silica in the soil and will provide light to the inside." They moved the builder a few meters over and the air shimmered again. A new block appeared that was seamlessly joined to the first block.

"The will of the gods is mighty, indeed," said Itok in amazement. He pushed the cart and helped move the builder into the next position. By the time the sun was directly overhead, they had finished three sides of the perimeter and were adding smaller blocks to the inside to form individual rooms. Interspersed here and there were slender columns that would help support the next level. By the end of day, they had nearly finished the ground floor and had finally depleted the matter in the containment vessel.

"It looks like the two of you have been busy!" said Rolli as he and Mardu pulled their trencher up to the temple. Lonni allowed Itok to assist him with swapping out the bottles and he was once again impressed with how quickly he caught on to everything. These people were clearly very intelligent, but not terribly inventive. Once again, Lonni and Rolli said their good-byes and walked back to the shore. Itok couldn't wait to show Mardu what they had built.

"Come, Mardu, let me show you the first floor of the temple." He led the way into the entrance and stopped inside. 'This is the main hall," he said, as he pointed to the vast area in the dwindling light. He walked to the right and entered a doorway, "This is the storage area for the wheat. There's another one on the other side as well." He went back out into the main hall and walked toward the back. He stopped and pointed, "Along the back are the offices and the service counters."

"Offices? Service Counters?" asked Mardu.

"That's what Enki said. I don't know what they are, exactly, but they have something to do with helping the people who will live in Eridu."

"What people? You mean, our people when they return from the hills?"

"Yes, and many others." He frowned, "It all made sense when Enki was explaining it. You and I will live here and be the spokesmen for the gods. When someone needs something, they will come to us for advice and assistance. We will have many people to help us with our tasks." Itok smiled, "You and I will be the High Priests of Eridu!"

"What have we gotten ourselves into?"

Itok laughed, "It is the will of the gods!"

February 2, 1438 A.D. - Strasburg, Germany

There was a loud knocking at the door and Johann stirred from his sleep in the rocker in front of the fire. He must have dozed off from the warmth of the fire in the hearth after his dinner. He shook his head to clear it as the knocking came once again.

"I'm coming, I'm coming," he yelled out as he rose up from his chair and walked over to the door. He opened it to see a stranger clad in a dark cloak that was gathered about him. "Come in, good sir," said Johann as he held open the door. "Come in from the cold and warm yourself by the fire."

"Thank you," said the stranger, "I think I will." He entered the room and walked over to stand in front of the fireplace. From his accent, Johann knew immediately that he was a foreigner, but he couldn't quite place where he might hail from.

"What can I do for you?" asked Johann.

"My name is Gottfried Schmidt and I want to hire your services for a year," came the reply.

"My dear fellow, I do not work that way. Perhaps you need some metalwork done? Simply tell me what you need me to do and I'll tell you how much payment will motivate me to do it. If you can afford it, then I will let you know when it will be done."

Gottfried pulled back his cloak and removed a small leather pouch that was fastened at his waist. Stepping over to the small table near the door, he tossed the pouch onto it where it landed with a loud thud. "That is yours if you will help me for a year. Maybe less if we make good progress. Regardless, you get to keep what's in there."

Johann looked at the stranger and then turned and picked up the bag. He undid the rawhide thong holding it closed and looked inside. Surprised, he shook some of the contents onto the table. Small teardrops of shiny metal spilled out onto the surface. He went to the mantel over the fireplace and picked up his lantern. He used a small stick from the fire to light it and then carried it back to the table. He sat and looked closely at the shiny pile on the table and then looked at Gottfried again. "Is that what I think it is?" he asked.

"You're a goldsmith," he replied. "I'm sure that you have the means to ascertain its purity and value. Assuming that it's pure gold, would that be enough to motivate you to help me out for the coming year? I promise you that it will be well worth your while."

Johann hefted the bag and thought quickly. He would check the gold, of course, but he sensed that Gottfried was serious about this. He didn't need a scale to know that the weight in his hand represented more money than he could possibly make in twenty years. Even twenty good years, at that. Without any obvious hesitation, he stood and shook Gottfried's hand, "When do we start?"

"As you may have already surmised, I'm not from around here and I will need a place to stay." He withdrew a smaller pouch from beneath his cloak and tossed it on the table next to the larger bag. "That is payment for my room and board if you will let me live in the loft over your workshop."

Johann picked up the smaller pouch and tested its weight. He hesitated for a moment and then replied, "I am sorely tempted by your offer, but for one tenth of this, you could live at the Waldenburg in style."

"I think it will be best if I stayed here."

Johann chose his words carefully so as not to offend this generous man, "I am a member of the guild and our methods are secret. I cannot allow you to be privy to my work. It is a violation of my oath."

"If you will allow me to collect my bags from outside the door, I think that I may be able to convince you that I have more to contribute to your craft than I might possibly learn from you."

Johann had to admit that he was intrigued by this stranger in the night who had shown up on his doorstep. "By all means, retrieve your baggage and I'll fix us some warm ale to drink." He turned and went into the kitchen to make the preparations as Schmidt exited the front door and returned with two leather cases. He placed the smaller one on the table and the larger one underneath, sat down in the chair in front of it, and waited for Johann to return. Johann entered with two ornate goblets and handed one to Gottfried. "Here," he said, "This will warm your belly as we talk."

"Thank you," said Gottfried gratefully as he took the offered drink from his hand. "May I call you Johann?" he asked.

"For the amount of gold you've given me, you can call me anything you want."

"Very well, Johann. And you may call me Gottfried," he said as he opened the case in front of him. Johann was impressed with the exquisite quality of workmanship evident in the hinges and latching mechanism. He would have to examine them more closely when he had a chance. The stranger reached into the case and removed several slender shiny rods and laid them on the table between them. Johann dragged the lantern nearer and picked one up to look at it more closely. Frowning, he stood up and retrieved a small box from the mantle. Opening it, he removed a magnifying monocle to get a better look. Placing the monocle in his right eye, he once again picked up the finger-length metal object and examined it closely. It appeared to be made of steel and was precisely shaped into a square rod. On the end of the rod was a raised detail that appeared to be the letter "e", but reversed.

"This is a letter punch," said Johann, "but I have never seen one so well made. Tell me, sir, how did you come by this?"

"I made it myself," replied Gottfried. He removed another object from the case and handed it to Johann. "Use this loupe if you would like to see it a little better."

Johann didn't recognize the word, but he immediately understood that it was a magnifying device similar to his monocle. He took it from Gottfried's hand and used it to once again study the punch. He picked up another one from the table and examined it as well. This one was identical except that it had the letter "t" on the end. He turned the metal piece over in his hand and cast his expert eye over it. He then looked up at Gottfried with amazement and new-found respect. "I am by far the best craftsman in the entire country, but I could never produce something as fine as this!" He studied it again before asking, "If you are capable of making this, what could you possibly want from me?"

Gottfried again reached into his case and removed a glass jar with a wide stopper sealing it and placed it on the table. "This is antimony. If it is alloyed with lead and tin, it will produce a superb casting metal that is hard and durable, yet has no appreciable shrinkage."

Johann's eyes glittered as he picked up the jar. Antimony was exceedingly rare and worth far more than gold. He couldn't even begin to estimate the worth of what he was holding in his hand. He set the jar down carefully. "For the moment, I'll take your word for it. If we're making a casting metal, I assume that there is something to be cast." He picked up one of the punches again. "Might I also assume that it has something to do with these letter punches?"

"Yes, you may. Here, let me show you," replied Gottfried who once again reached into his case and brought out a roll of parchment. He unrolled it on the table and anchored the corners with the punches. Johann could immediately see that it was a number of small drawings detailing the fabrication and construction of several separate devices.

Gottfried pointed to the upper left of the parchment, "This is an iron plate we will use to align the punches that will impress their shapes into a copper sheet." He pointed to the next group of drawings, "The dimples it makes will be used to align the hand mold into which will be poured the casting metal. The mold allows for varying thicknesses of the castings and sits directly on the copper plate." He continued with the next group of images, "The castings will be held in rows on this iron frame to form lines of fixed size and length. It will be fastened onto what is essentially a modified grape press that has another iron plate which will be used to compress paper onto the type." He pointed to what appeared to be a recipe in the lower right corner, "This describes a formula for an oil-based pigment that not only will adhere to the casting metal but will also adhere to the paper as well." He sat back and looked at Johann expectantly.

Johann looked at the drawings for some time, studying each of the details and noting how everything worked. He looked at Gottfried with obvious amazement. "I can't believe it's that simple," he said. "But only if this casting metal doesn't shrink, as you claim, and this oil-based ink does, in fact, bind to it."

"Trust me, the metal doesn't shrink and the pigment sticks," smiled Gottfried.

"Great God Almighty, man, do you know what you have here?" exclaimed Johann.

Gottfried grinned in response, "Yes indeed, Herr Gutenberg, I certainly do!"

Three Months Ago - Las Vegas, Nevada

Cassie exited the shuttle train at the main terminal and walked towards the baggage claim area. She had been more than a little surprised when Alex Montana had called and invited her to visit. She was well overdue for a vacation and had decided to take her up on her invitation. She saw Alex in the distance and waved.

"How are you?" asked Alex, drawing near. "How was your flight?"

"Totally uneventful, I'm happy to say. I've never really liked flying."

"Me either," came the surprising reply.

"But you're a pilot!" protested Cassie.

"When I'm the one behind the steering wheel, it's totally different."

They walked together to the baggage carousel and chatted while waiting for Cassie's luggage to appear. About ten minutes later, they were on their way out the door to the curb where Alex's SUV was waiting for them. Opening the rear hatch, Alex put Cassie's two small suitcases into the vehicle and slammed the hatch shut. Climbing into the passenger side, Cassie remarked, "It must be nice being able to park at the door!"

Alex smiled and pointed to the USAF sticker displayed prominently on the front corner of the windshield, "This little puppy lets me park pretty much anywhere I want." She started the car and pulled carefully into the flow of traffic around the terminal.

"I'm really glad I decided to visit, I feel less stressed out already. Thanks for inviting me," she said sincerely.

"I have to admit that I have ulterior motives. I have a little surprise waiting for you and I couldn't go into it over the phone." She looked at Cassie, "That doesn't mean that I'm not happy to have your company. I don't get out much and I don't have any friends."

"Oh, it can't be as bad as all that!"

"Yes, it can. But it's a natural outcome of my innate introverted personality coupled with my job. Loose lips sink ships, you know."

"So what's on the agenda?" asked Cassie. "The last time I was here it was for COMDEX where we hustled last year's product release."

"Funny that you should mention that," said Alex, cryptically. "I thought we would get something to eat first and then head on out to the homestead. Are you hungry at all?"

"Yes. All I had on the flight was a light snack." She grinned, "I hope that your idea of food involves meat and carbs!"

"Of course," laughed Alex. She took the on-ramp to I-15 and headed north. As they passed the downtown strip, Cassie was once again amazed at how much new development was in progress. She was in Vegas once or twice every year and was fascinated with the continual metamorphosis of the skyline where there was always something new appearing or disappearing. They took highway 95 to the northwest and stopped at a nondescript steakhouse located on the outskirts of Las Vegas. "I think you'll like the food here. It's relatively unknown to the tourists, but it's a huge favorite with the locals." She pulled into a parking spot not too far from the door. "It's also the last place to get a decent meal on this highway. I'm afraid that there's not much else where we're going." She and Cassie got out and walked up the sidewalk to the entrance.

+ + +

An hour later they were back in the SUV and headed northwest on 95 away from civilization. In response to Cassie's questions, Alex had refused to reveal the surprise she had alluded to at the airport. "All in good time," was the only answer Cassie could pry from her. After traveling for about a half-hour, they took the turnoff to the north at the town of Indian Springs. A few hundred yards up the road, they slowed down at a checkpoint and were waved on through by the two military guards on duty.

"We're entering one of the largest restricted areas in the world. The vast area to the north and west were used during the cold war for above-ground and below-ground nuclear tests."

"You mean like atom bombs?" asked Cassie.

"Yes, like atom bombs and other noisy toys as well," laughed Alex. "Area 51 is about fifty miles north of here and the so-called Desert Wildlife Range is further to the east.

As they drove north in the gradually fading sunlight, they quickly left the small town behind them and continued on the narrow blacktop for about another fifteen miles. Alex slowed down at one of the numerous dirt roads that intersected the two-lane and turned off to the east. For the next several miles, the road twisted and turned as it made its way up into the low hills and finally ended in a small gravel parking lot. Alex came to a stop and turned off the engine.

"Why are we stopping here?" asked Cassie, looking around.

"This is my home," she smiled. "Follow the path with your eyes up to the side of the bluff."

Cassie did so and suddenly realized that what she had at first thought was the blank side of the mountain was actually a cleverly camouflaged building built right into the native rock. The path led to the door of the facility.

"This is your house? Your homestead as you called it?"

"Yes. It was built by my grandfather in 1946 under a perpetual land grant drawn up by Woodrow Wilson himself. As long as a Montana lives here, it's all bought and paid for by the federal government even though it's technically private land." They stepped out of the vehicle and retrieved Cassie's bags from the back. They each carried one as they made their way up the path to the now-obvious doorway. "When I was little, my father would bring me to visit my grandfather. Even after I had gotten used to it, it always felt like I was crossing over into another world." As she said this, she opened the door into what looked like the foyer of a large manor house. There were several doors leading off to the side and to the back and on each side of the enormous hall was a grand sweeping staircase that apparently led upstairs. Cassie looked around and then looked back out the door they had entered as Alex pushed it closed.

"I see what you mean. We're a million miles from nowhere and suddenly we're back in civilization again," she said in amazement. "It *is* almost magical."

"Follow me up to the guest room and we'll drop off your bags," said Alex as she started up the winding staircase. It led into a long hallway running left and right. Alex walked down the corridor and opened the first door on the right. "Here you are," she said to Cassie. They entered a large room with a fireplace and several couches arranged nearby for easy viewing of the large flat-screen TV mounted on the wall. Alex set down Cassie's bag and pointed to the doorway at the rear of the room. "Your bedroom's that way with its own bathroom and walk-in closet. Why don't you take a few minutes to get ensconced while I wait out here." She sat down on one of the sofas and picked up the remote control from the low table in front of her. Cassie picked up her other bag and went into the bedroom. She had never seen anything quite like it in all her years of staying at various swanky resorts and hotels. The bridal suite at Caesar's Palace had nothing on this place. She dropped her bags at the foot of the king-size bed and went into the bathroom where she was once again amazed at the tasteful layout of everything and its understated opulence. She took in the sunken bathtub and the large dressing area before taking care of business. After about five minutes, she returned to the living room where Alex was using the remote to surf between the different news channels.

"Anything of interest?" she asked.

"Nope. Not a thing." She looked at Cassie, "Just the same old inane coverage of anything with video footage to watch." She pointed, "Like this kitten that fell out of a tree and was caught by a fireman. Luckily, there was someone there who captured it all with their smart-phone so that it could be shared with the whole world." She clicked off the TV and stood up. "How about we go down to the kitchen and rustle up some coffee?"

"Sounds good to me," said Cassie, hoping that she would finally learn more about Alex's surprise. They walked back down the spiral staircase and went through the doorway at the back. Cassie couldn't help but stare around at the large combination living room and entertainment center. They continued on through a large dining room with a table big enough to seat twenty people and pushed through a set of swinging doors into what was the most elaborate and state-of-the-art kitchen Cassie had ever seen. "Being a Colonel in the Air Force must pay pretty well," she commented and then immediately apologized, "I didn't mean it the way it sounded!"

"No offense taken," smiled Alex. "I make a little over $90,000 a year, but all of my room and board are paid for by the taxpayers." She laughed impishly, "Fortunately, they have no idea how some of their money is being spent." As she spoke, she opened a cupboard and removed a can of Maxwell House coffee. "Have a seat at the breakfast table and make yourself comfortable," she said as she began prepping the coffee maker.

Cassie sat down and frowned, "Don't you feel a little guilty about spending the taxpayers' money on all of this?"

"I did, at first, but I have no real say-so in the matter. If I choose not to live here, they'll turn it over to someone else and I just can't let that happen." Apologetically she said, "Given the grand scheme of things, I came to rationalize it as something beyond my control and simply accepted it." Alex started the coffee maker and went over to the sideboard. Opening the top drawer, she removed a large manila envelope and placed it on the table before sitting down. "In the back of my house, there is a hidden set of rooms that my grandfather used to store the things he could never explain. My father added to it as did I over the years."

"As I recall, you referred to it as your museum."

"Yes, and it's where I go sometimes just to look through the things gathered there and wonder what some of them are and what they're for." She picked up the manila envelope and extracted several sheets of paper. Turning them so that Cassie could read them, she slid them over to her, "About six weeks ago, I went into my museum and found this on my work table. As you can see, it's from Allen and he gave me very specific instructions to follow." Alex stood and went to the counter where she filled two cups with coffee and returned. As Cassie continued to read through the notes, she placed one of the cups in front of her before sitting back down in her own chair and waited patiently until Cassie finished.

Cassie finally looked up from her reading and said to Alex, "How is this even possible? If I find out that this is some sort of elaborate hoax, I'm going to be really pissed, you know."

"I assure you that it's not a hoax. No one else but me knows about my museum and if papers mysteriously materialize in there, then I believe with all my heart that it's the Others at work. And if Allen says I need to do what he tells me to do, I can only believe that it's for a benevolent reason."

"Do you know how this sounds? I mean, blind faith in Apple products is one thing, but you sound almost messianic when you speak of these Others." She frowned as she looked back down at the last item, "And we're supposed to meet with Allen in your museum in about ..." she glanced at her watch "... five minutes from now?"

"That what it says." Alex drained her coffee cup and stood up. "Come with me, Cassie, and let me show you my museum."

5320 BC – NW Persian Gulf Delta

"How much further do you think we have to go?" asked Faruk.

"I'm not sure, but it can't be much more, now that we've seen the sea," replied Akkad.

For several years now, Akkad and his village had heard various tales about the city by the sea where people lived all year around. The dwellers there no longer had to migrate with the seasons in order to survive. If the stories could be believed, the land was fertile and the crops were bountiful and everyone lived a life filled with abundance. The past two seasons, their own land had barely produced enough to keep their growing tribe fed and clothed and it was more out of desperation than with logic that he had convinced the others to make the trek to see the city for themselves. Three months ago, they had said a final goodbye to the lands of their ancestors and packed up everything that they could lash to their goats to hopefully survive the long journey eastward. Although they had managed to forage for berries and some small game along the way, they had found it necessary to begin rationing the food and water about three weeks ago. At that time, they had started to give up any hope of making it to the city, if it even existed at all. However, after only a week of half-portion meals, they met another group of travelers going the other way. These assured them that they only had about a two-week trek ahead of them before they reached the fabled destination. Noticing how malnourished Akkad's group had become, the strangers had insisted on sharing their own supplies and, killing two of their lambs, provided the nomads with their first real meal in months. Afterwards, they all sat around the campfire and had listened in awe to the tales of life in the big city. The next morning, they had started out with their bellies full and a renewed hope in their hearts that their journey was going to be worth it.

Akkad climbed the last bit of a small hill and stopped at the summit. Faruk caught up with him several moments later and stopped as well. Below them, as far as their eyes could see to the distant seashore, spread the city of Eridu. No longer a fable, but a real place. It was far larger than either Akkad or Faruk had imagined and it took them a minute or two to discern the thousands of people moving across the landscape to put everything into its proper scale. It was only then that they finally grasped the enormity of the city that stretched out before them and realized that it was much further away than they originally thought. On a high ground nearest to them rose a temple that towered over everything else. It descended in layers to a large open area surrounded by smaller temples. Outward and seaward around these spilled an organized vastness of reed dwellings. Encompassing it all was a high wall that spanned a ten-minute walk in each direction. Akkad compared its height to the people at its base and estimated that it would take fifteen men standing on each other's shoulders to reach the top of the wall. He tried to imagine how such a thing could have been built. To the right of them, spreading out from the wall and towards the sea stretched seemingly endless fields of irrigated farmland.

Akkad at last turned to Faruk, "Run and tell the others that we are here at last!"

Faruk turned and went down the slope at a quick trot. He couldn't wait to tell the others, although he was somewhat frightened and intimidated by what he had seen. The strangers that had fed them had repeatedly assured them that they would be welcomed and provided with a place to live. But that promise sounded somewhat hollow now and he worried that they might be taken into slavery instead. Or worse.

Akkad studied the city before him. The wall ran unbroken all around its perimeter. It appeared that the only way into the city proper was by climbing a single vast ramp up to the top of the wall and then another lesser ramp up to where the first of the temples were situated. Surrounding the base of the outermost ramp was a myriad of reed constructions with a number of people milling around them like bees around a beehive. Akkad wasn't sure about how they might be received by these people, but they would find out soon enough. While Faruk had his doubts, Akkad chose to believe they would be safe since he had no other reasonable alternative at this point. He studied the ramp with its buzz of activity and decided that his followers could wait off to the side while he and Faruk went up the ramps and into the city itself.

+ + +

Faruk and Akkad stared at the ramp that lay before them. It began a hundred-odd paces from the massive wall itself and rose at a steep angle to its top. They had walked down from the hills to its base with everyone in tow. As they neared the ramp, they had left the rest of their tribe and the pack-animals in a loose-knit group quite a way back before their final destination. Before they could begin to walk up the incline, however, a man ran up and intercepted them.

"I can see from the look on your faces that you are new here," he said. "Perhaps I can help show you around?"

"Is it that obvious?" asked Akkad.

"Everyone has the same reaction their first time. I've been here nearly ten years and I still marvel at everything. There is nothing like it anywhere." The man looked at each of them somewhat skeptically. "Got anything to trade?"

Akkad had been warned about people taking advantage of newcomers to Eridu. "We are poor and have little more than the shirts on our backs. If you can steer us in the right direction, we would be very appreciative. However, if you expect anything more from us than a 'thank-you', then you need to find someone else on which to prey."

The man laughed, "Please, my good man, put yourself at ease. My name is Yosef and I represent the Temple of Commerce. It's my job to welcome newcomers to Eridu and make sure that they aren't treated unfairly until we can get you properly registered as citizens."

Faruk frowned, "Citizens?"

"I assumed that you're here to start a new life. To leave the drudgery of your nomadic ways. That is what Eridu has to offer its citizens. If you are only here to visit our fine city, then we can issue a temporary permit for the length of your stay."

Akkad spoke up, "To be brutally honest, we were slowly dying off little by little whether we wanted to admit it or not. Each passing season brought more mouths to feed but less food than ever to feed them. The crops no longer grew where they used to and the fields were no longer filled with grass for the animals." Akkad paused for a moment before continuing, "Our trip here was more out of desperation than anything else. We place ourselves at your mercy."

Yosef pointed in the distance, "I assume that is the rest of your tribe over there? Would you mind if we go over and have you introduce me to them? I imagine that some of them, perhaps the women and children, are frightened to death not knowing what may happen to them."

Akkad glanced at Faruk who shrugged, "I see no harm in it. The sooner we all know what's in store for us, the better."

Yosef smiled and led the way to the group. As they drew near, Akkad went on ahead and told everyone that Yosef was here to greet them and welcome them to Eridu. He fervently prayed that he had made the right decision in coming here.

Yosef stood before the followers of Akkad and they crowded around so they could each get a better look at their first city dweller. He looked just like they did, but his clothing was unlike any that they had ever seen. Unlike their own brown garments, his robe was brightly colored like the blue of the sky and he had a sash around his waist that was a bright yellow. Also unlike their own clothes, his looked to be of a lighter material that hung well from his shoulders and yet conformed to his body. His hair and beard were also of a style and shape unfamiliar to their own fashions and was neatly trimmed which gave his bearded face a surprisingly clean look.

"Tribe of Akkad, on behalf of the High Priests of Eridu, and in the name of the Temple of Commerce, I welcome you to our bountiful city! If you choose to live here, life will be very different from what you are used to, but I think that you will find it far more rewarding than what you have known up until now. Once you have registered, each family will be given a place to live and a parcel of land to do with as they see fit. Each individual that is not part of a family will be given a smaller dwelling and a smaller parcel of land. You will learn more about this during your orientation session. That is, of course, if you've decided to live here as citizens." Yosef cleared his throat before continuing, "I traditionally like to welcome new tribes by giving the eldest woman a gift. Would the oldest woman among you please come forward?"

Amid some protesting on her part, a wizened old woman was moved towards the front of the crowd. Yosef stepped forward and welcomed her, "Come on out here and don't be bashful. You've earned the right to be the pride of your tribe." He waited until she approached him, "What is your name, might I ask?"

The old woman looked around at her friends and relatives and then gathered up her courage, "Ruthi," she finally said.

"It's a pleasure to make your acquaintance, Ruthi. Now come with me, please." He beckoned for her to follow him towards the base of the ramp.

She looked imploringly to Akkad who told her, "Go ahead and do as he says, Mother, I have a good feeling about all of this."

She nodded and struggled to catch up with Yosef who waited patiently before continuing at a pace that better suited her. As they strode out of earshot, the rest of the tribe milled around Akkad and pelted him with questions.

+ + +

Once again, Akkad and Faruk were ready to walk up the ramp and into the city. Yosef had returned with Ruthi and she had done nothing but talk non-stop about the stalls she had seen along the base of the ramp. Each of them, she claimed, had something that you could obtain by trading something else. She had spotted one glittering stall that offered decorative necklaces and was drawn to one in particular. It had a stone on a simple lanyard, but the stone was unlike any she had ever seen. The woman had offered to let her try it on and it hung from her neck and sparkled in the sunlight. She began to take it off, but Yosef stopped her and said, "This is my gift to you and I hope that you will enjoy it." He turned to the woman in the stall and said, "Please put this on my account," and acknowledged her nod in return. When they returned, she forgot how old and decrepit she was and ran the last little bit to rejoin their group. She couldn't wait to show everyone the necklace that Yosef had given her. Akkad appreciated Yosef's manipulation of his mother because it would make things much easier now. Whatever doubts the others may have had, they had been laid to rest by Yosef's shrewd actions.

Yosef had then offered to go with Akkad and Faruk to get them registered. As they began the long walk up the incline, Yosef told them, "We are headed to the Temple of Commerce where all manners of business are conducted. As part of the registration process, you will each get an account of trade that will initially list everything you currently own. As you get settled in and begin to integrate with the economy, you will register all of your transactions with the Temple as well. Again, I get ahead of myself. This will all be covered in the orientation session."

They reached the top of the wall and paused to look back. The ground was far below them and their tribe looked small and insignificant in the distance. They turned and continued up the next ramp to the temple that towered above them. As they crested the ramp and walked out onto the main plaza, they stared at all the people coming and going about their business. Whatever that might be. They stared ahead at the doors of the temple itself and marveled that a man four times their height could walk through them without stooping. They entered the great hallway beyond the doors and stared open-mouthed at the high ceilings and the vastness interrupted only occasionally by the massive pillars that supported the ceiling itself.

"When you're all done gawking, we'll go over to the Registration Counter and get you started. Once you've been through the process, you should be able to help the rest of your tribe get registered as well. Someone will be assigned to each account to help get you situated. You won't be needing my services anymore, but feel free to come find me at the base of the ramp, even if it's just to say hello." Yosef headed toward the right side of the vast expanse where a long continuous table-like structure was set out from the wall and ran nearly the full length of this side of the room. Yosef walked them over to what they assumed must be Registration and spoke to the man behind the counter, "This is Akkad and Faruk. They have sixty-four people in addition to themselves who will be registering. A rough guess is eight families of five, three families of four, and the rest singles. Twelve pack-goats and minimal property." He turned back to Akkad and Faruk, "This is Ramil and he will take care of you from here on out. I must say that it was a pleasure to meet both of you and your tribe. Again, I welcome you to Eridu!" He turned and walked away.

"Hey Yosef!" cried Faruk. Yosef paused and looked back, "Thank-you!" Yosef grinned and waved as he strolled out of the massive hallway.

Ramil smiled at Akkad and Faruk, "Okay now, which of you wants to go first?"

+ + +

Later that evening, Akkad and Faruk sat in the great dining hall. They were still somewhat in a state of shock at everything that they had seen and experienced on their first day in Eridu. All of the stories that they had heard were true and then some. Everywhere that they had been led or directed, everything that they had seen or heard, everyone that they met along the way, was something that they had never before encountered. Akkad was dealing with events more easily than Faruk, but even he was at a loss for words from time to time.

"This bread is simply amazing," Akkad commented to no one in particular.

Faruk nodded, "You keep saying that, Akkad."

"But it is! In all my days I have never seen or tasted anything like this. When I asked what it was made of, they told me it was made from ground wheat. Now I ask you, you've grown wheat your whole life and baked countless loaves of bread, did any of them ever turn out like this?"

"Of course not."

"When I asked how this was possible, they said that a temple priest showed them how to add yeast to the bread and wait for it to bloat up before baking." Akkad picked up another piece from the basket in front of them and broke it in two, "And this is the result." He bit into the bread and mumbled because his mouth was full, "Simply amazing!"

Faruk frowned, "All of this is simply too good to be true. What do they want from us?"

"You still don't trust them, do you?"

"No, I don't. There's got to be a catch somewhere."

Akkad didn't say anything while he savored the bread he was chewing. He swallowed and said, "I'm expecting that we will learn more tomorrow when we attend this orientation session they keep talking about. But from what I can understand so far, we have a two-week grace period during which food and a place to stay are, how did he put it?"

"On the house," replied Faruk.

Akkad nodded, "Yes, that's it, 'on the house'." He smiled at Faruk, "In the meantime, I suggest that we take advantage of their generosity and figure out what we're going to do once our two weeks are up." He sighed contentedly and reached once more into the bread basket.

+ + +

Mardu and Itok stood atop the Temple of Enki and looked out across Eridu. It had been twenty-one summers since that first one when they had built all of this with the help of the gods. They had stood at this very spot and gazed with awe at what they had created. Back then, of course, it was completely empty and devoid of life except for Mardu and Itok, who lived in the temple below. Today, however, it was a bustling hub of commerce that boasted nearly 20,000 citizens with the economic capacity to absorb 30,000 more.

Itok laughed, "Do you remember the look on Naim's face when he returned from the north?"

"Of course I do! How could I ever forget something like that? If you were in his shoes and you came back to find that someone had built this city in the six months that you had been gone, would you believe your eyes and your senses?"

"No, but I must say that he adapted pretty quickly. Although you and I heard what Enki and Nammu were saying about this place, it never really seemed to make any sense to either of us. However, when we explained it all to Naim, he was not only able to grasp its overall purpose immediately but also able to figure out how to get it all to work." Itok continued, "And don't forget how fast he picked up the writing of the gods as well. I'm still struggling with some of the bigger words."

Mardu smiled, "That's why he's the High Priest of Commerce and you're not."

They stood for a while longer, not saying anything. Mardu looked out past the city walls where he and Enkimdu had long ago dug all of the irrigation ditches that fed water to the vast fertile farmlands that they had created. He glanced at his brother and noted that he was probably thinking similar thoughts about the temples he and Enki had built. He looked back out over all the people that were working in the fields and then pictured those working in the various crafts and trades that occupied most of the dwellings within the city walls. And he also thought about the nearly 2,000 high and low priests and scribes of Eridu who were schooled in the ways of the gods and made sure that the city ran smoothly and productively.

Itok finally broke the silence, "I'm getting hungry. How about we find something to eat?"

"Sounds good to me," said Mardu. He looked out over the city and surrounding land one more time and then turned to follow his brother down the narrow stairway.

+ + +

"Our grace period is almost up, Akkad. Have you made up your mind about what we're going to do?"

Faruk and Akkad had returned to the hill from the top of which they had first seen Eridu. As they gazed out over the city before them once again, Akkad replied, "After spending the past week visiting each part of the city and talking to everyone that would lend me an ear, I'm more certain now than the last time you asked me."

"But have you actually told anyone else what you've decided?"

"Well, no," admitted Akkad. "Which is why I wanted to come back up here and explain it one more time to you before we tell the others."

"Let me try to explain it back to you first and then you can correct me and fill in the gaps of my understanding."

"Okay, I'm listening."

"We have been given a considerable allotment of land. We combine all of our allotments into a large area for growing crops and a smaller area for grazing animals. There's far more land than we will need for our own consumption, so we put the excess into the Temple of Plenty where we get credits on our account. With the credits we make from the crops, we build an oven and a place to bake this wonderful bread you're obsessed with and then we share it with others who then give us a portion of their credits on account."

Akkad looked surprised, "All this time, I didn't think you were listening to me." He pointed to the right toward the farmland nearby. "I was thinking that this land along here would do nicely."

"Why not something closer to the sea?" asked Faruk.

"From what I understand, each spring, the river floods most of the farmland. That's why there's a wall around the city. The land near here doesn't flood as often and sometimes doesn't flood at all. Periodically, the canals that bring the water need dredging and other maintenance from the flooding and we can minimize that with this location here." He pointed again for emphasis.

Faruk nodded his agreement, "Sounds good to me. I was also thinking about this place we're going to have where we will be giving people your marvelous bread."

"We won't be giving it to them, we will be putting it on their account."

"Okay, this place where people will be putting things on their account. I was thinking it might be nice to have some tables they can sit at and my daughter could cook them some food to go with it."

Akkad smiled, "And maybe you can brew up some of your famous barley malt to go with everything?"

"Yes. And put it on their account." Faruk frowned, "That's the part I don't really understand. What exactly is this account and what are these credits that go on it?"

"Do you remember when we first arrived and you said there had to be a catch?"

Faruk nodded.

"Well, in order to be able to do all of this, some of us are going to have to learn how to read and write the symbols of the gods."

"Read and write?"

"Reading is the manner of understanding the markings made by the scribes and writing is the manner by which these markings are made.

Everything that we do for someone or they do for us is noted on a clay tablet, somewhere, that eventually makes it into the master account. Periodically, the master accounts are reconciled by the high priests and a judgment is made as to how much we need to give to someone else and how much they need to give to us. We may feed someone on account for several months, but eventually they will give us something we need. Like a goat or maybe an ox."

Understanding came over Faruk, "And to make sure that our accounts are in order, we either need to learn how to read and write ourselves or to trust one of the scribes to do it for us."

"Exactly." Akkad pointed again to the land he had in mind. "Let's go down there and look it over. We have plenty of time to get to the Temple of Commerce today and register it as our allotment." Akkad turned and started down the hill with Faruk following close behind him.

Three Months Ago – Mount Ararat, Turkey

Allen reviewed what he was going to say one last time. He had to get it right the first time or the ripple effect might contain unforeseen consequences. Although he had repeatedly rehearsed the next few minutes in the simulator, he still had butterflies in his stomach. Allen smiled wryly at the thought that it was his fear of the Butterfly Effect itself that was the root cause of the butterflies fluttering below. His mind wandered as he thought back over the last six weeks and what he had finally learned about the past.

+ + +

Allen left the Council Chambers and headed straight for the room containing the Chaos Machine interface. He had read what he could in the instruction manual and couldn't wait to look back along the timeline. He had repeatedly scanned the next year of the future looking for answers and had finally decided that they could only be found in the past. He entered the chamber and sat down at the console. He experimentally slid the timeline forward a little and back to the present. Then he moved it in the other direction and, unlike previous times, it now slid backwards as well. As before, the current location along the scale was indicated by a green line. Additionally, there were occasional red and yellow lines that the manual indicated were branches and forks in the timeline. Bookmarks, Hazel had called them. Allen was already familiar with the yellow ones since they also cluttered the future timeline as well. He had even created a few of the trial adjustments himself to see how they affected the outcome. Moving backwards, they had no effect, but when moving forward, they were like signposts along the way. The yellow markers were points in time when a trial alteration was made to the inputs. Following the yellow timeline from that point forward projected future events that would occur if the alteration was, in fact, made. The red markers were points along the timeline where an alteration was implemented, forever pruning away the original sequence of events. The red timelines could be followed to see what history might have been if it had not been altered in some way. Allen noted as he scrolled back further and further in time that, while there were many, many yellow lines, there were almost no red ones to be found.

Rewinding the past, the first red marker that Allen encountered was when Wyatt had kidnapped him from his office bathroom. He was curious to see what would have happened if he had not been spirited away and was now sitting at a console underneath Mount Ararat pondering what might have been. Moving a month, two, five, and finally a year into the alternative future showed him having yet another press conference with Cassie while introducing their new product at the precise moment that the Earth exploded. Jumping back to his current location on the timeline, he began to scroll further back into the past. After a few dozen swipes of his finger produced no more red markers, he decided to change the scale. Where previously each swipe of his finger scrolled back one year, he was now able to page back ten years at a time with each swipe. He quickly encountered the next red marker in 1947 on July 4th. Allen was at a loss as to what it indicated since there were no notes associated with the change that was made. Unlike the previous red marker that he knew was connected to his disappearance, this one seemed unrelated to anything that he could determine. Following the red line forward allowed Allen to visit different times and places, but it wasn't until he browsed to the present in this timeline that he realized that there were no cell phones or computers or internet. Or any of the myriad other devices that everyone takes for granted. While trying to figure out what change might have happened to cause such a huge difference, he made one of his famous dissociative leaps of mind when he suddenly realized that the Roswell Incident had never occurred in the original timeline.

Finding Roswell, New Mexico, was easy enough and Allen followed signs to the site in the present timeline. Rewinding back to the date of the crash, he watched in fascination as a huge fiery weather balloon smashed into the ground with its attached payload. Unable to actually touch anything to investigate further himself, he advanced the timeline until he could watch the local RAAF MPs uncover a shiny gloss-black softball-sized sphere that had embedded itself halfway into the protective casing of the payload. By carefully moving back into the past and moving upwards at the same time, Allen was able to back-track the path of the balloon until the moment the glowing sphere passed at meteoric speed through the balloon igniting the hydrogen gas before smashing into the hard case of the instrumentation package. After pausing the moment, he switched to the original timeline and watched as the balloon continued its upward journey without interference. No softballs; no

Roswell Incident; no transistors; no micro-electronic revolution. One tiny small change that forever changed the course of history. Somewhere over New Mexico in 1947, a butterfly had flapped its wings. Allen didn't know how or where the softball had come from, but he had a pretty good idea who had set it in motion. And he was determined to see what became of it.

He glanced at the time and gave a slight start as he realized that he had been trying to track down this one change for a little more than four hours. As he scrolled back further into the past, he encountered more red timelines for 1929 and then 1881 and, prior to that, 1828. Offhand, they didn't ring any bells, other than maybe 1929 having something to do with the stock market crash. While being able to virtually go anywhere and anywhen, he still had to painstakingly search until he found a newspaper headline or a newscast or something to try and understand what was different. He had no way of actively looking up information as a passive observer and the odds of finding someone who happened to be Googling something he might want to know were miniscule at best (even if the internet still existed in the timeline of interest). Somewhere there had to be a change log to document the rationale for the change and describe it in detail. He made a mental addition to the top of the FAQ list he was readying for his next meeting with Hazel and then turned to finding out when the void in Iraq first appeared. Before he had his next little sit-down with the Chairman, he wanted to have enough answers in order to ask the right questions and he wasn't going to give up until he had them.

Sliding the scale multiplier to the maximum setting, Allen was rewarded with a timeline that stretched more than 7,350 years into the past. Fine red lines crowded the beginning of the timeline and slowly fell off in frequency as it progressed to the present and beyond into the next year. There were also several white lines at wide intervals about which he had no clue. Thinking about the two changes he had explored, it was almost incomprehensible how much had been done to what should have been the un-edited history of the planet. His planet. Who in the hell were these people and what the hell was really going on? Allen closed his eyes and slowly counted to ten while breathing slowly and deeply. He opened his eyes and proceeded to zoom in on the beginning of the timeline until it had expanded to show the first ten years of the Chaos Machine. He navigated to the location of the void under what was back then the northwestern-most tip of the Persian Gulf and discovered what he knew he was going to find all along. He moved the controls and checked Mount

Ararat as well, but the void that existed today was not there in 5,342 BC. Jumping 100 years at a time along the timeline, he was able to determine that the none-ness surrounding his current location appeared some 2,500 years later. Clearly they were related, somehow, but Allen knew he would get the answers to his growing list of questions much, much more quickly directly from the horse's mouth himself; or he was going to tell Hazel to pound sand and then go back home to await the End of the World (probably at yet another press conference). He put the console into sleep mode and stormed off to find Hazel. After randomly looking for Hazeltine in a few of his favorite hangouts, Allen belatedly settled himself into his office after being told that he was on his way there and would meet with him shortly.

+ + +

After about twenty minutes, there was a knock at the door and Hazeltine poked his head into the room. "Hi, Allen. Did you want to see me about something?"

"Yes, I do." It took some effort for Allen to keep his voice calm. "Do you have a few minutes to come in and sit down and go over several things with me?"

"I assume this has something to do with what you've learned in the past few hours at the console? The full Council has unanimously agreed to hold nothing back at this point. I've cleared my calendar indefinitely so that I can fully answer any new questions you may have. If a technical explanation is needed, Minerva will be more than happy to give you all the gory details, of course."

"But, of course." Exasperated, Allen went on, "This may sound a little harsh, but try to see it from my perspective. A month-and-a-half ago, you kidnapped me and brought me here and overwhelmed me with all this magical technology and convinced me that the end is nigh. An end that will be brought about by something buried beneath the ground in Iraq. Something that was placed there more than 7,000 years ago. You've asked for my help when it looks like you're part of the problem." Allen took a deep breath to calm himself a bit before continuing, "Care to fill me in on a few of the minor little details you might have neglected to mention before? Like, who are you guys, really? And where are you from?"

"Are you hungry at all, Allen?"

"What?"

"I think we need to sit down over a nice meal while I fill you in on the rest of the story."

"Thanks, Hazel, but I want answers. Now."

"The meal is an integral part of the answer. You've never seen my kitchen, have you?"

"I didn't even know you had a kitchen. As a matter a fact, I have no idea where you live or sleep. Or *if* you sleep. You're always just around when I need you."

Hazeltine beckoned to Allen. "Come with me. It will be a dinner that you will never forget. I promise." He turned and stepped into the hallway where he waited patiently for Allen to follow.

Allen sighed and stood up to comply. What was it about Hazel that kept extending his natural trust for this man? He shook his head as he walked toward the door, "You and your promises!"

They walked down the short hallway that led to the teleportal and crossed over into a nicely appointed kitchen and dining area that flowed around a large round table surrounded by seven chairs. Along the wall was a counter with several industrial-looking appliances that Allen didn't recognize. The lighting was indirect and, while muted, provided a bright glare-free environment. While not overly large, the enclosed area was spacious and yet somewhat cozy at the same time.

"Where are we?" asked Allen.

"Welcome to the *Pride of Fridu!*"

August 7, 1828 – London, England

"Hendricks! Where are you, Hendricks?"

"Right here, sir. What can I do for you?"

"My wine glass seems to have gone empty again."

Hendricks was too much the gentleman's gentleman to allow his emotions to show, but inwardly he frowned to himself. "Perhaps now would be a good time to go upstairs and go to bed." He made a show of taking out his watch, looking at it, and then putting it back into his vest pocket again. "It's well past your usual time to retire."

"Bloody hell. It's been five years now and we can't even get the first three stages working right. It's always one damned thing after another."

"Mr. Clement says that he's found the problem and that he can have the replacement gears ready by early next week."

"Yes, yes, I know. But it's always one bloody thing after another. I thought by now I would at least have some type of fully functioning prototype. Enough to show that the design is sound and that it can be built to the exacting specifications that are required."

"It's a very ambitious project, sir. Nothing like this has ever been built before. I'm sure that Mr. Clement will return next week and your prototype will work like it should."

"You're a lot more optimistic than I am, Hendricks." He sighed and stared wistfully into his empty wine glass. "Perhaps you're right. I should go to bed now."

He began to stand up unsteadily and Hendricks quickly moved to assist him up the stairs to his bedroom.

"Good night, sir. I'm sure that things will look much better in the morning light."

"Good night, Hendricks. I hope that you are right."

+ + +

The next morning, Hendricks had breakfast waiting by the time his employer made his way down to the dining room. Impeccably dressed and on-time as always, he bore no sign of the excess alcohol that he had consumed the previous evening. After seeing him to his place, Hendricks first brought him his morning cup of tea and his Friday copy of The Daily Universal Register. As he laid the paper in front of him, he pointed to an article on the front page that mentioned a new weaver opening her shop nearby.

"Look at this, sir. They've set up one of the newest Jacquard looms just a couple of miles down the lane. Have you ever seen one in action?"

"Not personally, no. One of the Society fellows has gone on at length about the devices and the processes involved, but I dare say that it has little practical use beyond making fancier shawls at a cheaper price."

Hendricks returned to the kitchen and came back with a small silver rack with several pieces of toast and a crystal bowl full of warm marmalade with a serving spoon. Setting them to the side of the plate, he said, "Might I suggest an outing, sir? It might get your mind off of other things. I, for one, would like to see this loom and, if I'm not mistaken, I think it would be of interest to you as well."

"Since I don't have anything better to do while waiting for George to come up with the new parts, I think that sounds like a smashing idea. If you wouldn't mind bringing the carriage around to the front after I'm finished eating, we'll go and take a look."

"Very good, sir," replied Hendricks, smiling to himself, as he left to fetch the rest of the breakfast.

+ + +

After he had cleared the plates and poured a second cup of tea, Hendricks went outside to the rear of the carriage house and began the process of harnessing the ever-cantankerous horse. While not one of his favorite tasks, he had developed a tentative working relationship with the beast and found it tolerable after a fashion. If all went well with this outing, he would finally be able to take his leave and return home. The thought cheered him considerably, although the past few years had been enjoyable enough and Charles Babbage was a fascinating person to be around during this age. After coaxing the horse to back up to the carriage, he successfully maneuvered the harness and traces into position and then paused for a moment to stroke its muzzle. Reaching into his pocket, he pulled out a lump of sugar and held it out on his palm where it was quickly licked up by the equine's tongue. He wryly reflected that it was indeed unfortunate that horses didn't just naturally want to pull wagons for a living. Things would be much better for everyone involved. Until then, however, he had learned that a little bit of bribery worked best. Climbing into the driver's seat, he released the brake and drove the carriage around to the front of the manor where his erstwhile employer was waiting expectantly. Hendricks jumped down and opened the door to the carriage proper and waited until his charge was properly seated before climbing back up into the driver's seat and setting off.

The shop was a bit further than Hendricks had let on, but they arrived in less than half an hour. Hendricks tied the horse to the post in front of the shop and spoke to the young man sitting on a bench outside. "Here's a shilling for you, laddie, if you'll keep an eye on Mr. Babbage's carriage. And there'll be another one for you if you stay until we return."

"Thank you, kind sir. I'll make sure it's well watched over. You can trust me, sir, just ask anyone. Me name's Mickey."

"That won't be necessary nor do we expect to be gone very long." He stepped to open the carriage door and helped his employer out onto the store stoop in front of a door which bore the legend in gilt:

Analytic Designs, Ltd.
Mlle. DuBois
Proprietoress

Hendricks knocked twice on the door and then held it open as Babbage entered before him. As the door closed behind them, a merrily tinkling bell sounded their presence. A small woman with long black hair piled high on top of her head emerged from the back of the shop and greeted them at the small counter that occupied about half of the space.

"Good morning, kind sirs. How can I be of assistance?"

"Please allow me to introduce myself. My name is Charles Babbage and this is Hendricks, my majordomo. I have an interest in various mechanical contrivances and I am led to understand that you have one of the new Jacquard looms in your shop?"

"Why, yes, I do. And allow me to introduce myself as well. I am Sylvie DuBois. I am hoping to use the loom to develop custom scarves and tapestries for the higher-end London market." She smiled brightly at him. "Perhaps I can design one for you? Something in a silk brocade, maybe? I think you'll find that my rates are quite attractive."

Babbage mused to himself that the rates were not the only thing that was attractive about Miss DuBois. "To be perfectly honest, I've heard a lot about these Jacquard looms–even studied some drawings–but I've never had an opportunity to see one in person." He looked about the shop before replying. "Would it be too much of an imposition to ask for you to show me around?" Anticipating her reaction, he continued, "I would even be willing to pay a nominal fee for the privilege of the excursion."

DuBois smiled back at Babbage, "I sense that you are more interested in the loom itself than the works of art that it can produce." She turned and gestured toward the doorway behind the counter, "Follow me and I'll show you how I marry art with technology to create something new and exciting."

Babbage fell in behind her as she walked down a short narrow hallway toward the back of the shop followed closely behind by Hendricks. Opening the door at the end, they stepped into a large square workroom that was about sixty feet on a side. Numerous skylights set above in the roof allowed a plentiful amount of natural light to shine down onto the large assemblage that occupied the center. Along one of the walls were two much smaller devices with numerous stacks of thick cardboard slats that appeared to be arranged somewhat at random. Standing in another corner was a large drafting table with a roll of paper that lay across the top that was covered with a myriad of markings.

"What do you think of my loom, Mr. Babbage? Isn't she a beauty?"

Clearly fascinated, Babbage moved toward the loom and slowly circled it while studying it intently. The main frame, as well as almost all of the structural components, was constructed of a light wood with a finely polished sheen. From the middle of it all rose a chaotically ordered mass of strings that had to number into the hundreds. They swept upward into an enclosure that sat atop the loom nearly ten feet off the floor. Hendricks smiled to himself as he watched the expression of intense concentration on his employer's face as he studied the Jacquard invention. He had seen that look many times before and knew that Babbage was firmly hooked.

"It's unbelievable! It's like the antithesis of one of my own creations. Whereas mine are almost entirely constructed of metal and precise down to the thousandth of an inch, this thing is almost entirely made of wood and looks like a veritable rat's nest with all of these threads everywhere." He paused and smiled apologetically to Sylvie, "I didn't mean that like it sounded. I'm not sure what I was expecting, but I was unprepared for anything like this."

"Well, I must say that your timing is impeccable. I was just getting ready to make a trial run of my newest design. If you would like to stay and watch, I'll be more than happy to give you a demonstration of what I call analytic weaving."

"I'd like that very much. I must confess that I can't make heads or tails of exactly how this thing works just by looking at it." He craned his head back to look up, "I gather that those drapes of punched cards somehow feed into that mechanical assembly up top, but it's not clear what happens at that point."

Sylvie laughed, "It's not as complicated as it looks. If you will give me a moment to lock the front door, I'll check the fire and make sure that the boiler is up to pressure."

"Boiler?"

"Oh, surely sir, you didn't think I would require myself to actually perspire by working the loom by hand?" Her eyes twinkled merrily, "Let me go lock up and I'll be right back to give you my dog-and-pony show. Feel free to look around all you want, but please don't touch anything." She turned and went through the door leading to the front of the shop.

For the first time, Babbage noticed the door at the back of the room and the heavy wooden shaft that passed overhead through a small square hole in the wall. The other end buried itself into the rectangular iron box at the very top of the loom. Hendricks noted that his countenance was approaching something like true rapture and he smiled outwardly in spite of himself, "It's a fascinating device, is it not?" Babbage didn't reply, but he was clearly entranced.

DuBois returned and interrupted his train of thought, "If you would like to see my power plant, come with me." She strolled smartly across the shop to the door at the rear. Opening it, she held it so that both Babbage and Hendricks could precede her. Attached as a separate building, the steam room contained a large boiler about four feet tall and three feet in diameter. But it was the giant rocker arm and flywheel that dominated most of it. A wide leather belt connected the flywheel to the shaft that Babbage had previously noted in the other room. DuBois moved to the coal bin, but Hendricks beat her to it.

"Allow me, mademoiselle. I'll be more than happy to shovel the coal for you, if you'll just tell me when to stop."

"Why, thank you, Hendricks, that's not necessary, but I appreciate it." She glanced at the gauge affixed to the side of the boiler, "If you'll just add two full scoops to what's in there, it should be more than enough. We've already got enough head to start it up." As Hendricks picked up the shovel to comply, she stepped over to the large valve on the pipe connected to the steam cylinder and slowly turned it while keeping her eye on the gauge. A slow chuff-chuff sound began that matched the rotation of the flywheel as the steam engine began building up speed. After about thirty seconds, she stopped opening the valve and watched the gauge intently for another full minute. She turned to Babbage and smiled once more, "While we're waiting for Antoine to stabilize, allow me to give you a quick overview of what's about to happen." She led the way to the door leading back into the shop.

"Antoine?" asked Babbage as he followed through the doorway.

"Yes, I named my little steam engine after a friend of mine. Like most men, he can be very temperamental." She closed the door and walked over to the drafting table. "Here is where it all starts. I first create a drawing of what I want to weave and then transform my design into the appropriate pick patterns that are needed to weave it. For this piece, I first created an India ink portrait of the customer who has commissioned me to make this for them."

"Why, that looks just like Lady Pemberley!" exclaimed Babbage.

"It turned out to be a very good likeness, indeed," she replied modestly. "However, I would appreciate it if you would keep her name to yourself. I take my pledge of the confidentiality of my customers very seriously."

"My lips are sealed, I promise. Please continue."

"I next scribe horizontal and vertical lines across the drawing. How many lines I use and how close they are drawn depend on both the material and the size of the final product. At each intersection of a vertical and horizontal line, I make a mark denoting whether it will show the warp or the woof." She paused to make sure that her audience was with her before she beckoned them to follow her over to the machine next to the piles of cardboard slats. "Once this is done, I transpose the tick marks into holes that I punch into these cards and the patterns of the holes determine which warp threads are lifted in sequence." She picked up a blank card from the table and inserted it lengthways into the press. "Here, let me show you how it's done," she said as she sat down on a stool and placed her fingers into the machine. "I can specify the pattern of eight threads at a time by pressing and holding these keys and stepping down on the treadle below." A loud thump emanated from the punch as she said this. "I simply look at each group of eight as I move across the pattern and mimic the tick marks with my fingers." Another thump issued from the punch. "For this work, there are 400 threads in the warp which means I need to punch fifty patterns of eight in each card." She emphasized this with yet another step on the treadle.

"Why eight holes at a time?" Babbage asked.

She laughed and held up her hands, "Because I have eight fingers." She stood up and moved to the loom itself and pointed out the hanging chains of cards, "Once I've punched the cards, I stitch them together so that they can be fed into the Jacquard Head. Each card lifts the appropriate threads of the warp and the shuttle is then sent through to form the pattern required."

"There must be hundreds of these cards!" Babbage exclaimed. "Good Lord, woman, how long did it take you to punch all of these?"

"There's 1,136 cards all-told and it took me about three months from start to finish. As I mentioned earlier, your timing couldn't have been any better since I only just finished the last card this morning." She looked at both Hendricks and Babbage expectantly as she walked over to the side of her loom, "Well, gentlemen, are you ready to see automated weaving at its finest?" Without waiting for an answer, she reached up and pulled down on a long lever that engaged the idler pulley on the shaft that was slowly turning above. With a slight jerk, the various threads began to lift and fall as the shuttle flew back and forth across the loom. As the weaving progressed, it was taken up on a roller that advanced with each pick. "It takes about three seconds for each cycle or twenty picks a minute. With 1,136 picks, it should be finished in a little under an hour."

Babbage said nothing as he stared in fascination while, minute by minute, the likeness of Lady Pemberley slowly appeared on the face of the cloth. He started suddenly when DuBois reversed the drive lever and the loom suddenly stopped. Like he was awakening from a trance, he turned to her and remarked, "Is it done already? I completely lost track of time there for a while." He turned back to the portrait and leaned forward for a better look. "It looks like she has some sort of bug on her face," he said, as he pointed to an obvious blemish in the material.

"In spite of how careful I am when punching the cards, I sometimes make a mistake. However, this is normal. Each pick is numbered and corresponds to the numbers on the cards. All I have to do is to find the offending cards and replace them." Her infectious smile lit up her face again, "Once that's done, I just run the cards through the loom again and the bugs go away." She pulled a small, ornate timepiece from her apron pocket and glanced at it, "I would normally be more than happy to entertain you further, but I'm anxious to get this completed so that I can present it to my customer on Monday morning. I'm afraid I'm going to have to ask you to leave so that I can focus on finding and fixing the errant cards."

"That's quite understandable, Miss DuBois. I can't tell you how much I have enjoyed watching your loom for the past hour or so. Its operation is quite mesmerizing." Babbage smiled apologetically, "I want to pay you for your time and was wondering if I might be able to have one of the cards to take with me?"

In answer to his question, DuBois walked over to the pile of cardboard slats and picked up two from the large pile and another two from a much smaller pile. Turning back to Babbage, she held them out, "Here are a couple of blank cards as well as a couple of my bad punches for souvenirs. As for paying me for my time, I insist that the pleasure has been all mine. It's not often I have someone visit me who shares such a passion for mechanical contrivances."

"One more question before we take our leave, if you don't mind. What happens to the cards when you've completed Lady Pemberley's scarf?"

"In this particular case, I deliver the cards to the customer along with my creation. If their purchase gets soiled or otherwise damaged, they can bring the cards back to me and I can create a new replacement for a nominal fee. Nominal, that is, compared to the original charge." She smiled deviously, "On the other hand, if they only pay enough for the first run itself, I retain the right to send the cards to Paris where I have the products mass-produced for sale in the French fashion market." She continued speaking as she led Hendricks and Babbage to the front door of the shop, "I'm afraid that my next project isn't quite as challenging as this one, but you are more than welcome to come back any time to view its progress over the next few months." She paused as she passed the counter and retrieved a small pasteboard. Handing it to Babbage she said, "Here's my card. And, please, let me know if you would like to commission one of my analytic designs. I promise that you won't be disappointed."

"I'll keep that in mind. And thank you once again for taking the time to demonstrate this remarkable device. I'm sure that I will see it again in my dreams." With that final comment, he opened the door and stepped out onto the stoop followed by Hendricks.

"Take care! I look forward to seeing you again!" called out DuBois as she shut the door and locked it behind them. Hendricks could see that his employer was lost in thought as he helped him into the still-waiting carriage. He turned to the expectant lad that was standing nearby and handed him a shilling. "Here you are, Mickey, just like I promised. And here's another since we were inside much longer than we thought we would be."

"Thank you, guvnor! Bless you, kind sir! If you ever need me for anything, just ask around."

"I will certainly do that. And I'll make sure to tell everyone how reliable you are," said Hendricks as he climbed up into the driver's seat. He released the brake and began the return trip to Babbage's manor. He would wait until after dinner to show Babbage the letter from his "mother" that would necessitate his immediate departure from Babbage's household. He shook the reins to hasten the horse to move a bit faster.

+ + +

The next morning, deep inside Mt. Ararat, Hazeltine met with Gabriel for his debriefing. "I want to compliment you on a job well done. Your role was played with perfection, as usual. Hopefully, it won't be too terribly long before we will need you on the stage again."

Gabriel smiled, "Thank you, sir, but when you're born to the Guild, the talent comes naturally. All I did was follow the scripts that you provided. However, I'll miss my dear friend Charles after spending so many years with him. I'm afraid he didn't take my resignation very well at all. He's quite a character, you know."

"Yes, that he is."

Hazeltine stood and Gabriel took this as a sign that the meeting was over. As he left, he wondered for the umpteenth time what it was all about. He had played one role or another over the years, but was never quite sure why he was asked to play certain parts. He mentally shrugged and reminded himself that the reason was immaterial and looked forward to the next time Hazel might need him.

After Gabriel had closed the door, Hazeltine once more reviewed the change log and added another note. Without Gabriel's periodic sabotage, Charles Babbage would have completed his difference engine in 1825 and sparked the beginning of a mechanical steam-powered future where electricity would take second seat for more than another century and a half. Vast calculating machines would have followed with more and more complexity as they advanced even further with the punched cards introduced by Babbage's analytical machine in 1827. Having proven that the technology would work, its implications quickly spread to other inventions and devices and monopolized most of the scientific development until late in the 1900s. However, that was a moot point now. Hazeltine reflected on how accurately Gabriel's actions had followed the projections. Maximum deviation from target was less than one part in two-hundred trillion which was more than sufficient for the change that was made. Hazel made one last addition to the log, closed it out, and then left to find something to eat.

Three Months Ago – Mount Ararat, Turkey

"Ten-minute warning ..." The alert interrupted Allen's train of thought and he returned his mind to the present. In ten more minutes, he would no longer be inside a shielded area for the first time since he had vanished from his executive bathroom. As explained to him by Minerva, without the shield, anyone who was actively using the Chaos Machine would cause a feedback loop that would oscillate out of control in mere nanoseconds. Like the high-pitched squeal of a loud speaker system, anyone using the console would be influenced by the projections which would then cause the projections to immediately change which would then, once again, influence the behavior of the observer. This explained the presence of the smaller void that Allen had discovered. The larger void in Iraq served a similar function, but that was ancillary to its main role. Allen's thoughts returned again to when he had first learned its true purpose only a month and a half before.

+ + +

Hazeltine smiled at Allen, "Welcome to the *Pride of Eridu!*"

"Eridu? Like the ancient Sumerian city?"

"Not exactly, but the two are indeed related. As you have already surmised, I am not from around here. My ship, and the legendary city, are both named after the capitol of the planet Shoomar."

Allen could only stare at Hazeltine in response as the reality of his wildest speculations slowly soaked into his already numbed mind. This man wasn't a man at all. He was an alien. And his kind had been interfering with Man's development for nearly 7,400 years. He suddenly felt a need to sit down and did so in the nearest chair at the table.

Hazel frowned with concern, "I can see that you're somewhat surprised, but I was sure that you had already figured things out." He sighed, "Don't you trust me, Allen?"

Allen exhaled as he suddenly realized he was holding his breath, "Yes, I trust you, dammit. I don't know why because it goes against every fiber of my being. I can only conclude, at this point, that you are exhibiting some kind of alien mind control over me."

Hazeltine laughed, "The only mind control involved has simply been giving you access to information that has influenced how you see me. In the past three months, I have made many promises to you and I have kept every last one of them. Is that not true?"

"Yes, this is true," replied Allen somewhat grudgingly.

"I also promised you a meal that you wouldn't forget." As he said this, he turned to one of the appliances set into the countertop alongside the kitchen area and deftly ran his hand over the faceplate. Almost immediately, a tray bearing a large dish with food and a tall glass cylinder of blue liquid appeared which he carefully placed in front of Allen. Smiling expectantly, he continued, "I created this especially for you. I think that you will find it to your liking." Hazel walked around to the opposite side of the table and sat down facing him, "Eat up, Allen, while I tell you a story."

Allen was distracted by the food that had been placed in front of him. The smell was quite unlike anything he had ever experienced before. He suddenly realized that it had been almost seven hours since he had last eaten anything and his salivary glands took on a life of their own. He transferred the plate and glass to the table, along with the oddly emblazoned flatware, and pushed the tray aside. Peering at the food in front of him, he glanced up at Hazeltine suspiciously. "It looks like prime rib and baked potato, but the color's a little off. What is it?"

"The meat is the finest in the known universe. It comes from an animal that is remarkably like your native cow, but whose species originates from a planet we call Amarron. The baked potato is prized for its flavor and comes from a tuber grown only on Winnerk." He assured Allen, "Both are fully compatible with your metabolism and have, in fact, been tuned to your natural preferences."

"And this anti-freeze here?" Allen pointed to the glass.

"That's something that I concocted myself. Unlike alcohol, it merely enhances your natural endorphin levels so that everything is more enjoyable. Also unlike alcohol, it doesn't cloud your judgment nor does it leave you with a hangover due to its lack of toxicity." Hazeltine warned Allen as he picked up his knife, "Be really careful with that, it's a lot sharper than it looks."

Allen looked closely at the knife's edge and wisely decided not to test its sharpness with his thumb. He used it to effortlessly cut off a small piece of the faux prime rib while thinking that a surgeon's scalpel was dull by comparison. After putting the chunk of meat in his mouth and chewing it slowly, a look of pure pleasure lit up his face. He swallowed and took a small sip from the blue liquid to chase it down. "Omigod," he moaned and proceeded to cut off a much larger piece for his next bite.

Hazel laughed, "I always keep my promises." He cleared his throat, leaned forward on his elbows, and continued, "A long time ago, in a galaxy far, far away, a young boy wanted more than anything to be the captain of a space-faring freighter. His father was a freighter captain as was his father's father and so-on going back nine generations before him. For several million years, Shoomar had been known for the reliability of its shipping industry and he wanted to be counted among its elite corps. He, himself, had been born and raised on a freighter much like the one we're on now. Hauling freight from port to port was all that he had ever really known and he had worked at every possible ship-board task that might have been required over the years. When he finally reached his year of maturity, he took his life savings, plus the generous gifts from many encouraging family members, and made a down payment on a ship. It was an old worn-out clunker that he had found in a junk-yard and he was only able to afford it because it was being sold at scrap-value rates. In spite of the generous financing he was able to arrange, he was barely able to keep up with the payments by working as a day laborer. But he spent his nights working on the ship. He first re-furbished everything that only required his labor and nominal materials while saving up for the new and used parts he needed for the controls and mechanics. Having grown up on a similar class ship, he knew what was needed to make it reliable and space-worthy. When he was finally finished, it passed its certification with flying colors and was commissioned into service. While he had been working to get the ship ready, he had formed an alliance with six others who had agreed to enter into a partnership with him in the freight-hauling business. For many, many years, these six individuals had followed their captain through countless jumps from one point in the universe to another as they carried freight to and from thousands of different worlds. Until one day when their dilator valve ruptured in mid-jump and they found themselves in orbit around the planet you call Earth."

Allen had put down his knife and fork a few moments earlier and took a hefty slug of the blue water, "Wait. Back up just a bit. We're on a spaceship?"

"Yes. In the mess hall, actually."

"And you're the descendant of one of the people who crashed here?"

"Not exactly, Allen. The story I just told you is my own. I'm the captain of the ship in my little tale and, before you ask, I'm a little bit younger than thirty-five-thousand of your years." He smiled wryly, "And I've spent the last seven-thousand-odd of them trying to figure out a way to get back home again." Hazel gestured at the remaining food on Allen's plate, "How's the meal, by the way?"

"This is incredible. I've never had anything as remotely satisfying. And the baked potato, or whatever it is, I could die for."

"Continue eating, if you're still hungry, while I finish my tale." Allen cut another bite off of the meat and stuck it in his mouth as Hazeltine leaned back in his chair, "I've been blessed by having one of the best pilots one could ever hope for. You've met her, but you haven't been properly introduced. Her name is Sparta and she is one of the Council members. This ship was never meant to land on a planet. The only local propulsion we have available are our maneuvering thrusters. While more than sufficient to move us into and out of planetary orbits, they are nowhere nearly powerful enough to slow our descent to any noticeable degree. Normally, in such a situation, we would use our escape capsules to land safely, but Sparta came up with another idea. While it was a risky gamble with an uncertain outcome, she convinced us to go for it and deliberately used our thrusters to drop us out of orbit into the shallow end of a body of water. At the very instant we would have slammed into the sea at 500 kilometers per hour, Sparta diverted all of our available power into the inertial dampeners while simultaneously firing all of our ventral thrusters on full throttle. The net result was that we were effectively weightless for a fraction of a second before all the circuits blew out. However, that fraction of a second was all that was needed for the surface tension of the water to bring us to a dead stop before we sank slowly beneath the waves. It took a couple of days to repair the damage and get everything working again, but we were still alive and kicking. We had originally planned to wait things out until we either died of old age or we were rescued. However, we re-purposed our backup navigation system into what would ultimately become our Chaos Machine. With its projections, we saw that the race of beings, your Mankind, would slowly die out over the next thousand years. Although it goes against our Rules of First Contact, we decided that we couldn't just stand idly by and watch your species wither away. So we began to interfere with the natural order of things, but only enough to prevent the eventual collapse and extinction of the human race."

Swallowing his last piece of meat, Allen said, "And the end of the world? What's up with that? Is that something you were saving for us just in case we humans made it this far?" Without waiting for an answer he turned his attention to polishing off his baked potato.

"I don't blame you for being sarcastic, Allen. When you're finished eating, I'll give you a tour of my ship. The explanation of what you call my 'doomsday machine' lies within."

Allen ate the last little bit of potato and followed it by draining the tumbler of liquid. He subconsciously rubbed his stomach as he sighed out loud. Pushing the chair back and standing up, he smiled and said, "Let's go take a look at this ship of yours, Hazel. To be perfectly honest, after a fabulous meal like that, I can hardly turn you down. Once again, you have lived up to your word."

Hazeltine cleared the table by piling everything up on Allen's tray and then sliding it into what was obviously some sort of waste disposal unit set into the wall. He indicated that Allen should follow him as he led the way to the teleportal. "Bridge," intoned Hazel and the door opened into a circular control room. He stepped onto the bridge proper and it came to life as various display screens brightened and stabilized and numerous control panels blinked their readiness. "The void you noted underneath Iraq is the force-field that surrounds this ship and keeps it from being crushed. When we first crash-landed here, this area was all water and we sank into the muck at the bottom. Over time, the sediment carried by the Tigris and Euphrates rivers has built up and effectively moved the shore nearly thirty kilometers to the south."

Allen looked around the room in fascination as he tried to make sense of the array of readouts and control surfaces. Some of them looked generically familiar, but others were truly alien in appearance. The cryptic symbols that covered some of the displays only enhanced this perception. Hazel touched one of the consoles and Allen let out an involuntary gasp and stepped back a pace as a large sphere winked into existence and hovered in the air several feet in front of him.

"This is a projection of my ship," said Hazeltine. "It's a little over six-hundred meters in diameter and its highest point is currently nearly fifty meters underground. But you knew that already." He touched the face of the console again and the sphere became transparent revealing the arrangement of the inside decks. "At the center of the ship is the radiator that maintains the force-field protecting the ship itself." As he spoke, a small yellow dot lit up in the center of the projection. "This, in turn, is powered by our generator located here." A larger red dot appeared and was connected to the yellow one with a green line as he continued, "The red dot you see is our main power plant. The red color indicates that it is nearly exhausted. Under normal circumstances, it would maintain its output for about 500,000 years. However, the force-field was only intended to block the occasional meteor or other space junk. It was never intended to stave off the crushing pressures it has been under for the last seven thousand-odd years. " Hazeltine touched something and the projection winked out as suddenly as it had appeared. "As a result, this power unit will fail in a little less than one year from now. When it implodes, it will force a collapse of the dark matter that makes up its storage cell which will essentially result in a micro-nova." Hazel looked sadly at Allen, "And when it does, of course, it takes everything in this star system along with it." He looked down at his feet for a long moment before bringing his gaze level again, "This is your doomsday machine, Allen, and the end is nigh."

+ + +

"Two-minute warning ...."

Allen gave a slight start and reviewed his lines once more. He stood up from his desk, picked up the small package lying on top, and walked through the doorway leading out into the hallway. Still trying to calm the butterflies in his stomach, he strolled down to the end and through the teleportal where he found himself in a large room lined with shelves and a work table positioned in the center. Occupying the shelves were numerous objects carefully arranged side-by-side and neatly labeled with large cards that were filled with fine print. Allen set his package on the table and waited expectantly as the teleportal closed behind him. Thirty seconds later, right on cue, the door opened in the nearest wall.

Three Months Ago – Near Indian Springs, Nevada

Cassie stepped through the doorway ahead of Alex and involuntarily cried out "Allen!" as she spied her boss standing near the center of the room. She impulsively rushed over and gave him a hug for a moment and then suddenly stepped back a couple of paces. She peered at him suspiciously, "It is you, isn't it? And not some alien clone or puppet or something?"

Allen laughed, "Yes, it's me, Cassie, in the flesh. Now how about finishing that hug?" He expanded his arms in the universal sign. "And then maybe you can introduce me to Alex?"

Cassie stepped forward and hugged Allen again. "It's so good to see you, boss. I really missed you." She sighed loudly for effect and turned to Alex, "Alex, this is Allen." She pivoted back, "Allen, this is Alex." Clearly exasperated, she continued, "Now that we've got the formalities out of the way, do you mind telling me ... us ... what's going on? Where the hell have you been?" She glanced around the room and continued, "And how in the world did you get in here, of all places?"

Alex spoke for the first time as she stepped forward and extended her hand, "It's a pleasure to meet you, Mr. Brookstone. I've been looking forward to this for some time now."

Allen gave her a firm handshake and replied, "Please, call me Allen, and the pleasure is all mine. Your blind loyalty to those you call the Others has enabled a plan to go forward that will literally save our planet from certain destruction." He looked from Alex to Cassie and then back to Alex again. "If that sounds a bit overly dramatic, I apologize, but the actions of both of you are necessary to ensure that this plan continues successfully." He intoned dramatically: "The fate of the world hangs in the balance!" He paused for effect and then laughed, "I always wanted to say that."

"I think he may have experienced some sort of schizoid break," Cassie said in a whispered aside to Alex, "It's probably best to humor him." Putting on her best motherly expression she said, "That's really nice, Allen. And what can Alex and I do to help you save the planet?"

"I would be terribly disappointed if you weren't skeptical, Cassie. That's one of the reasons I asked Alex to bring you here, instead of somewhere else." Allen strolled over to one of the nearby shelves and pointed to a brown and tan rock. "Alex will tell you that this rock was discovered during a recent excavation near the Persian Gulf. It had jammed the rollers of a 30-ton rock crusher and required the partial disassembly of the machine to remove it. After passing through a number of hands, it ended up on Alex's desk." Allen smiled mischievously as he asked, "And what have you been able to learn about it, Alex?"

"That it's incredibly old and it's impervious to any type of analysis. Can't cut it open, can't see inside it. Alpha, gamma, magnetism, inductance. Nada." A pensive look crossed her face, "I don't suppose you can tell me how you knew about this? Or maybe even what's inside my little Easter egg?"

"Your Easter egg, as you call it, is about 7,350 years old. It was synthetically created by one of the Others and contains a teleportal beacon that allowed me to transport here. It's protected by a molecular plating that both renders it virtually indestructible as well as shields it from almost all types of radiation." Allen moved to the left end of the shelving and pointed to another item, "These two half-shells comprise the casing from a satellite put into orbit by the Others. It's over 100,000 years old and was deliberately crashed into a weather balloon over Roswell, New Mexico, in 1947. Your grandfather removed the power transistor and passed it on to the folks at Bell Labs."

Alex stared incredulously at Allen, "I knew it! You've actually been with the Others. You really have! There's no other explanation for how you could possibly know these things." She smiled hopefully, "I don't suppose you could arrange for me to meet them? I mean, after we save the planet, of course."

Even though he knew in advance what Alex would say, he laughed genuinely when he saw how earnest she was when she said it. The simulations had been convincing, but they were still not quite like the real thing. Continuing on-script, he replied, "Not only will you get to meet them, but you're also going to help them go home again."

"What are you talking about?" interjected Cassie.

Allen turned to her and continued, "And you, my dear, get to play the mystic magician and amaze the world with your new magic tricks." He turned to the package sitting on the table and opened it. Removing two large manila envelopes, he handed one to Alex and the other to Cassie. "Unfortunately, I don't have time to stay and chat right now, although it's what I'd really like to do. When you have a chance, sit down together and read through the contents. I know that I can count on you both."

"And the Others?" asked Alex. "What about them?"

"They're counting on both of you as well." Allen stepped over to firmly shake Alex's hand goodbye before turning back to Cassie and giving her a fatherly hug. "Hang in there, Sunshine. I'm sorry I can't spend more time with you right now, but the laws of chaos are very unforgiving. I'll be back in touch soon. I promise." Allen stepped back several paces and tapped his left breast, "Beam me up, Scotty!" He smiled apologetically, "I always wanted..." and disappeared in mid-sentence without a sound.

Alex sighed contentedly, "That's what I like best about my job, there's nary a dull moment."

"I must say, I didn't see that coming," replied Cassie.

"What's in the box?" Alex stepped over to the table, lifted the lid, and peered into it. "Looks like some kind of USB flash drives." She picked one up and turned it over and about in her hands. "I think this is your new MicroStash product that Allen mentioned in his video."

"What makes you say that?" Cassie joined her and reached into the box to pick one up to see for herself. The package was about the size of a small matchbox with generic black-on-white copy:

MicroStash
USB Infinity Drive
It Never Fills Up!

Flipping it over, she read:

Another fine ACME product!

"Who, or what, is ACME?" asked Alex, raising her eyebrows slightly.

"I have no idea." Her curiosity growing, Cassie used her finger to slide the tray partway out of the matchbox. Nestled inside was a small USB thumb drive that appeared to be made from black obsidian. An exquisite silver infinity symbol graced the side. She stared at it for a few moments before sliding it closed again and placing it back into the box on the table. "I think we better go get some more coffee and read the instructions before we do anything else." She pointed to the drive that Alex held, "Bring that with you and let's leave the rest here for now."

"I think that's an excellent idea. I can't wait to see what's in these envelopes." She paused at the doorway to let Cassie precede her from the room before leaving and closing the door behind her.

2842 BC – NW Persian Gulf Sea Floor

Altair looked around the dinner table at his crew members and smiled. He didn't remember whose idea it was originally to hold anniversary parties for important dates, but it had become an event that everyone looked forward to with excitement. The more important the milestone, the more elaborate the party. This one was far more notable than any previous anniversary because it marked the 2,500th year since they first became stranded on this planet. They all felt that a quarter of a deca-millennium was certainly worth an extra special effort, even by their standards. Lonni had found a collection of party-favor templates and had apparently drawn upon every one of them for this occasion. He reached up to make sure that the festive hat was still perched in place on top of his head. Each of their hats bore the Guild designation of their respective professions. The only exception was Tommi, who had donned his chef's hat as the self-appointed maitre d' for the evening. The dining area had been festooned with several hundred meters of brightly colored ribbons that drooped across the ceiling and dangled down the walls. Altair beamed with satisfaction, "That was one of the best meals we've had in a long, long time. Nicely done, Tommi!"

Tommi blushed as the rest chimed in with "Here! Here!" and followed up with a long round of applause and cheers.

"Aw, you're just saying that because you didn't have to do any of the work."

Ferta smiled placatingly, "Of course we are, Tommi, but that doesn't change the fact that it really was quite a stellar meal. Any of us can punch up a meal from a template, but no one can mix and match the way that you do to keep coming up with some new taste sensation."

Rolli stood up and walked over to the food processor, "How about I fix us another round of soothies to take to the entertainment room and we can find out what Mirta's got waiting in store for us."

"Sounds like a plan to me," said Sparta.

All but Altair stood and pushed their chairs under the table before entering the teleportal. He sat looking thoughtfully at nothing in particular within the surface of the table.

"Aren't you coming along, Cap'n?" asked Rolli, as he balanced a tray with seven slender drinks arrayed upon it.

"I'll be right there, Rolli, I was just reminiscing about the past." He sighed somewhat resignedly, "It's something that seems to come to mind every time we celebrate another anniversary."

"You and me both, Cap'n." As he entered the teleportal he turned and said, "Don't be too long though, we don't want you to miss anything."

"Give me five minutes and I'll be there. I just want to savor the moment."

"Aye," said Rolli and he saluted smartly as the doors slid shut.

Altair grinned at his flashy exit. He wasn't often given to nostalgia and introspection, but he had become fascinated with the ongoing development of the indigenous species. In spite of his reservations about blatantly violating the Primary Directive of First Contact, he had found enormous innate satisfaction in watching the natives of this planet develop with only a little prodding now and then. A lot had happened since Mirta's early projections showing that Homo Sapiens would die out in less than 1,000 years. Eridu had become a font of knowledge from whence it flowed in the language of the gods. Within only three generations, the ability to make markings in clay and be able to read them was commonplace. When Mardu died the year after Itok, Mardu's meme was placed on a slender column of gold in the Temple of Enki. From all over the known world, people made pilgrimages to the Oracle at Eridu and addressed their questions to the god Marduk. Sometimes Marduk answered and sometimes he did not. When he chose to do so, it was always in the native language of the asker. Sometimes he spoke slowly and distinctly to no one at all and the scribes in attendance for that very purpose would dutifully note what was said and deliver the pronouncements to the High Priest. Over the next hundred years, volunteers from the larger families in Eridu went forth and built more temples along the rivers to the north and west. It was a good start and Mirta's projections of their survival extended farther and farther into the future. But they still showed a death spiral in less than 1,500 years.

Altair reflected back on their party for the 500th anniversary of their arrival. Two-thousand years before, it was much like this one except that Lonni hadn't yet discovered the party-favors and decorations. As they sat around the table enjoying their after-dinner aperitifs, Mirta, Ferta, and Sparta cheerfully announced that they were pregnant. They seemed greatly amused by the reactions of the others, especially Altair. After the initial shock and surprise wore off, they were inundated with questions.

"Are you serious!?" exclaimed Rolli.

"Who's going to look after the babies?" asked Lonni.

Tommi looked especially pained, "I signed up for a freighter, not a nursery!"

"Whatever were you thinking?" queried a still-astonished Altair.

Mirta was the first to reply, "The latest projections of the survival of the natives is actually worse than it was 300 years ago. In spite of all the progress we've made in spreading the word, it hasn't been enough to sustain their species for more than a couple of thousand years." She frowned slightly, "Their lazily feral nature keeps getting in the way."

Ferta chimed in, "We decided that if we're ever going to save these people from themselves, we need more help."

"And the best way to get more help is the good old-fashioned way," added Sparta.

Tommi stared incredulously at first one and then another, "The three of you got knocked up in order to help save the planet?"

"Not the planet, silly, just my people," responded Ferta.

Altair gave a loud sigh of exasperation, "Good grief, Ferta, they are *not* your people. We know how much you love them, but your hobby is bordering on becoming an obsession." He gestured around the table, "*We* are your people, Ferta. Technically speaking, we shouldn't have done anything to help these poor souls at all. Ever."

"Technically, you're 100% correct, Cap'n. But, not to put too fine of a point on it, we are no longer the crew of a Shoomaran freighter and we haven't heard anything from the rest of the Universe in 500 years." Ferta looked to Mirta for support.

Mirta picked up the thread, "Whether we adopted this planet or it adopted us, the three of us feel that we need to help these 'poor souls'— as you call them—to survive. Worst case, we all die on this planet within the next sixty-to-seventy-thousand years or so. Best case, we somehow get to go back home again. We can either wait for the unlikely chance of someone stumbling upon our distress beacon or we can help these people survive and thrive and progress enough to help us fix our dilator valve so that we can leave on our own."

Sparta joined in, "What she said."

Altair was clearly bemused by their logic. "I see," he replied. "And how does getting pregnant help to accomplish this miracle?"

Sparta and Ferta both looked at Mirta who answered for them, "The extremely short lifespan of these 'humans'—as I call them—condemns them to prioritize the short-term over the long-term. Strong leaders arise who spend their life trying to make things easier for the next generation. Each subsequent generation produces less and less and consumes more and more until everything is gone. Then they either die out or attack a neighboring tribe to continue their lifestyle. These anarchistic periods are followed by strong leaders arising to restore a semblance of a civil society again. And every time the cycle repeats, the people struggle more than their forefathers ever did until the clock finally runs out in about 500 more years." She smiled wryly, "You know the old saying, one jump forward and two jumps back."

"Did you say 500 years?" asked Lonni. "Not too long ago, you said it was more like 1,500 years."

"The control unit for the nav system is limited in the amount of data it can process. Normally this isn't a problem, but as I explained not too long ago, it uses a lossy compression scheme that is more than sufficiently accurate for navigational purposes. However, when it's applied to the use we're putting it to now, it tends to average out some lows and gives more emphasis to the peaks. A projection made today shouldn't be any different than one made yesterday or tomorrow. Unless something changes, that is."

"I recall you saying something about them fluctuating a while back," remarked Altair.

"Yes," replied Mirta. "It turns out that the changes are caused by our leaving the ship from time to time. Every time we leave our shielded environment, the nav system begins to assimilate our very thoughts into its repository. This causes the projections to be skewed because we look around us and our minds wander into the realms of what if and why not. As a result, the projections incorporate events that won't actually happen because we're only thinking about them happening."

Tommi interrupted, "So the projections are getting better because we want them to get better?"

"Something like that," replied Mirta. "In other words, the only way we can get accurate projections is to confine ourselves to the ship."

"For how long?" asked Rolli.

"For as long as we want accurate projections."

Altair cleared his throat, "Assuming we stay on-board, how accurate are the projections actually going to be? As I understand it, even without our dreams and wishes being incorporated, the data is still a bit fuzzy."

"I didn't want to say anything until I was sure. About a month ago I started with a number of replicated nav control units and have finally finished merging them together to handle the necessary bandwidth."

"So that's why you've been spending so much time in the shop lately," interjected Lonni. "Every time I asked about it, you managed to change the subject."

"As I said, I wasn't exactly sure what was going on and I wanted to confirm my suspicions before sharing them with everyone else." She looked around at the group, "Last week, I finally finished all of the modifications and swapped out the systems. After a reset, the system came up and showed the planetary environment as before. Unlike before, however, the last human dies in a little less than 507 years from now. Over the next five days, I ran the projections again and again and they each agreed with the others to all significant sexagesimal places. However, after I teleported to a deserted beacon and back, it had jumped to 1,033 years. As of an hour ago, the end of life estimate had decreased by only a few seconds."

"So what's the big deal?" asked Tommi. "Every time we go out and about, we'll just come back here and reset the console."

"We can do that, but we'll lose the referential history of everything that occurred prior to the reset each time." Mirta frowned slightly, "I know I have a mild obsession with data storage and integrity, but my gut says we shouldn't keep throwing the data away every time we simply want to go ashore." She smiled, "And if it's any consolation, a side effect of the modifications I made apparently causes an interaction with the field surrounding our moly-plated beacon on the beach. Somewhere between the fourth and fifth harmonics, the effect dies out, but it essentially blocks the reach of the nav system for a radius of about five meters."

"So, you're saying that we can go for a stroll on the beach as long as we don't stray more than a half-dozen steps from the beacon?" asked Rolli.

"Or we can make some more and just carry them with us!" Tommi added.

Mirta started to answer, "Yes, but there are some caveats ..."

Altair spoke up, "I don't mean to interrupt this conversation, but, as I recall, you were telling us why the three of you decided to get pregnant. I don't think I quite got an answer to my question."

Mirta looked somewhat chagrined, "Sorry, Cap'n, I got a little carried away." She cleared her throat before continuing, "The modifications I made not only provide us with a finite model of this star system, but it also allows us to project exactly what will happen in the future. With a little more work, I'm positive I can provide a way to modify the inputs and be able to see the results of any changes we might choose to effect before we actually put them into motion."

"Changes?" asked Altair.

"If we don't want them to die out in five-hundred-odd years, we'll need to help them in more ways than we have so far. And I mean a lot more. Due to the short lives of these humans, they need leaders that will survive from one generation to the next in order to insure sustainability and growth. These leaders will also need to be able to trans-morph from generation to generation as their roles in society continually change and adapt. Our long lives make us suitable candidates, but we can't leave the shielded environment without affecting the nav system. However, if there were more of us, some new crew members that didn't know anything other than what they've been told, they could live and work among the general populations and gently make minor changes when needed. And their lack of knowledge of what if and why not wouldn't affect the nav system one iota."

"Let me guess, you're hatching members of the Actors' Guild," chipped in Lonni.

"Close enough," replied Mirta.

Ferta spoke up, "Two male actors and a female scientist, to be precise. My baby's going to be named Gabriel."

"Mine's going to be named Methuselah," added Sparta.

"And I'm naming my own daughter Minerva," finished Mirta. "And before you ask, we're going to raise them on one of the supercargo decks where they'll grow to maturity without any exposure to outside influences. Once Gabriel and Methuselah are of age, they'll go out into the world and play the parts we write for them based on the projections of changes we can make."

Altair frowned, "And these two actors will then save the planet?"

"Oh, no, Cap'n! As soon as we decant these babies, we're going to make more," gushed Ferta. "A lot more!"

Altair smiled to himself as he recalled the conversation. In the centuries that followed, their actors had gone forth and laid firm foundations for the beginnings of sustainable major civilizations on nearly every continent. Wherever there was a large source of fresh water, they had founded temples around which future civilizations would develop. Outside of the Eridu Valley, the next most advanced settlement was at the mouth of the large northward-flowing tributary about 1,000 kilometers to the west. The periodic flooding of this river replaced the vast irrigation systems that they had built here. With the introduction of sea-faring vessels came the ability to go ever farther and farther afield. As they continued to spread their influence, they established numerous trade routes that allowed the surpluses in one region to be exchanged for the surpluses of others. This allowed each settlement to grow beyond the limited resources of any one area. Current projections indicated that the humans were well on their way to growing and expanding while the relatively recent introduction of bronze smelting had apparently awakened an industrial mentality that rivalled that of the boat builders. They were still trying various scenarios in order to both stabilize this trend while continuing to accelerate its development before proceeding to the introduction of iron smelting.

Altair was suddenly jolted out of his funk by the strident sound of the collision warning siren. "That can't be right," he thought as the distinct rise and fall of the alarm continued, "We're on the bottom of the sea!" He activated his comlink, "Battle stations, everyone!" he ordered as he jumped up and headed for the lift.

Sparta responded first, "I'm on my way to the bridge."

"On my way to Engineering," chimed in Lonni.

The rest of the crew quickly checked in as they scrambled in response to the alarm. They all knew the drill and by the time Altair reached the bridge himself, everyone else was already at their emergency stations.

"Status report!" commanded Altair to Sparta who was busily running her fingers across the various controls and displays.

"Incoming asteroid, Cap'n. It's about 400 meters in size and coming in hot."

"But we're on the bottom of a drekkin' ocean!" exclaimed Altair.

Sparta ignored his profanity, "The closest approach point of the vector is about 5,000 kilometers, but that's close enough to trigger the warning system."

"Permission granted to turn it off."

Sparta didn't bother with a reply, but the clamor immediately ceased. "Time to closest approach is a little less than 22 minutes."

"That's not much of a warning," said Altair. "How come we didn't know about this sooner?"

"The range of the beacon's sensors is limited to about 300,000 kilometers. It was already inside the orbit of the moon before the proximity monitor detected it."

"Ferta! Can you tell me more about what's going on?"

"Working on the projections now, Cap'n. The nav system has the point of impact about 5,000 kilometers due south in the middle of the ocean." A few long moments later, they could all plainly hear her sudden gasp of dismay.

Altair responded, "What is it, Ferta? Are we in any danger?"

A muffled sobbing was all that came back over the comlink.

"Sparta! You're in command of the bridge!" He stepped into the lift and headed to Navigation where he found Ferta with her head down on the console and her shoulders heaving in concert with her sobs. Above her floated a view of the Earth from about 10,000 kilometers out that displayed a slowly rising mass from a point in the ocean to the south. Spellbound, he watched as the sea boiled away in an ever-increasing billowing cloud that was slowly growing and spreading. Altair watched the projection play out with a mixture of awe, fascination, and then horror as he realized the implications. While he didn't know exactly what was going to happen, he knew for sure that they only had about twenty minutes to do something about it, if anything. "Sailor! On deck at attention!" bellowed Altair. The command had its desired effect of jarring Ferta back to semi-coherence as she instinctively stood and saluted. "Report!"

Although there was a noticeable catch in her voice, Ferta was able to force her reply, "The asteroid appears to be on a hyperbolic trajectory traveling about 230 kilometers per second. At this speed, it will pass through the outermost atmosphere and plunge to the bottom of the ocean in only a couple of seconds. Most of it vaporizes and what's left will impact the ocean floor where the silt provides enough of a cushion so that it doesn't actually crack the mantle of the planet." She choked back another sob before continuing, "I'm sorry Cap'n, I couldn't bear to watch it after that. I know it's not good."

"That's okay, Ferta. This doesn't fall under your assigned duties and I'm glad you were here to quickly gather all of the basics. Now I want you to go pull yourself together and be in the mess hall in ten minutes." He smiled encouragingly, "Okay?"

Ferta sniffled a little as she replied, "Aye, Cap'n, I'll see you in the mess hall in ten."

As she left, Altair spoke over the comlink, "Mirta, I need you in Navigation. Everyone else can stand down from alert status. I want everyone in the mess hall in ten minutes for a conference." He continued to watch as the boiling cloud grew ever larger. He couldn't fault Ferta for her reaction since she literally couldn't help herself. Her genetic makeup included a healthy dose of empathy that was necessary in her secondary role as ship's Surgeon. His chief Science Officer, on the other hand, had almost none.

Mirta stepped into the room and flashed a grim look at Altair, "I heard Ferta's summary and it sounds pretty bad. On the other hand, Ferta says that it didn't crack the mantle which would have been much, much worse." She paused and looked at the projection still playing out above the console, "Give me a few minutes with the nav system and I can get a more precise idea of what we're dealing with."

"I need an immediate, short term, and long term impact analysis. You have eight minutes to get it done and get to the mess hall so that you can brief the rest of us."

Mirta was already seated and running her hands across the control surfaces. Without looking back at Altair, she replied in the affirmative, "Aye, aye, Cap'n!"

Altair headed for the mess hall by way of the bridge to pick up his notepod and then his cabin to freshen up before the meeting. By the time he arrived, everyone was there except for Mirta. It was apparent from the looks on everyone's faces that Ferta had filled them in on the imminent threat and he sat down to join them. "Mirta will be here in a few minutes to give us a better idea of what we're up against." He slowly looked around the table making sure he made eye contact with each of them–most importantly–including Ferta. "Until we get some facts, there's no point in worrying about it." He had expected no response from his shocked crew, so he wasn't disappointed when none came. They continued to sit in a palpably gloomy atmosphere until Mirta entered the mess hall.

She didn't take a seat, but remained standing and faced those seated around the table, "We don't have a lot of time, so I'll get right to the point. As you already know, a rogue body is about to impact the planet. Its trajectory is almost exactly vertical with respect to the surface. From the galactic perspective, this is a perfect bulls-eye dead-centered on the planetary disk. Although it's fairly small, its velocity is 227 kilometers per second which is an order of magnitude faster than the typical velocities encountered in planetary collisions. At 0.075 percent light-speed, the kinetic energy that will be dissipated is enormous since it increases with the square of the velocity. Due to the range limit of the nav unit, my back-tracking stops at the outer asteroid belt, but this came from way beyond that. In order to acquire a velocity of this magnitude, my best guess is that it got itself slingshot around some black star somewhere some million or so years ago."

"How long before we feel something here?" asked Altair.

Mirta glanced at the chronometer on the wall before replying, "Impact is at 19:39:21 which is just under nine minutes away. The first sign will be a bright flash below the horizon which will block most of the radiation that will be unleashed. About ten minutes later we will get a severe earthquake as the tectonic impact spreads" She smiled only slightly as she continued, "The good news is that we won't be affected at all, other than a mild shaking that I'll negate with a tailored power curve applied to the inertial dampeners."

"And the bad news?" asked Sparta. "I've read about impacts like this before. There'll be huge waves in the sea like the ripples caused by tossing a pebble into a pond, but on a much larger scale."

"Normally, that would be the case, and the ripples, while large, would not be much of a problem." Mirta paused and looked down as if collecting her thoughts before continuing, "Almost all meteors and even the smaller asteroids burn up in the atmosphere before they can hit the planet's surface. And even the larger ones generally lose most of their mass and slow substantially before impact. But that's because they are typically traveling at only ten to twenty kilometers per second before they enter the thermosphere and begin to burn up from the friction. In this case, however, at 227 kilometers per second, the body passes through the four-hundred-and-fifty-kilometer thick atmosphere in only two seconds before it hits the sea. Unlike slower traveling bodies that push the atmosphere aside and heat up from the friction generated, our body will literally compress the molecules in front of it faster than they can move out of the way. By the time it hits the last twenty kilometers where eighty percent of the atmosphere is concentrated, it will have compressed enough matter in front of it to start a massive fusion reaction. This reaction grows exponentially and will reach a temperature of several million degrees before it hits the sea one tenth of a second later.

The heat will instantly vaporize the sea for about a twenty-kilometer radius as it hits the ocean bottom and sends a goodly portion of the seabed about ten kilometers into the air as a result of the impact."

Lonni spoke up, "How come we didn't know about this? Like the last two times?"

"As you already know, the range of the nav system only extends somewhat beyond the asteroid belt. The two major impacting bodies that we dealt with before originated from there. From the moment we began to get good projections, we've known about them and the others yet to come. In this case, however, the meteoroid only came into range about four weeks ago. Without any major changes in the works and our recent real-time monitoring activities, no new projections have been run for over six months. If it weren't for the collision detector in the distress beacon, we wouldn't have found out about it until the earthquake jolted us out of our seats in the rec room in, oh, about six minutes from now."

"While it's comforting to know that we're not in any danger, how bad is it going to be for everyone else?" asked Tommi. "I mean, how big of a wave are we talking about?"

"In about five-and-a-half hours, the first compression wave will reach inhabited land. Instead of picturing a pebble in a pond, picture something more like firing a 10mm slug-thrower straight down into a mud puddle." Mirta paused for a moment, "I wish I had some easy way to break the bad news, but I think it would be best to just show you what's going to happen next." She turned to Rolli, "Why don't you bring another round of soothies to the rec room and I'll play the projection for everyone there." She glanced at Ferta, "And I think you should make the soothies really, really strong. We're all going to need it."

The Chaos Machine

Three Months Ago – Mount Ararat, Turkey

"... to say that!" finished Allen as he materialized in the doorway of the teleportal. While he was confident that everything had followed his carefully rehearsed script, he hurried down to the end of the hallway to see the results. He entered the console room and sat down in his now well-worn chair. Running his fingers over the control panel, he backtracked to the time that he entered Alex's museum. His main concern was the thin white line that indicated an unknown state for the machine. This was the result of the interference field surrounding the moly-plated beacon on the shelf in the museum. During the time that he had spent in its close proximity with both Alex and Cassie, no data had been acquired by the machine. Once they had left the room, however, the machine re-integrated the before and after and was able to assess the accuracy of the transition. If Allen's interaction with Alex and Cassie went according to plan, then the resultant outcome would match what had been predicted. Allen manipulated the controls to home in on the two co-conspirators as they left the room together and followed them to the kitchen where they poured themselves some more coffee and sat across from each other at the small table.

+ + +

Almost at the same time, Cassie and Alex opened the clasps of their respective manila envelopes and removed a thick sheaf of papers. Looking at the top of the first sheet, again at almost the same time, they glanced at their watches and then looked up at each other in disbelief.

"How is this possible?" asked Cassie.

Alex continued reading the rest of the first page before responding, "If you're looking at the same thing I am, it appears that we have just now called to order the first meeting of the ACME Corporation with two-thirds of the board in attendance and you having Allen's proxy vote."

"Yes, but the time and date? It's ... well, it's one minute ago, now, but how did he know when we would pull these out to look at them?" She frowned in thought, "I mean, what if we had opened them later? Or sooner?"

Alex laughed, "Welcome to my world, Cassie, where truth is stranger than fiction." She smiled, "Just a few minutes ago, we saw your boss poof out of existence from a hidden underground room. And now you're surprised that he can appear to predict the future?"

"Well, no, not as much surprised but also wondering how he could possibly do it."

"Maybe he's a time-traveler from the future so he already knew the exact moment we would open the envelopes," replied Alex. "Or maybe someone from the future told him when it would happen."

"It's just spooky, that's all." Cassie continued reading down the meeting agenda, "There are no minutes to go over, so I guess we can jump to the first item which is 'Saving the Planet'."

"Has Allen always been so melodramatic?"

"Oh yes, for as long as I've known him. He says it adds to the zest in life. Me? I get eye-strain from rolling my eyes."

Alex removed the large paper-clip holding the pages and removed the first three sheets which were stapled together. "At least it's only three pages long. Should we take a few minutes to each read them through?"

"Sounds good to me," replied Cassie as she began reading to herself.

+ + +

Allen smiled. According to the overlay analyzer, the original hypothetical future mated perfectly with the newly projected timeline with zero deviation. He breathed a heavy sigh of relief. As Hazel had explained it, some deviation was okay, but most required some sort of follow-up change to steer things back on track. The further the timeline projected into the future, the more pronounced the effects of the deviation. Allen once again turned his attention to the console. He changed location and timeframe to a meeting in the war room underneath the Pentagon and listened in for a few minutes to their conversation. Satisfied with the outcome, he moved on to a briefing of the President by Alex. Convinced that everything was going according to plan, he browsed various places a month or so out to get a feel for the impact of the new USB drives that were going to start shipping soon. Even further out, he viewed the distribution of the ACME food processor and drink dispenser. And, for the first time, the timeline extended far, far into the future; well beyond the previously projected end of the world. He sat back in his chair and reviewed the sequence of events for the umpteenth time, trying to poke holes in the logic or spot any unforeseen fallacies. His gut told him that it would work and the Chaos Machine seemed to confirm it, but, as Hazel had pointed out, the sooner he spotted a potential flaw, the better their chance to rectify it. So one more time, he started back at the point when he finally grasped the real problem on board the *Pride of Eridu*.

+ + +

"This is your doomsday machine, Allen, and the end is nigh," said Hazeltine.

"I don't suppose you've thought about turning it off, or anything?" asked Allen.

Hazel gave a wry laugh, "I wish it was that simple. There's a series of safety interlocks that prevent it from being disabled except by a properly qualified technician at a certified service center. Like the ones around Denorra or Plenidad."

"And they don't make on-site calls, I assume?"

"Actually, they do, and for a reasonable fee, I might add," said Hazel. "But in the case of a Bad Jump, of course, there's no way to call tech support in the first place."

"Bad jump?"

"I'm sorry, Allen. Up until now, I haven't filled you in on a lot of background information because I felt it was more important for you to understand our Chaos Machine first." Hazel motioned to the doorway, "Let's go back to the mess hall and get some soothies and I'll give you a tour of the rest of my ship. Along the way, I'll try to explain what life is like in the more-civilized part of the Universe."

As Allen followed Hazeltine to the mess hall, his mind was slowly becoming less and less numb and starting to function more normally again. He had suspected that Hazel was indeed some sort of alien, but he didn't really believe it until now. Having now accepted this, he began to slowly wrap his mind around this new information.

Hazel handed Allen a tall glass with the electric blue liquid that Allen still thought of as antifreeze. "How about we start with the navigation room? Its console is almost identical to the one you've been using for the last few months and it should make you feel right at home."

"Right at home? A hundred meters below Iraq in an ancient spaceship from another solar system?" Allen snorted, "You have a really odd sense of humor, Hazel."

"That has been said of me by many before you," Hazeltine replied seriously. "And, technically speaking, we're from another galaxy. The term 'solar system' is a bit colloquial, don't you think?"

Allen ignored him and responded with more questions, "What's a bad jump? And why can't E.T. phone home?"

"Navigation," intoned Hazeltine as they entered the lift. He turned to face Allen and answered, "Do you remember Minerva's explanation of the Chaos Machine? How it's synchronized with the singularities surrounding the Earth?"

"Yes, of course I do." Allen smiled, "And I like to think that I actually understand it, as well."

As they exited the lift into the small navigation room, Hazeltine continued, "Do you also understand how our teleportal works?"

"Not entirely, but I grasp that it's a variant way of manipulating the singularities underlying everything. Like your food processor."

As when they earlier entered the bridge, the room came to life as multiple displays lit up. A simulacrum of the Earth appeared, suspended in the center of the room. Allen walked over to the nearer console and glanced at it momentarily.

"You're right, as usual, Hazel," mused Allen. "I *do* feel right at home here. I can't make heads or tails of all these screwy labels, but the controls and their layout is pretty much identical to what I've been using for the past few months."

"When this system was fully operational, it was a key component of our jump technology. Each ship contains two paired quadro-trilithium crystals that are effectively mirror twins of each other. One is housed in the navigation system and the other is housed in the dilator valve. However, the fields that contain them interact in distinctly separate ways." Hazeltine paused for a moment, "I won't pretend that I fully understand how it works, but the gist of it is that we can set up the field in the navigation system to a potential location and then the field in the dilator valve emits or absorbs the energy required to swap the singularities between moments. The force-field radiator is coupled to the dilator field in such a way as to provide the envelope of singularities to be exchanged and all of it, of course, is powered by our energy source."

"I think I follow you. The teleportals must do the same thing between the source and the destination fields," observed Allen.

"Exactly!" exclaimed Hazeltine. "Since the development of the jump technology, there have been only six times when a ship has jumped and never arrived at its intended destination. Never heard from again, we call this a Bad Jump where the two words are capitalized as a formal moniker. It is the boogieman that haunts the dreams of all Universal travelers."

"And now there are seven Bad Jumps?"

Hazeltine sighed before continuing, "I take no pride as a ship's captain in saying that, yes, we are the seventh Bad Jump of record in the entire history of jumps."

Allen was thinking about how much time had passed since this ship had been stranded, "Umm, just out of curiosity, how long ago was the first jump?"

"In round numbers, let's see, it was about three, no make it three-and-a-half million of your years ago."

The feelings of insignificance that were previously hovering around Allen became almost palpable as he sensed them closing in around him. He shook his head to shake off the feeling, not entirely succeeding in the effort, "So what caused your particular Bad Jump? And how did you end up here?"

"From the very beginning of jump-drive development, the interaction of the fields between the navigation system, the dilator valve, and the ship's hull itself has always had to be perfectly synchronized or bad things might happen. The combination of the rigorous alignment of these fields must be always coupled to a sufficient power source which is why I can't turn it off or otherwise disable it. By design, it's a closed system to prevent unauthorized tampering and can only be serviced within a proper stasis field to maintain the singularity envelope."

"So, if everything's so damned foolproof, what happened to your ship?"

Hazeltine literally hung his head in shame. After a bit, he raised his head again and explained, "We knew that our dilator valve was overdue for replacement. It was only a matter of time before it failed, but we didn't have enough credits to get it serviced." He sighed, "If we had completed the jump as planned, we would have collected more than enough payment to get it replaced. But it failed in between moments and we ended up here."

Allen frowned as he tried to picture this and what it might mean, "So what state are the singularities actually in when they are between states? Between moments?"

"You'll have to ask Minerva to explain it. As I understand things, no one really knows for sure and there are several competing theories.

Suffice it to say that, in our case, we were orbiting Shoomar one moment and then orbiting your Earth the next. Other than a few minor discrepancies, your entire star system and galactic neighborhood are eerie doppelgängers of our own home galaxy." Hazeltine paused before continuing, "Our best guess is that we came out of the jump here because it's such a close duplicate to where we were. Theoretically, if we jump but provide no net change of energy to the dilator valve, we should remain right where we started. However, we *could* conceivably end up somewhere else if no net change of energy was required to jump there, but that's only a hypothetical."

Allen smiled, "I would say that it's clearly more than hypothetical at this point." He thought for a moment and then continued, "So, logically speaking, if you can't shut down this doomsday bomb, and you can't remove it, the only other solution is to somehow move your ship somewhere else."

Three Months Ago – Area 51, Nevada

Cassie finished reading the project overview before Alex did, so she went back and re-read some of the details for a second time. Finally, Alex looked up and said, "Seems reasonable to me, don't you agree?"

Cassie stared at her for a moment before she realized that Alex was kidding, "Yes, for something he calls 'Saving the Planet', I have to say that it sounds perfectly reasonable to me as well." She frowned slightly, "Does your copy say anything about what we're actually trying to save the planet from?"

"Not a clue."

"This is so typical of him. The exact phrase he used was 'save our planet from certain destruction' but then he doesn't bother to tell us from what." She sighed, "The worst part of it all is that I don't really have any option but to go along with his crazy plans."

Alex grinned, "So, moving on to the next item on the agenda, I get to read 'Tasks for Alex' while you're reading 'Tasks for Cassie' and then we get to compare notes afterward."

Cassie looked perplexed, "Well, mine's pretty simple. It just says to do whatever Alex tells you to do."

Alex shrugged as she began to read her own task list. After a few minutes she looked into the envelope and dumped its contents onto the table. For each of them there was an identification card and a credit card with their names on them.

"Looks like I'm the new Vice President of Manufacturing for the ACME Corporation with a gold AMEX card to boot!" exclaimed Alex.

Cassie frowned at her ID card, "And I'm the new Vice President of Magic for the same." She rolled her eyes, "At least I get a gold AMEX card as well."

"Have you ever been to Area 51 before?" asked Alex.

"What? No. Why?"

Alex stood up from the table, "Get your purse and bring along the USB drive, we're going on a road trip!"

$+++$

The SUV pulled up in front of a large non-descript hangar adjacent to a modern runway. While the distance from Alex's domicile was only about twenty miles, it had taken them nearly half an hour to drive the winding road through the hills to reach their destination. Alex and Cassie stepped out into the baking Nevada heat and looked around.

"I thought that there would be a lot more security around here," remarked Cassie. "This place looks deserted."

"Well, it *is* the weekend," explained Alex. "Besides, most of what goes on here is out of sight and hence out of mind." She led the way to a normal-sized door set in the wall of the hangar. "As for security, we've been under constant surveillance ever since we entered the checkpoint at Indian Springs. Nothing goes in and nothing goes out without someone logging the activity." She opened the door and held it for Cassie, "Trust me, I set it up myself." Alex left the door open while she found the breaker for the lights and switched them on. A low hum filled the hangar as the sodium vapor lights began to glow softly. After a moment she closed the door and she led the way across the floor as the lights grew steadily brighter.

"Do you come here often?" asked Cassie.

Alex stopped and turned around a full three hundred and sixty degrees before replying. "This is my first time in this particular hangar, but it's pretty much like all of the rest of them." She pointed to a large machine near the back of the vast area, "Except for that thing over there." She walked towards the object in question as she spoke, "Allen said we were to come to this hangar and we would find the equipment necessary to make billions of these USB drives and distribute them around the world."

"I'm sorry, did you say 'billions'?"

"Yes. Allen seems to think that everyone on the planet needs one," answered Alex. "And he wants us to start shipping them next week."

Cassie followed Alex in silence until they stood in front of what would pass for a very large vending machine. Dangling from a bright gold cord was a thick manual with "RTFM" stamped boldly in red across the cover. Alex walked over and untied the cord holding the manual, "I'll be more than happy to volunteer to read this, if that's okay?"

"Knock yourself out," replied Cassie. "You're in charge of manufacturing, not me." Grumbling, she continued, "I'm just a lowly magician."

+ + +

Two hours later, they were sitting on the floor in front of the machine, each engrossed in their own work. Cassie was busy with her tablet making notes while Alex had nearly reached the end of her manual. They were both startled when a loud pounding came from the door near the front of the hangar. Alex's face lit up, "That must be the pizza I ordered for us." She continued, "Would you mind getting that while I finish? I'm almost done and can't afford to lose my train of thought."

"Pizza? Here?"

"But of course. Meat Lover's Delight!"

Cassie got up and walked to the door as the pounding repeated itself. "I'm coming! I'm coming!" she yelled.

"No tipping allowed, by the way," Alex called out after her.

Cassie was expecting someone in a pizza delivery uniform of some sort when she opened the door. She was not expecting the four men in military uniform that were standing rigidly outside.

"May we come in, ma'am?" inquired one of the young soldiers.

"Do you have pizza?" asked Cassie.

He moved aside so that she could see the cart behind him, "Yes, ma'am, we do."

"Well, then, come on in!" Cassie held the door for them as they wheeled in not one, but three carts and proceeded toward the rear of the hangar. Closing the door behind them, Cassie followed the small procession across the football field-sized floor to where Alex sat engrossed in her reading. The four soldiers stood stiffly in place while waiting for Alex to notice them. She finally closed the manual with a triumphant smile before looking up.

Surprised and clearly embarrassed, Alex said apologetically, "Sorry guys, I was so wrapped up in what I was doing, I didn't even know you were there."

"Yes, sir." The one who had spoken to Cassie continued, "We have the supplies you requested. We would have been here sooner, but some of the things you wanted were a bit difficult to acquire on such short notice." He looked around, "Where would you like us to set up?"

"There's an outlet over there to the right. I'd like the counter set up there with the coffee maker. The work table can go here where we are right now with the work-lights set up on the four corners of the area." She paused for a moment, "How about setting up the chairs first over to the side here so that we can dig into the pizza. It's been a while since we last ate and we're both famished. At least, I am."

"Me, too," chimed in Cassie.

"Yes, sir. We'll get right on it." Without further ado, the four men in uniform proceeded to unpack two softly padded office chairs and set them facing each other followed by two folding trays that were set next to the chairs. Next came napkins and plates for the pizza along with the question "What would you like to drink, ma'am? We have coffee, Coke, and water."

"I'll take the water, please," replied Cassie. She noticed that he didn't ask Alex what she wanted but placed a Coca-Cola in a bottle on her own tray. She felt weirdly out-of-reality as the uniformed soldier held open a pizza box while she selected two slices to put on her plate.

She looked questioningly at Alex who only smiled back with twinkling eyes as she spoke to one of them, "We're good, for now, Thompson. If you can get the rest of the stuff set up, I can take it from here. I'll let you know if I need anything else."

"Yes, sir." He turned to the other three as they were finishing up and the four of them wheeled the three carts out the door only a couple of minutes later.

Alex waited until the door was shut before she burst out laughing. "Oh, Cassie! The look on your face was priceless! I would've thought you had a much better poker face than that." She continued to laugh as Cassie started laughing as well.

"I'm sitting in a top-secret hangar in Area 51 eating pizza served by a guy in uniform in front of a machine that looks like a prop out of a 'B' movie while reading instructions from the future handed to me by my boss who's a vanishing alien puppet and who needs my help to save the planet. Forget poker face, I'm lucky to be holding onto my sanity at this point." She raised her eyebrows slightly as she continued, "And why did those guys call you sir? Do you outrank them or something?"

"Yes, or something." Alex had finally quit laughing, "But, seriously," she pointed to the machine, "We definitely have something right out a grade 'B' science-fiction movie alright. I may not be one hundred percent up on the theory behind this thing yet, but I understand more than enough so that we can start using it." She smiled once more, "I've got that Christmas morning tingle going again!"

Cassie sighed loudly to express her frustration, "Well, do mind filling me in on it, too?"

"Sorry, Cassie, I didn't mean to keep you in the dark. It's just that when I'm reading something technical, I get into this zone where I tune everything else out and focus only on absorbing the information." She leaned forward in her chair as she continued, "I just realized I haven't said anything at all to you in the past couple of hours." She looked at the piece of pizza in her hand, "Except to ask you to get the door."

"That's okay, I had plenty to keep me busy trying to figure out exactly what it is we're trying to do here from Allen's notes. He mentions a number of 'props' I will need to do 'my magic tricks.' Do you have any idea what these props are that he's talking about?"

Alex pointed, "Look at the machine here. What do you see?"

"It looks like one of those 'claw' machines you see where you put your money in and try to grab a stuffed animal from the pile. Except three to four times as wide and tall as one of those. And also no claw and no stuffed animals."

"Did you ever see a magician make a woman disappear and reappear? Some of them use a glass cabinet like this one to make them disappear and reappear by using one-way mirrors and special lighting. For a magician, this would be called a prop and it would be necessary in order for them to create the illusion of magic."

"Of course! Sufficiently advanced technology!" She laughed, "So says the VP of Magic!"

"Let's move over to the work table and I'll get us some coffee. It should be ready by now." Alex stood up and pushed her chair over to the low table where she set down her plate and half-eaten slice of pizza while Cassie followed suit.

"I don't mean to sound like a whiny teen or anything, but my tablet has no cell phone or network connection available," whined Cassie.

"Oh, Cassie, I didn't even think of that. What kind of host am I not to provide Wi-Fi service for my guests?" She pulled her own phone from her pocket, "What's the MAC address of your tablet?" As Cassie read the hexadecimal numbers off to her, she punched them into her handset. "Wait for it ... wait for it ..." she said and got a confirmation chirp from her phone. "Sorry about that, you should have said something sooner," Alex said apologetically as she began to pour coffee into the two cups provided for them.

"Well, this being Area 51 and all I just figured it went without saying," Cassie assured her.

"Here's your coffee. Let's sit down and I'll fill you in on what we're going to do with this machine." She smiled, "According to the instructions, we have a bona fide replicator on our hands!"

"Replicator? Like the things that almost wiped out the galaxy in the *Stargate* shows?"

"No, silly. Like the cafeteria in *Star Trek* where they push a button and get dinner and drinks," replied Alex. "But bigger."

"So we can make really large instant dinners? Like a giant microwave?"

Alex laughed, "Okay, now I know you're pulling my leg. As I said before, I don't understand exactly how this does what it does, but the process is simple enough. We put in raw material and it rearranges the atoms into molecules and the molecules into whatever we want. As long as it can fit inside the volume of the enclosure."

Cassie looked dubious, "Anything we want?"

"Well, as long as it's in the template library. We can replicate anything in the library as long as we have the raw materials and the energy required to produce it."

"So how do we turn it on or start it up?" Cassie stood up and walked over to the machine. "And what are we going to make with it first? It's really unfortunate that it's too small to make a Ferrari."

"Allen says we need to make a miner first to gather the materials we'll need to make more USBs." Alex glanced at Cassie, "Do you have the USB drive that Allen gave us? It turns out that it's the key to turn this thing on. And it has the template library we need as well."

Cassie went back to the table and retrieved the USB stick from her bag. As she handed it to Alex she said, "What's a miner? The one that's spelled N-E-R and not N-O-R?"

"It's the first of your magic props, of course!"

Two-and-One-Half Months Ago – Pentagon Sub-Basement 12C

The four career officers knew each other well. They rode the elevator down together and entered the small conference room, taking their places at one end of a long table designed to seat twenty. The dim lights had turned on when they first entered and they left them that way as their clandestine meeting began. Each of them wore the four-starred uniforms of their commands: Army; Navy; Air Force; Marines. The Chiefs of Staff were officially termed, respectively, CSA, CNO, CSAF, and CMC.

"Now that we're all here, do you mind telling us *why* we're here?" asked the CSA.

The CSAF spoke up, "I'm assuming that this has something to do with Montana's latest shenanigans?"

"You got that right," replied the CMC. "I overheard the Secretary complaining about their meeting with the CIC. Seems like the she-bitch wants a bunch of your cargo planes for one of her pet projects and the Secretary was told, in no uncertain terms, to approve the request."

"Yes, I know. The reqs came across my desk last week and I had a fit, to put it mildly. I refused to approve them and passed them up the chain hoping someone else would turn them down. In spite of my pointing out the serious crimp that this will put in our supply chain, I was told to give her whatever she asked for." The CSAF apologetically continued, "As you know, I couldn't say anything to you about it. You know the rules."

The CNO spoke up, "Rules or no rules, I want to know what she's up to. I had one of my NCIS operatives look into her activities, but even he wasn't able to learn what's going on at that damned base of hers. However, he did find out that she's got the AG's pet guard dog running interference for her."

"The Dragon Lady? I thought that she had retired," said the CSA.

The CNO replied, "Retired from public service, maybe, but she went to work for Allen Brookstone."

"Speaking of Allen Brookstone, I hear that no one's actually laid eyes on him since he disappeared. Aside from a couple of videos, who's to say that he's even alive?" The CSAF laughed, "The FBI says 'nothing to see here ... move along' and suddenly the Dragon Lady quits and goes to work for that Stevens woman. And now they're both somehow tied up with Montana and whatever she's up to now."

"How many planes did she ask you for this time? Three? Four?" asked the CMC.

"I wish. She asked for six C-17s and nine C-5s and wanted them within 48 hours. I was going to stall on their delivery using lack of availability or needing maintenance, or some such, but she had requested them by inventory number and damned if they weren't all conveniently already queued up for immediately deployment." The CSAF paused before continuing, "Somehow, she knew which planes were immediately available and I couldn't come up with a defensible reason to delay them." Smiling slightly, the CSAF continued, "However, she had the gall to ask me to have them re-painted before delivery and when she found out that would delay them for a week or more, she said that she would paint them herself." Sighing heavily, "The request came in on Wednesday and, by Friday, she had her frickin' planes. All we can do is bend over and take one for the team."

The other three nodded in agreement. The CMC spoke for all of them, "So, once again, Montana's voodoo operations trump common sense ... and, as usual, there's nothing that we can do about it."

Two Months Ago – Franklin, Tennessee

Harold had finally reached the last stoplight on his way home from work. After nearly an hour of stop-and-go traffic on I-65 during the Friday afternoon rush-hour, he was bushed. His work week had been particularly stressful since it had mostly been filled with useless meetings where everyone sniped at each other over why the project was so far behind. "TGIF!" he said out loud to himself. He had been expected to put in another couple of hours at work, but he had left promptly at 5:00pm with the explanation that he had a package waiting for him at home and he needed to make sure that it didn't get stolen. He had checked the tracking information at lunch time and had seen that it had already been delivered. As the traffic light turned green, he smiled at the thought that, in just a few more minutes, he would be able to start playing with his latest e-toy. Pulling into his carport, he could see the box with the Amazon smile on its side sitting behind his trash container. He locked the car and eagerly picked up the carton before getting the mail from the mailbox. Fumbling with his keys, while trying to juggle the box and the senseless pile of junk mail, he finally got the door open and dumped everything on the couch in the living room before entering his alarm code. As a matter of habit, he glanced through the pile of mail and pulled out two bills that had arrived. Everything else would go in the recycle bin–except for the *Hammacher Schlemmer* catalog, of course. Perfunctory duties now out of the way, he was free to devote his time to his latest purchase. Grabbing a knife from his cutlery drawer, he sat down at the kitchen table and carefully slit the tape holding the box closed. He removed the bubble-wrapped item and cut the tape securing it. Inside was a matchbox sized package holding his new Infinity Drive. Using the point of his knife, he picked at the shrink-wrap and then peeled it from the matchbox. He flipped it over and read the instructions printed on the back:

* Insert Infinity Drive into any USB port
* The end will first glow RED and then turn GREEN when the drive is ready to use
* The drive may be removed at any time while the end is GREEN
* Do not remove the drive while the end is RED – To do so may cause a loss of the last transaction – In no case will the drive become corrupted

* See the READ.ME file located in the root of the drive for more complete information or visit our website FAQs

Harold pushed the tray out of the box with his finger and picked out the simple-looking device. He held it toward the overhead light so that he could see it better and gave a low whistle of appreciation. The drive itself was about an inch-and-a-half long with the width and thickness not much more than the USB plug itself. The inky black case looked like obsidian, but Harold found himself lost in an illusion of depth within while the polished silver infinity symbol looked like it was floating in a sea of black glass. "It's absolutely beautiful," sighed Harold to himself. Although he had previously ordered several things from Amazon, he had never signed up for an account until now. For at least the first few months, the USB drives were only being offered to registered Amazon account holders and limited to only one per street address per account. The drives were technically free, but there was a $4.95 charge for shipping and handling. Harold had immediately created an account in order to be one of the first to get his hands on one of these magic drives. He stood up from the table, pushed his chair into its place, and went into his home office where he eagerly woke up his computer and plugged in the drive. He opened his file browser and saw what many others had already seen firsthand. For the last two weeks, Harold had obsessively read and viewed everything he could find about the new drive that was rocking the world of portable data storage. He saw the new drive whimsically labelled *MyStuff* and opened it to the root level. Double-clicking on the READ.ME file, he opened it up and quickly scrolled through it noting that it appeared identical to the ones he had already read on-line. "Nothing to see here ... move along," he said out loud. "Now to put it to the test," thought Harold as he clicked on his main volume and started a copy of it onto the new drive. Thanks to having already downloaded the recommended accelerator from the ACME website, a friendly little progress bar popped up and estimated that the time remaining was about three hours. Harold had read about how fast this drive was and had watched a number of YouTube videos of people copying massive amounts of data onto them. However, seeing a one terabyte drive being copied in less than three hours in person was another thing entirely. According to what he had read, the copy rate was only limited by the speed of his hard drive. Memory to USB copies were even faster and a number of early users had already configured the USB drives as ginormous virtual RAM drives with simply amazing results. Harold sat and watched hypnotically as the bright green progress bar slowly crawled across the screen. It would take a lot longer to copy down his stuff from the cloud due to the speed limitation of his Internet connection, but he would eventually have every bit of his digital data on his new toy.

Two Months Ago – Somewhere West of the Rockies

Announcer: *"We have 'Bob' on the wildcard line who's calling in with an update on the ACME USB drives. Go ahead, Bob."*

Caller: *"Hi George, it's good to talk with you again."*

Announcer: *"You, too, Bob. I know I speak for my listeners when I say that we're all looking forward to hearing what your sources have learned about these new USB memory sticks that are flooding the market."*

Caller: *"When I called in last week, I indicated that two of my contacts in highly restricted research labs were going to let me know what they learned about the USBs, as everyone is calling them."*

Announcer: *"Yes, Bob, please continue ... the suspense is killing us."*

Caller: *"They both claim that they have subjected the USBs to every conceivable test and have learned absolutely nothing about them. How they work, how they're made, what they're made of ... nothing! It's absolutely incredible!"*

Announcer: *"So you're saying they haven't been able to dissect one of these to find out what's inside?"*

Caller: *"I'm saying that one lab tried a fairly large laser with enough power to vaporize a diamond and it just ignored the energy entirely. The other lab tried packing C4 around it inside a safe with nary a scratch to show for the effort. They can't see into them or through them ... they can't cut them open or melt them or anything."*

Announcer: *"That's unbelievable!"*

Caller: *"I also haven't had much luck in tracing the origins of this mysterious ACME Corporation, but my money's on Allen Brookstone being behind it somehow. What's more interesting, however, is that the USBs are apparently coming from Area 51, or at least are being shipped from there."*

Announcer: *"Area 51? Are you serious?"*

Caller: *"Very serious. I've had confirmation from multiple sources that planes are being loaded with pallets of USBs from several hangars at Area 51 and from there they are flown to various Amazon distribution centers around the world."*

Announcer: *"And this has been confirmed?"*

Caller: *"Oh yes, at least indirectly. The planes are white with the red cheatline and they use 'Janet' as their call sign when entering and leaving civil airspace. Their arrivals and departures have been noted at various terminals that facilitate Amazon shipping services and match up with the distribution of the USBs themselves."*

Announcer: *"That is fascinating! Aside from the many speculative acronyms folks have come up with so far, have you found out what ACME stands for?"*

Caller: *"Not definitively, no, but if you ask me? I'm pretty sure that the 'A' in the name stands for Alien!"*

Four Months Ago – Mount Ararat, Turkey

Allen had somehow found himself in a large circular room that had hundreds of doors set into the continuous wall. He couldn't recall how or why he was here, but he knew that he had to find a way out. He ran to the doors that were closest to him and tried turning one of the large brass knobs, but no matter how hard he tried, he couldn't budge it. He tried pounding on the door, but the sound was deadened as if he were pounding on the door of a bank vault. He moved to the next door to the right and tried the knob for that one with the same negative results. Moving from door to door, he tried countless knobs before it dawned on him that he didn't know where he had started. Had he been around the room one complete time, or more, and tried all of the doors? Or did he still have some untried knobs left to turn? Almost mechanically, he moved to the next door and was surprised to see it had an ornate brass nameplate adorned with cryptic symbols. As he stared at it, the symbols blurred and seemed to move as they transformed themselves into the word "ALTAIR." Allen reached for the knob and it turned easily in his hand. Opening the door, he saw nothing but blackness beyond. With his pulse racing, he stepped through the doorway, into the blackness, and began falling into what he somehow knew was a bottomless pit.

Allen awoke from his nightmare in a cold sweat. As the dream faded, he realized that he had fallen asleep in his easy chair reading the tablet that Hazel had given him. It had been nearly two weeks since Hazeltine had taken him on his tour of the *Pride of Eridu* and Allen was still trying to un-boggle his mind from the experience. After leaving the navigation room, they next visited the engineering room which was surprisingly sparse compared to what Allen had expected. Hazel had explained that there really wasn't much to their jump-drive in the first place and all of it was locked away behind the secondary shields. The lone console in the small room displayed various parameters including, as Hazeltine pointed out, the dwindling level of their energy source. Their next stop was the ship's machine shop which was quite large by any standards and was filled with numerous small work areas that seemed to be oriented around specialized equipment. Hazel had bragged that they could make anything in this shop that they needed to keep the ship running and up-to-date. Almost everything had a template that they could use to replicate any part needed and the other equipment gave them the ability to make or modify something that wasn't already templated.

"Except for your dilator valve," needled Allen.

"Yes, all except our dilator valve," replied Hazeltine.

Allen couldn't resist adding, "And your power supply, of course."

Hazel had laughed wryly at this, "Yes, and our power supply, of course."

Hazeltine had explained that from time-to-time they took on passengers. While they primarily were a freighter, they also carried super-cargo when the price was right. Three whole decks were dedicated to the creature comforts of whatever alien races may have need of the space for transit. Occupying the central levels of the ship, each circular deck was six hundred meters in diameter and dynamically reconfigurable as the requirements might change. Allen had marveled at how clean and new everything looked as they toured some of the room cabins, the dining and entertainment areas, the gymnasium, lounges, and parks spread throughout what was literally acres and acres of space. The medical facility was the next to the last stop and was filled with specialized equipment that Hazeltine proudly proclaimed as second-to-none for any shipboard contingencies. Their last stop was Hazel's private cabin which was surprisingly warm and comforting in its size, layout, and decor. It was here that Hazeltine presented Allen with a stylish tablet that he explained was unique in several ways. First and foremost, it contained a complete copy of the ship's log, which, as Hazel explained, was an anomaly in itself. Ship's logs were reserved for the captain's eyes and were only passed along upon death, sale of ship, or retirement. They were never, ever copied ... until now. It was also unique because Hazel had tasked Minerva with translating everything into English for Allen. This was particularly challenging not only for the sake of the Captain's Log, but the vast amount of encyclopedic data that it contained as well. Data that was in written, verbal, and holographic formats describing, as Hazel put it, "everything worth knowing about the Universe." Before he handed it over to Allen, he gave a brief tutorial on how to navigate the information and to perform basic searches. It was when he told him that the password for the Captain's Log was "ALTAIR" that he learned that Hazeltine had a first name.

Since then, Allen had spent every waking moment trying to absorb an almost bottomless pit of information, which clearly was the root cause of his dream. He would read and listen and watch and learn until he literally dropped from exhaustion. When he would groggily awaken some hours later, he would pick up where he left off. From time-to-time he would nibble half-heartedly at some food, but even the bacon-ultimate cheeseburgers failed to distract him from what he was learning. As he gradually pieced together a working model of a completely alien society and their technology, a plan began to bubble up from deep in his subconscious. The more he learned from his new tablet, the more his searches narrowed in on a possible solution to their problem. To everyone's problem. As he lifted the tablet up to use it, the front lit up with the words "Don't Panic!" in large, friendly letters. Hazeltine had explained that it was something Minerva had added, insisting that Allen would appreciate it. It replaced the ship's crest that normally adorned the splash screen and caused Allen to inwardly smile each time he saw it. Thus cheered ever-so-slightly, he once more dove earnestly into the black hole of information, convinced that the answer lay somewhere within.

2342 BC – Mount Ararat [Turkey]

Altair and his crew had decided to celebrate their third millennial anniversary in spite of it evoking never-to-be-forgotten memories of how their last celebration had ended. Unlike previous times, when they had gathered in the mess hall aboard their ship, they were now seated around a large table in a small dining room deep underneath an extinct volcano. Five-hundred years ago to the day, almost all of their efforts had been wiped from the face of the planet by the massive upheavals caused by the rogue meteoroid strike. What had taken them nearly two millennia to get in place and working, had vanished almost overnight. Although, at the time, they were able to help thousands of the natives escape the worst of it, it was only a small fraction of the millions of deaths that were unavoidable. They all felt as if they had lost their own children, their own kin, somehow. Literally, in Sparta's case, whose firstborn child, Methuselah, perished in spite of their best efforts to rescue him. They mourned his loss most of all and gave him a proper Shoomaran burial when his body had been recovered.

Altair looked around the table with pride. In spite of all of the things that they had been through in the past three-thousand years, his crewmates had held it together and taken it in stride. Even Ferta, hit the hardest of all by the devastation, had finally shaken off her depression and turned once more to saving "her people." Since the deaths of Mardu and Itok, she had been forced to accept how short the lives of these people really were and no longer seemed to get as emotionally attached to any particular individual. But they all felt the loss, nonetheless.

"Can I refresh your drink, Cap'n?" asked Rolli.

Altair swished what was left in his glass, eyeing it critically, "Sure, why not?" He handed the glass to Rolli who filled it from the carafe in front of him and passed it back to him. "Thank you, kind sir," said Altair. He raised his glass in front of him, "Here's to the past five-hundred years gone by and to the next five-hundred years yet to come!"

"Here! Here!" replied the rest of them in unison. "I'll drink to that!" The familiar toast got them to laughing and Altair once again marveled at how fortunate he was to have such a wonderful crew. A ship's captain couldn't do any better than the six sitting around the dining table with him.

"These parties are always so much fun," Tommi spoke up. "Maybe we should start having them every hundred years instead?"

"But, if we did that, wouldn't they eventually become less special?" asked Mirta. "I think that some sort of supply-and-demand curve would apply."

"There you go, Mirta, you're always dousing our enthusiasm with facts and numbers," laughed Lonni.

"At least this one should end on a much happier note than the last one," said Mirta.

This reminder of the catastrophic ending to their last party cast a pall over everyone as they each reflected upon that day and those that followed.

+ + +

The first jolt of the seismic shockwave was the most severe compared to the countless aftershocks that continued over the next few days. Relatively speaking, it was merely a mild precursor for what was to come from the sea. The first compression wave hit the gulf about five-and-one-half hours after impact. It gradually flooded the shore and slowly surged up the valley, but not far enough to cause any immediate damage. After about ten minutes, it had reached its highest point and had begun to recede back out away from the shore. As the enormous hole in the ocean created by the vaporization of nearly five-trillion cubic meters of seawater backfilled, it collapsed upon itself and sent a much, much larger shockwave back out. Eight hours later, the rebounding swell reached nearly two kilometers high and swept across the floodplains. Rushing back up the valley once more, it showed no sign of stopping and continued onwards spreading across the hills and lower mountain ranges. Outward from the point of impact spread this watery pulse that covered two-thirds of the land masses on this side of the planet. Twelve hours later they met on the far side of the planet inundating the land masses there before rebounding back towards the source. The ejecta that had been hurled into the atmosphere on impact spread at high altitudes and blocked a substantial amount of the sunlight while seeding the vast storms that swirled for nearly a year-and-a-half afterwards. Almost every coastal settlement around the world had been washed clean and any boats, whether at sea or berthed, were transformed into kindling and swept along with the rest of the flotsam and jetsam. With the supply chains destroyed and much of the land and water tainted with salt, death, famine and disease spread in the aftermath.

On board the *Pride of Eridu*, Altair and his crew had a grisly preview of the destruction to come. Immediately, they set about contacting their emissaries to bring them to safety, sending runners after those who had strayed from their beacons. Before the second onslaught hit, they had managed to bring aboard everyone except Methuselah who was nearly a day's journey from the nearest teleportal. Along with their own, they had also managed to rescue nearly three thousand of their human priests; bringing aboard not only the natives, but many of their livestock as well. Several of the lower decks became home to the refugees while several others were converted to stables for the animals. In order to minimize the potentially traumatic experience of teleporting from temple to ship, the floors, ceilings, and walls of the decks housing everyone had been rendered to look like natural stone caves. Along the walls of the many corridors and common rooms were placed flaming sconces to provide illumination as well as open-pit fireplaces to complete the illusion. As far as the natives were concerned, they had simply descended a series of stairs into the bowels of their respective temples while the animals were led directly onto another level. If they happened to notice that the straw bedding was a bit too uniform or wonder at the quality of the food that was provided for them, no one said anything about it. The one-hundred-and-fifty actors assigned to their new roles worked to provide as comfortable an environment as possible for the refugees.

After having done what little they could do with almost no real planning, Mirta turned her efforts to using the navigation system to probe once more into the future and the near-infinite possible alternatives. Altair and the rest of his crew were still reeling at the suddenness of it all and numbly went through the motions doing what was needed to feed and care for the three-thousand humans and five-hundred animals that they were now sheltering. The projections showed that the violent electrical storms that were swirling the surface above would continue for more than a year and the world that waited to greet their guests was drastically different from the one that they had left. Especially those for whom they had no ready means by which to return them to their original locations; most of their beacons now lay buried under too many meters of rock and silt to be used. The few temples that survived the massive series of earthquakes and aftershocks, were mostly leveled by the mega-tsunamis that followed. Even their flagship temple, the *Temple of Enki*, had been shoved off its foundation and flipped end-over-end, breaking apart in the process. The meme of Marduk that had resided in the temple was swept away to the far north and disappeared down the lava tubes of a dormant volcano. The network of large inland lakes centered around Atlantea to the west had suffered one of the worst of the seismic upheavals and had sunken far enough to form one giant inland sea into which the subsequent surging overflow poured. As a side-effect of this process, the large forests to the south of the new sea were completely leveled by the water, forever poisoned by the saltiness and subsequent acid rains. Within a hundred years, it would only exist in the tribal lore as it was replaced with endlessly shifting sand dunes. The severe alteration of the landscape by the cataclysmic tidal waves, in conjunction with the chaotic storms that followed, rapidly changed the pattern of hydrologic redistribution around the globe. Regions that had previously been prolific in greenery and abundant life turned into deserts while other less hospitable areas became more habitable.

It was Ferta that first suggested re-locating to where Marduk's meme had finally landed. Having explored the depths underneath the volcano using the nav console, she suggested placing a force bubble deep within and then proceeding to establish a new home. She pointed out that their ship was now fully buried under the runoff from the flood and reminded them that they had all expressed an oppressive sense of being buried alive. With nearly an entire shipboard lifetime of being surrounded with essentially nothing, the smothering perception of claustrophobia was something of an anomaly for them. She also pointed out that it would be a natural point of egress for those survivors who could not be returned to their origins since the bulk of the cone-shaped mountain had sheltered the fertile land immediately to the northeast. It was this area to which they would direct the refugees and assist them with becoming self-sufficient again. That would have to wait, of course, until the storms had abated and forecasts could be made in earnest, once again.

Over the next five-hundred years, they had restored or replaced most of their beacons and had once more deployed their actors around the world. The scripts that had been worked out for a millennium before the asteroid hit were modified to fit the new order of things. If Ferta was disappointed in how far and how fast "her people" had slipped back into anarchy and tribalism, she didn't show it. However, she spent almost all of her free time running new forecasts of what if and why not and had gradually assembled a new path to a successful future for the human race.

Three Months Ago – Yucca Flat, Nevada

Cassie always enjoyed taking helicopter flights, especially when they took her from one place to another with more efficiency than any other mode of travel. However, until now, she didn't fully realize how spoiled she had become from flying in the corporate aircraft. It was only her third day of using the miner that Alex had cheerfully provided to her and she was already bored to tears with the routine. As the marine helicopter jolted to a landing at the bottom of a shallow bowl-shaped depression, she sighed to herself for the umpteenth time. She had jumped in with both feet and, while she no longer had any second thoughts about doing what Allen had asked of them, there *were* some third and fourth and fifth doubts that followed. She pulled the lever in front of her to lower the miner to the desert floor and pressed the button on the handle. Alex had tried to explain how it basically worked, but most of it went over her head. She had finally been comfortable with comparing it to a camera that she was using to take snapshots of the various places. When she was done, she brought the "camera" back to Alex for "developing" and went back out with another "roll of film." Having taken her "picture" here and raised the miner again, she clicked the mike button, "Got it. We're good to go."

The reply came back from the pilot even as the rotors spun up to speed, "Hang on ma'am, ETA next crater is about one minute." Before he had even finished his sentence, they were airborne and tilting forward as the ground raced below them only fifty feet away. Cassie avoided looking out the side window whenever they moved on to the next site since the angle and nearness of the ground gave her vertigo. After a few more nearly identical hops, it was close enough to lunchtime for Cassie to suggest that they head back to base. The pilot acknowledged her request with a "Roger that, ma'am" followed by "ACME control, we are en route to decontam ... ETA twelve minutes."

She heard the reply as it came back over her headphones, "ETA acknowledged. Decon team standing by." The brief communication was a stark reminder that this was no ordinary day job. Compared to her normal duties behind a desk, she was a fish out of water. As her mind wandered back to their first use of the replicator, she realized with a slight start that it had only been five days ago.

+ + +

Alex inserted the USB key into the receptacle on the side of the replicator and, after a slight delay, the machine beeped once. "Is that it?" asked Cassie. "I was expecting something a little more dramatic."

"Well, looky there!" Alex said, pointing to the floor of the machine. Cassie turned and glanced into the enclosure in surprise. Where previously there was nothing, there now lay two devices that resembled computer tablets on steroids. Alex opened the door and picked one of them up. "Allen says that they are personally keyed to the first person that picks one up." She stood back so that Cassie could reach in and pick up the other one. As she did so, she was surprised at how light it was and stared in fascination as the display screen lit up:

Welcome to your new
ACME *NotePod, Cassie!*

Please acknowledge the
<u>End User's License Agreement</u>
by placing your right thumb
on the square below:

"Seriously?" asked Cassie, glancing up to see Alex smiling at her reaction.

"I didn't bother reading it ... I just went ahead and activated it." She turned her tablet so that Cassie could see the large, friendly letters, "Don't Panic!"

"Well, I never sign anything I haven't read," she replied, as she tapped what appeared to be a link for the EULA. She was rewarded by a popup that literally hovered above the screen:

You may not view the
End User's License Agreement
without first acknowledging the
End User's License Agreement

As she finished reading the notice, it faded and she was once again presented with the original screen. With one of her trademark sighs, she placed her right thumb in the square and was immediately rewarded with the same "Don't Panic!" splash-screen. She giggled as she turned to Alex, "Did I happen to mention that my boss has a weird sense of humor?"

"You did allude to that, once or twice." Laughing along with Cassie, Alex led the way to their work area where they sat down in the chairs to examine their tablets. "I have a confession to make." She pointed to the instruction manual laying open on the nearby table. "Initially, everything we are going to do, and how we are going to do it, is in there." She lifted her tablet for emphasis, "And the rest of it is in these notepods."

"So you already knew what would happen when we inserted the key? And when we picked up the tablets?" Cassie saw Alex's smile, "And you already knew about the EULA, as well!" Cassie snorted. "You could have at least warned me."

"But what would have been the fun in that? Your reaction was priceless!"

"Did I happen to mention that you have a weird sense of humor as well?" Cassie tried to glare at her with her best daggers-from-the-eyes look, but couldn't keep it up for more than a couple of seconds. Finally, she broke into a wry smile, "So when are you going to let me in on the Big Secret?"

"Now's as good a time as any. I really don't know much more about Allen's plans beyond how to create the notepods and a simple 'getting started' tutorial. Now that we have these, I think that all will become clear soon enough." She leaned forward and held her tablet so that Cassie could watch her as she swiped her finger across the screen. Three large rectangles appeared to hover about a quarter of an inch over the face of the screen:

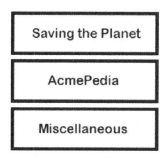

Alex pointed to the rectangles, "The first of these has all the gory details of who, what, how, and why we're doing this. The second is a reference for everything we need to know in conjunction with whatever's in the other two. The last one is apparently a catchall for Allen's personal notes, random observations, and some useful tools."

"OMG! It's like our own *Hitchhiker's Guide to the Galaxy*!" exclaimed Cassie. She immediately tapped the second box and was surprised when her finger hit a hard surface that was clearly above the surface of the screen. She was presented with a search box and what appeared to be a full-size keyboard that floated over the bottom of the device. As she typed in the word "miner" on the virtual keyboard she was startled that it looked and felt like a real keyboard. "This is simply amazing," she said as she hit the enter key.

Alex saw her expression and explained, "The virtual keyboard construct is embedded in a shaped field that simulates the presence of a tangible, physical object."

Cassie laughed, "Whatever ... as far as I'm concerned, it's all magic to me!" She read the disambiguation choices and selected "Singularity Containment Vessel" from among the other more mundane uses of the word miner. She had only read a few lines into the article before turning the tablet around so Alex could see it. "Here's a picture of this miner I get to play with, but the explanation for it degenerated into Greek after only a couple of sentences." She looked helplessly at Alex, "I still don't know what it's for or what it does."

"I think we should start with 'Saving the Planet' before we do anything else. Allen indicated that there is a common narration with linked sections specific to each of us. In the 'Miscellaneous' section are tools for collaborative annotations, video conferencing, and Internet access, among other things."

"You're right, of course. Let it be said that I've never been known for my patience." Cassie tapped the red box with an X and the screen reverted back to the three rectangles again. This time she chose the first one and began reading while Alex did the same.

+ + +

Cassie was literally jolted from her mental musings by the landing of the helicopter on the specially constructed decontam grillwork. As soon as the blades had stopped completely, the craft was rocked to-and-fro by streams of high-pressure water from the six water cannons mounted atop the small pylons evenly spaced around the landing pad. After a full minute of being deluged, the water stopped and the pilot started up the rotors. Once they were up to speed, the helicopter lifted off back the way they came and flew full-out in a broad arc to finally land on the pad next to the hanger now known as ACME 1. Although they could have flown in a more direct path, the pilot had previously explained that the maneuver was similar to driving down the freeway after washing your car. As Cassie exited the helicopter, she was greeted by two privates who were armed with Geiger counters and proceeded to wave their wands over her first before proceeding to the pilot and the rest of the aircraft. After removing the miner from the mounting brackets, they scanned it as well and gave a thumbs up to Alex who was nearing the landing pad.

"How was your flight, Cassie?" she yelled over the slowing turbine. "You're back a little earlier than I expected."

Cassie suppressed the urge to raise her middle finger instead of her thumb, but she knew it wasn't Alex's fault that she was the one assigned to collecting the nuclear waste. She grinned her best and gave a thumbs up as well. On approach, she had noted the white cargo plane backed up to the main entrance doors, but she had not really appreciated how large it really was until she walked toward Alex to greet her. From the depths of the hanger stretched two conveyor systems that led into the maws of the cargo plane itself. Large pallets of shrink-wrapped Infinity drives were moving steadily from the hanger and into the C-5. "I see that you've been busy, Alex! So how long until we're ready to ship our first official production run?"

"Actually, we're almost done ... about five more minutes should do it. However, we're way ahead of schedule, and since the departure time is more than six hours away, I thought we'd go off-base and grab a decent lunch for a change." She pointed to the much smaller C-21 that was now visible once they had moved closer to the hanger. Until now, it had been obscured from view by its massive big brother. "Guess who's here?"

"Vivian!" yelled Cassie as she ran to greet the red-haired figure descending the still-unfolding steps from the plane. She knew that Vivian would be riding shotgun on the delivery run, but she hadn't known for sure when she would arrive. She waited until Vivian was fully deplaned before grabbing her hand in a welcoming handshake. Vivian responded by pulling Cassie close and giving her a heartfelt hug.

"It's good to see you, Cassie!" she exclaimed as she released her and began walking with her toward Alex and the hanger. "For the past few weeks, I haven't been able to talk to a soul about what I've been doing and why I'm doing it." She laughed, "I must say, however, that I've never had so much fun and intrigue in a long, long, time!"

Alex joined them, "Are you guys hungry? If your bellies can hold out, I thought we would hit the diner in Indian Springs." She grimaced, "It's more than an hour's drive, but I honestly don't think that I can handle another pizza or the commissary, at this point."

"How about that steakhouse we stopped at this side of Vegas?" asked Cassie. "That was awesome!"

"Well, it's about twenty-five minutes further than the diner, can you wait that long?"

"Sounds good to me," answered Cassie.

"Me too!" chimed in Vivian.

"Okay, then. I can see that they're finished with the loading ... let me wrap things up here and get something from the motor pool and we'll be off."

+++

Once the trio was settled into a booth in the back corner of the steakhouse and had placed their orders, Alex set her scrambler in the middle of the table and activated it. Cassie noted the puzzled look on Vivian's face and explained that it would block the sounds of their voices to prevent any possible eavesdropping.

"So you can continue filling me in on things while we eat?" asked Vivian. "You were just starting to tell me some tall tale about aliens living and working amongst us when we pulled into the parking lot."

"Yes, I was." replied Alex. "While growing up, I've labeled them as 'the Others' and always thought of them as leprechauns, or some-such, like from Middle-earth. But Allen says that they are actually from a planet they call Shoomar."

"Shoomar? Where's that?"

"Well, it turns out that no one really knows. The Others first appeared in 5342 BC after their jump-drive failed in transit and left them in orbit around the Earth. Since they have no idea where they are, they can't point to where they came from, apparently."

Cassie interjected, "Tell her about the bomb."

"Bomb?" asked Vivian.

Alex explained, "Well, not a bomb, *per se*, it's actually their ship's power supply which is about to run out of juice."

"It's a bomb," insisted Cassie.

Alex conceded the point, "Cassie's partially right. When the power supply runs down all the way it implodes and wipes out our entire solar system."

Cassie looked smug, "Like I said ..."

"Sounds like a bomb to me. I'm not much on astronomy, but won't that wipe out the Earth, too?" asked Vivian.

"Well, of course," answered Alex. "Which is why we have to help the Others get somewhere far, far away before it collapses."

Vivian sat there for a moment while digesting this new revelation. She didn't doubt the wild story her two co-conspirators were telling her, but this "bomb" made terrorist threats pale by comparison. For the past few weeks, she had been following her own detailed instructions that she had discovered on her desk when she arrived one morning. It was from Allen and it gave her specific tasks to accomplish before eventually arriving at Groom Lake. The last item on the list told her that, shortly thereafter, she would be fully briefed by Alex and Cassie over lunch at a steakhouse and to do whatever Alex told her to do. And now here she was, with yet another of Allen's mysterious "prophesies" fulfilled. She was, by nature, a very patient person, but she couldn't wait to find out what lay in store for her.

Cassie assured her, "Don't worry, Vivian, Allen has a plan to save the planet!"

Alex suddenly said "Shhh!" as she reached over and pressed a button on the scrambler. Their food had arrived and they made small talk while waiting until the server had left the vicinity. Alex turned the screening field back on before continuing, "Allen is working with the Others to fix their jump-drive so that they can make it to the asteroid belt. From there he thinks they have a shot at returning home. Or at least jump to some other galaxy where we are no longer threatened by the implosion."

"But what about the Shoomarans, the Others, won't they still die when their power supply finally runs out?" asked Vivian.

"If they can make it to a repair facility before that happens, they'll be fine. If not, the end result won't be any different for them than if they stayed here. Allen says that the Others are willing to give it a shot."

Vivian frowned, "I'm a little confused. How does making these USB drives you've been telling me about help to accomplish this?"

"Allen's been a little vague on that topic. He's given us detailed instructions on how to make them and distribute them through Amazon, and eventually others, but he hasn't really explained *why* it needs to be done."

Cassie piped up, "He says that we need to collect a boatload of singularities anyway, so we might as well put some of them to good use."

"Singularities?" asked Vivian. "You've really lost me now."

"Don't worry," laughed Cassie. "I don't understand it either, but Alex does, so we don't have to!"

Three-and-One-Half Months Ago – Mount Ararat, Turkey

Allen was sitting at the small conference table that occupied the corner of his office while viewing a holographic projection from his notepod. He heard a slight knocking on the door and paused the display while he stood up and crossed over to the entrance. Opening it wide, he wasn't at all surprised to see Minerva standing there since he was expecting her.

"Come in, come in, Minerva," said Allen. "It's good to see you again!"

"Chairman Hazeltine said that you wanted my assistance. How can I help you?" replied Minerva.

Allen motioned to the chair on the other side of the table as he returned to his own. "Have a seat and let me show you what I'm trying to understand." He terminated the current display and turned to her as she sat down opposite him.

"By the by, I wanted to tell you that I looked up that phrase you used with which I was unfamiliar," she volunteered brightly. "It was very appropriate, I thought."

Allen looked confused, "Which phrase was that?"

"I'm sorry, I should have been more specific. It's the only question you've asked me out of 7,322 of them that I couldn't answer." She tilted her head slightly as if listening to some silent voice as she continued, "I had asked you, 'So how many singularities can fit in a small volume, a pea perhaps?' and you had responded with, 'How many angels can dance on the head of a pin?'"

Allen laughed, "I remember now, you looked very confused by my response."

"Outside of yourself, I've never had anyone answer one of my questions with another question. The correct response should be either the correct answer or a simple 'I don't know'." She frowned slightly, "It should never be another question."

"So, if I ask again, 'How many angels can dance on the head of a pin?', what would your answer be now?" prompted Allen.

"That's easy ... as many as are needed." She smiled, "Just like the singularities."

"Speaking of singularities, that's why I've asked for your help. I've spent the last few weeks trying to immerse myself in your technology and culture and I've been able to learn most of what I needed to know.

Or so I believe." He grinned, "I've also learned of lot of amazing things that have no bearing on our problem, but are, nonetheless, still amazing." He paused, "If you don't mind my asking, how old are you, Minerva?"

"Why do you ask?" she replied with a straight face before continuing, "Do you see how annoying that trait can be?"

"Yes, point made. You appear to be about thirty years old, but I'm beginning to suspect that you're a lot older than that."

If Minerva was annoyed, she didn't show it, "In our culture, it's considered impolite to ask someone their age, but suffice it to say that I'm about 6,900 years old, by your measurement."

"That's what I thought. Otherwise, I would have asked Hazel for an older, hence more knowledgeable, person. He said that if you couldn't answer my questions, no one could. I hope you don't mind me diving right in?" Allen tapped his notepod and an image sprang up between them. "Here's a diagram of the ship proper." He tapped again, "And here are the schematics for the Chaos Machine." Tap. "And the primary navigation system." Tap. "And the jump-drive." Tap. "And, finally, the dilator valve."

"I'm with you so far." Minerva smiled impishly, "Was there a question in there, somewhere?"

"No. Yes. I don't know." Allen ran his fingers through his hair before he continued, "It appears that you have a PL-103-B jump-drive and two PL-203-A navigation systems, one of which has been repurposed as the Chaos Machine, of course." Seeing Minerva's questioning look, "The manual for the jump-drive says that it may only be used with a PL-203-B navigation system, or higher, but that's not the case. Why is that?"

"I don't know," replied Minerva, "But we can find out." She laid her own notepod on the table and tapped on it a couple of times. "The service log shows a letter upgrade to the PL-103-A drive a while back."

"What's a while?" asked Allen.

"Umm ... a rough conversion of the service timestamp places it about 10,000 of your years ago, give or take." She continued reading, "Ah, here's your answer, the upgrade to the jump-drive was free under the maintenance plan, but the dilator valve was retained as a PL-103-A until the navigation systems could be upgraded as well." She tilted her head slightly, "I remember my mother telling me that they were going to get the nav systems and dilator valve serviced after their last jump. Their original destination would have landed them at a certified shipyard where they had an appointment scheduled." She sighed, "Ironic, isn't it?

If the dilator valve had worked as it should, I would have never been born." She smiled again at Allen, "So, moving back on track, next question."

"What's the difference between the crystal at the heart of the dilator valve and those at the heart of the nav systems? Do more angels dance on the head of one pin than on the other?"

"Well, technically, they're identical, but inverted mirrors of each other. That's why we can't simply copy one of the crystals in the nav systems to make a crystal for the dilator valve. And due to proprietary reasons, we don't have a template to make a replacement, either." If she was exasperated, she didn't show it, "We've been over this before and there's no way to get it working again."

Allen persisted, "So, if the dilator valve is actually a PL-103-A, what happens if I replace the crystal in the dilator valve with the one in the Chaos Machine?"

"I don't know. I don't think it's ever been done before. At least not the way we've re-purposed and modified things." She tapped on her notepod, "Hmm." She tapped again, "Well that's interesting."

"What's interesting?"

"If we were somehow able to replace the crystal as you suggest, the ship, in theory, could jump to anywhere within the reach of the Chaos Machine using the original navigation system." She looked puzzled, "I'm not sure how that would help, even if there were some way to swap the two crystals. Since that can't be done, the outcome is immaterial, in any case."

"Hypothetically, let's say that, somehow, the crystals could be swapped. Obviously, I've never used one of these nav systems, so I can only go on what I've read in the owner's manual."

"I've never used one either, if it makes you feel any better," Minerva said.

Allen sighed, "Not really. I was hoping to talk to someone that has had some tube-time with the actual interface."

"For that, I think we should get my mother involved. After all, she was the one who originally built the Chaos Machine." She tilted her head, "She says she would be more than happy to join us. I hope you don't mind that I invited her, she should be here in few minutes."

"I don't mind at all. Your mother is Mirta, right? I've seen her a couple of times, but we've never been properly introduced."

"Be forewarned, she doesn't speak your language so she'll be communicating through a translator device that she developed herself," Minerva said apologetically.

"Not a problem. I'm really looking forward to meeting her." Allen tapped his notepod again, "While we're waiting, I wanted to ask you about using a quadro-trilithium crystal to store data. It seems to be a common practice, like the memory in this tablet."

"Yes, of course. As you may recall, you twice asked why the crystals never fill up. Do you remember the answer?"

"Yes, I do. At the time, I didn't fully get it, but the reading I've done in the past few weeks on the basic theory behind the singularities, has clarified things a lot. As I understand it, when properly annealed, the singularity history is reset and begins folding states into the time-intervals themselves from that point forward. A single singularity can be used to store serial data as binary states along the time-interval-axis; all that's needed is some way to track the interval points to read the data back again." Allen smiled, "It doesn't fill up because there's nothing to fill up. Where I start getting confused again is how the singularities are stored in a crystal in the first place and how they are differentiated from the singularities that, of necessity, must make up the quadro-trilithium itself?"

It was Minerva's turn to laugh, "Think about your angels, you can have none or many, as needed. You just need to give them a pin on which to dance." She suddenly stood up, "My mother's here ... I'll let her in, if that's okay?"

"Of course," said Allen. He stood as well and followed her to the double doors. Minerva opened the door and Mirta entered a few steps and stopped. She held a small cube in her hand and smiled at Allen.

"Allen, this is my mother, Mirta."

Allen instinctively held out his hand in greeting and Mirta responded in kind. She spoke in the language that Allen had previously heard in the council meetings, but this time a pleasant sounding voice emanated from the cube in her hand. "It's a pleasure to properly meet you, Allen. I offer my humblest apologies for not having mastered your language. Minerva says you have some questions about our nav system that she can't answer?"

"Yes, I do. Please come have a seat at the table," said Allen as he walked to the nearest chair and pulled it out, holding it for Mirta.

She looked flattered by the simple courtesy, "The Captain said that you were a gentleman, but I had no idea. Chivalry died out a million years ago in our system." She sat down and assisted with Allen moving her chair in place. "Thank you, Allen."

"My pleasure, ma'am." Allen and Minerva returned to their chairs and sat down as well. "I appreciate you taking the time to help me understand things better."

Setting her translation device on the table in front of her, she said, "Minerva says that you were wondering what would happen if we swapped the crystal in the dilator valve with the one in our Chaos Machine. She seems to think that it would effectively make our drive functional again, but only within its sphere of influence. I tend to agree." She continued, "However, she also says she pointed out that we have no way of swapping the crystals in the first place."

Allen was a bit mystified, "Just out of curiosity, how did you know what Minerva and I talked about in such detail?"

Minerva answered for her, "We each have embedded implants that allow us to chat sub-vocally, although we generally prefer face-to-face conversation since body language accounts for a not-insignificant portion of our communications. Most of our people prefer their comlinks, but Mirta already had one for her work with the computers so I opted for one as well."

"Ah, that makes sense. I remember coming across references to your implants, but I skipped over that part in my learning." Allen turned to Mirta, "As I understand it, from the manuals I've read, you basically navigate the nav console to where you want to be and then the jump system inserts or removes energy so that the states of the singularities within the volume of the force field of the ship swap places with the singularities of the destination."

"Yes, that's a good description of what ultimately happens," replied Mirta.

"So, hypothetically speaking, if the crystals were somehow swapped out, the nav system could be used to jump beyond the asteroid belt to a relatively empty region."

"Hypothetically, yes. But I don't see how that would help things in the long run."

"Is it possible to configure the jump-drive to jump somewhere else that requires a specific net change of energy in the system?" asked Allen. "All of the instructions show how to select a destination for which you have sufficient energy available to make the jump, but they don't seem to have any provision to allow it to pick a destination based on net-energy expenditures."

Mirta looked thoughtful before replying, "I think that could be done, but I don't understand why you would want to do so. If you specify an infusion of, say, ten units, the number of destinations available are near infinite. Specifying something like a million units would result in many fewer destinations available, but they would still number in the thousands."

"What if you were to specify zero units and jump to a destination that requires no energy transfer at all?"

Minerva interjected, "With no net energy, you wouldn't jump!"

Mirta clarified, "The gravity-well topology dictates the amount of energy that needs to be supplied or gained. Moving from a less-dense region to a more-dense one requires energy while the opposite direction gives up energy." She paused while she seemed to think for a moment, "I see what you're getting at, Allen. She turned to Minerva, "Statistical random distribution of singularities should theoretically result in a number of regions having identical gravity-well topologies. Can I see your notepod for a moment? I didn't bring mine."

"But, of course," Minerva replied as she slid the tablet over to her mother who proceeded to rapidly navigate through a number of screens before looking up at Allen.

"When we first arrived here, we noted that this region of your galaxy is identical in every way to our home system within a fifty light-year radius. Beyond that distance, things aren't quite the same, but become negligible due to the inverse square relations. One moment we were in orbit around Shoomar and the next moment we were orbiting Earth. My best working hypothesis, at the time, was that we ended up here because it had an identical gravity-well topology. As unlikely as that might be, the scans of your nearby star systems confirmed that it was so."

"So, again speaking hypothetically, you could execute another zero-energy jump and land back in your own system?" asked Allen.

"Or somewhere else equally unlikely to have the same neutral topology," replied Mirta. "But, once again, we can't swap the crystals so we can't jump to orbit in the first place."

Allen sheepishly continued, "I don't pretend to understand everything about your technology and certainly not in the area of these singularities, but please humor me for just a little longer." Allen tapped several times on his notepod and projected an image over the center of the table. "This is what you call a Singularity Containment Vessel, correct? It looks like it can be used to gather and store singularities until needed. Like what might be needed in your food-processor, for example."

Minerva spoke up, "Yes, it breaks down matter as we know it into singularities and then stores them as a single singularity with many attributes. Within the containment field, the singularities have no mass, but can be transmuted into whatever atoms are needed later."

"If you're thinking of using one to transfer the crystals from one device to another, it won't work. You can break down the crystals from one and create a replica, but it will no longer be any more a copy of the original than if you just created one from the singularities that are already stored," added Mirta.

"Well, I'm way out of my league here, but it would seem to me that you could merge two containment vessels back-to-back, so to speak, and effect a transfer of singularities between sources. Or destinations. As I understand it, they only get corrupted when they are broken down for storage. If you're not storing anything, it seems like they would simply swap places intact."

Mirta looked at Allen with clear admiration, "That's brilliant! Your terminology is a bit off-base, but what you're describing certainly isn't. It's a wonder we've never thought of that!" She turned to Minerva and excitedly started speaking in tongues, or so it appeared to Allen as her translator had fallen silent.

Three Weeks Ago – *Pride of Eridu*

Allen sat at the table in the mess hall and looked around the room, smiling to himself as he did so. He just loved it when a plan came together. He looked over to where Alex was in an animated discussion with Ferta and Mirta. Cassie was talking to Rolli and Tommi in front of the food processor, while Vivian sat with him at the table with Hazel and the rest of them. With help from Sparta and Lonni, Hazel was explaining to Vivian how laws were enforced in Shoomar and how that compared to other systems. Each of them now sported comlinks that allowed them to understand one another without the need for a separate translator. As Lonni was explaining the various sentences for smuggling and their effect on the shipping business, Allen's mind wandered back only a week earlier when he sat at this very table discussing the final plans.

+ + +

"Thanks to Allen, it looks like we really have a shot at getting home again," said Mirta. "Without his oblique views and insight into our systems, I can truly say that we would have never come up with this idea."

Allen literally blushed at the compliment, "I just hope it works."

Mirta replied encouragingly, "As you know, we were able to successfully swap out the crystals in the dilator valve and the console. As of an hour ago, Ferta and I finished every test and scenario we can think of without trying an actual jump. We have green lights across the board. As far as we can tell, it looks like it will work as advertised."

"I only wish we didn't have to sacrifice the Chaos Machine," said Ferta.

"Perhaps it's for the best," replied Hazeltine. "It's already going to be dicey explaining where we've been and what we've been up to for all this time. If they catch wind of the fact that we've helped an alien race in violation of First Protocol, we'll all end up in prison. Or worse. I think it's best if we have no record of our stay, other than the log in the primary nav system."

"Which conveniently terminates with our jump from Shoomar," added Sparta. "If we replace the dilator valve with a replica, it will simply look like it's the original after it failed..."

"...and no one will ever be the wiser," finished Tommi.

Allen quietly concurred for a different reason. Anticipating the imminent demise of the Chaos Machine, he had spent the last few weeks exploring all the changes that had been made over the millennia and followed as many alternate timelines that he could find. His frustration at not knowing why a change had been made was easily eliminated when Minerva showed him that he only had to hold his finger on the help screen instead of tapping it. Having kicked himself for not trying that on his own, he found that it opened up the changelog for each of the branches. Not only did it specify what change had been made, it also documented the rationale and the various alternatives that had been considered. The things he learned about the actors that had been placed on the Earth thousands of years ago, and the prominent places they had held in man's religious history, was unsettling to say the least. Almost any one of them would destroy one or more of the fundaments upon which every modern religion was based. In Allen's opinion, it was best to leave sleeping dogs lie. Besides, there was a lot more at stake than upsetting a lot of apple carts.

"Does everyone agree with this?" There were nods of assent from everyone around the table. "So, we leave in thirty days," said Hazel. "We jump beyond the asteroid belt and hide in the shadow of Aurora where we won't risk being seen by Earth telemetry. It's also an equivalent region of our Shoomaran system that is extremely unlikely to be occupied. At the instant we jump, the void we leave behind will be replaced from the buried containment vessel that Allen has filled with the singularities he's gathered. This will prevent the severe earthquake that would otherwise result."

Allen interjected, "Actually, it was Cassie that gathered up the singularities from all of our toxic waste sites." He smiled, "A whole boatload of them, as a matter of fact."

Hazel laughed, "Yes, Cassie, of course. I must say that I'm looking forward to meeting her in person." He glanced at his notepod, "Where was I? Oh yes. Assuming we jump successfully beyond the asteroid belt, Ferta will set the parameters for another jump that requires no energy ... and then we will see what happens. As you already know, the others were unanimous about staying behind. Having been born here and having led a satisfied and happy life up until now, they see no reason to leave. They have assured us that they are happy to live out their natural lives underground and avoid interaction with the rest of the world, other than helping Allen with his endeavors."

Allen smiled at Hazel, "If I haven't mentioned it before, I want to thank you for letting our 'alien' race continue to develop using your advanced technology. Having read your First Contact protocols, I can fully appreciate the trust that you've placed in me. I promise that it is warranted."

"If we hadn't interfered in the first place, we wouldn't be having this conversation today. You've bailed us out of a real jam, Allen, and for that we're forever indebted to you. We all agree that if you're smart enough to figure out our problem, then you're wise enough to use our technology. It's unfortunate that, if we do succeed in returning home, we won't have any way to ever return or contact you again. At least not until your system is someday discovered by one of the exploration teams."

Allen responded, "I speak for all humanity when I say that we are also in your debt. I've followed countless timelines where mankind did not survive for one reason or another. And while the choices you have made for us were painful for many of those in the generations that followed, with 20/20 hindsight, I have concluded that you ultimately chose the best outcome of all possible paths. We owe our very existence to your meddling in our affairs. We thank you!"

+ + +

"Aren't you having something to drink, Allen?" asked Cassie. "These soothies are out of this world!" Allen gave a start and looked up in surprise at Cassie, "Aha!" she said. "Your mind was somewhere else, wasn't it?" She sat down next to Allen and said, "I knew it. Come on and join the party. It won't hurt you any."

"Sorry about that, Cassie, my mind sort of wandered for a bit. So what do you think of this place?"

Allen and Cassie both looked around the mess hall together. Lonni had been in charge of decorations and the room was nearly filled with garlands, streamers, and balloons. Across the far wall stretched a banner printed with cryptic Shoomaran symbols. Underneath, in English, it said "BON VOYAGE!" Ferta had insisted that they have a coming home party before they left. When Allen had pointed out that it was technically a going away party, she had replied that it depended entirely on your perspective. So, as a compromise, they decided to celebrate both. Since the party only included the ship's crew and the four humans, it was held here instead of in the entertainment room. And besides, all of the food and drink was much closer at hand. Everyone seemed to be of good cheer and having fun.

"A penny for your thoughts, Allen," said Cassie.

"I was just thinking that it's only three more weeks until D-Day," Allen replied.

"D-Day?"

"Departure Day, of course," replied Allen. "Until now, I hadn't truly realized how much I'm going to miss Hazel." Standing up, he continued, "I think I'll go and get one of those soothies now."

Departure Day – *Pride of Eridu*

The four humans joined Hazeltine and his crew one last time in the mess hall to say their goodbyes. Both groups were very somber and subdued; after all that had been said in the past few days, there was nothing more to be said now. After brief hugs all around, Hazeltine spoke up. "When we were first stranded here, seven-thousand-odd years ago, I never thought I would ever see Shoomar again. While the odds were not exactly zero that we would somehow be rescued, they might as well have been. I had long ago resigned myself to living out my life on this planet for the next sixty-thousand years or so." He turned to Ferta, "All of this time, I worried about Ferta and her obsession with your species. She was bound and determined not to let you die out and was convinced that you would someday be able to help us go home again." Altair smiled, "Turns out, she was right. Your species has the ability to learn, process, and synthesize new ideas. All of which place you very high on the Tantry Scale, according to Mirta. You are still ignorant of many things, but you are certainly not stupid. Ignorance can be remedied with knowledge, but, alas, stupidity has no cure."

Lonni spoke up, "I wasn't terribly happy to have ended up here, but I, too, had resigned myself to being here for the rest of my life. We are still a crew, we have our health, and, most importantly, we now have a chance to go home again. Even if we never come down from the jumps we're about to make, the possibility alone bestirs hope within me. Hope that had long ago faded from my mind."

"Me, too," chimed in the others, almost in unison.

"I hate to run you folks off, but I think that we should get going," said Hazeltine. He shook Allen's hand once more before walking with him to the lift, "Take care, Allen."

Joining the other three in the lift, Allen turned and said, "Godspeed, Hazel!" just before the door slid completely shut.

Shortly after they landed on Earth, Hazel had removed his captain's cap, since they were no longer a space-faring vessel. For the first time, since then, he placed it on his head before turning to his crew. Altair addressed them, "Unless there are any objections, I want to jump in five minutes. There's no point in putting it off any longer. We'll either make it to the asteroid belt or we won't."

"It's going to work, Cap'n," said Mirta. "Everything checks out."

"Well, we won't find out by just standing around here, will we? Everyone to their stations; we'll jump on my mark."

A couple of minutes later, Sparta sat at her place on the bridge while Altair anxiously paced back and forth. "Navigation: do we have a course laid in?"

Ferta replied, "Yes we do, Cap'n. Course is locked and ready."

"Engineering: how are the power systems and electricals?"

"We're good to go, Cap'n," responded Lonni.

"Communications: status check!"

"We have green, green, and green, sir," said Mirta.

"Everyone ready? On my mark: three ... two ... one ... mark!" As he spoke the last syllable, Sparta tapped her console and the display screens in front of them filled with the backlit view of an asteroid. "Navigation: location?"

"Right on the money, Cap'n, we've jumped to where we wanted to be!"

Altair allowed his crew a few moments of wild cheering and yelling before saying anything. Inside, he felt the same joy, but remained focused on the next step. "Okay, okay, everyone. Now that we are back in space, need I remind you that we are once again a Shoomaran freighter? And that we are now underway?"

He could almost hear the chagrin in their voices as they each replied, "Aye, aye, Cap'n!"

"Mirta? Can you let Minerva know what's going on? Assuming your implants still have the reach?"

"Already done, sir, she's with Allen and the others," came the reply.

"Is everyone ready for the next jump?" asked Altair.

"Good to go, Cap'n!" said Rolli.

Tommi chimed in, "Ready, sir!"

After the rest finished their affirmations, Altair asked, "Navigation: do we have a course laid in?"

Ferta tried not to laugh, "Yes we do, Cap'n. Well, we sort of do, that is. Power levels are locked to zero; destination unknown."

"Okay then. On my mark: three ... two ... one ... mark!" Once again Sparta tapped her console in concert with Altair's words. As he and Sparta expectantly watched the display screens, their hearts sank. Nothing had changed; everything still looked the same. They hadn't jumped anywhere, after all.

Mirta spoke up first, "Cap'n! We're being hailed on the ship's channel!"

"Pipe it through so that we can all hear it, Mirta," ordered Altair.

As she did so, they all heard a Shoomaran voice demanding, "... identify yourself. Again: hailing unknown ship ident alpha, charlie, mike, easy, three, seven, niner, niner, six, zero. Please identify yourself."

"This is Captain Altair Hazeltine, of the *Pride of Eridu*, requesting assistance. There is no emergency. All hands on board are safe and sound. I repeat, there is no emergency."

"Please say again, Captain. It sounded like you said the *Pride of Eridu*. Please note that it is a crime under our laws to claim false registry. Such a crime may be punishable by fines, prison and/or work farms."

Altair tried to keep a straight face as he ordered Mirta to activate the video link as well. Looking into the view-screen, he saw a relatively young woman peering back at him. "As I said, this is Captain Altair Hazeltine, of the *Pride of Eridu*, requesting assistance." He smiled at the screen, "Are you going to honor my distress call? Or has protocol changed since we've been gone?"

"My apologies, Captain, it's just that this is highly irregular." The Shoomar controller looked to the side at another display, "The *Pride of Eridu* was lost a long time ago in a Bad Jump." She frowned at the display, "Long before I was even born, as a matter of fact." Turning back to face Altair once more, she continued, "Emergency Field Service has been dispatched to your location and should arrive in a few minutes. Now, do you want to try again and tell me who you are?"

Altair laughed, "It's a long, boring tale, but we are, indeed, the *Pride of Eridu*, and we have returned from our Bad Jump."

The controller shook her head, "If what you say is true, then this is *way* above my pay grade. I'm handing you off to the director herself." She looked aside for a moment and tapped on another console, "Please change your communication channel to four-two-seven and stand by for further instructions." Looking back to Altair, she said sincerely, "Good luck with trying to sell your story to the director, Captain. Shoomar Control out."

+ + +

While Altair was speaking with Shoomar Control, Ferta left Navigation and entered the engine room. She checked the settings on the containment vessel that was aligned to the dilator valve and tapped her notepod. Smiling at the results, she was satisfied that anyone examining the valve would conclude that it had failed during their last jump. Conveniently, of course, that would mean losing any locational information of where they had jumped from. Checking the settings on the containment vessel again, she hauled it down to the cargo deck and entered the combination on her personal storage locker. Without waiting for the door to completely retract, she ducked in and carried the containment vessel to the rear of the locker and set it down. Next to it was its twin brother aligned to her replica of the secondary nav console. Covering the console and the containment vessels with a tie-down mat, she exited her locker, making sure that the door was secured behind her. Returning to her station, she sat down and, according to their plan, notified Altair it appeared that the dilator valve was totally shot.

+ + +

After twenty minutes, Sparta noted, "No sign of Emergency Field Services yet, Cap'n."

"What a surprise," he said sarcastically. "And no word from Shoomar Control, either."

As if on cue, Shoomar Control came alive on channel 427, "Attention ship ident alpha, charlie, mike, easy, three, seven, niner, niner, six, zero: please stand by for Director Wexalen in 60 seconds."

In the thirty-thousand or so years that the crew had been with their captain, they had never heard him laugh so hard or for so long. "Oh, this should really be good," he finally managed to gasp out as he brought his breathing under control. "Mirta, is there any way that you can record this? Both sides?"

Mirta sounded somewhat puzzled by his request, but responded by running her fingers over the communications console, "Recording everything we can everywhere we can, Cap'n."

Only a few moments later the display screen came alive again. This time it was an officious-looking woman in the uniform of Shoomar System Security. Before she could say anything, Altair said, "Hello, Athena, it's good to see you again." He smiled, "Did you miss me?"

Departure Day – Mount Ararat, Turkey

Allen sat at the conference table in his office with Minerva. This time, they were joined by Cassie, Alex, and Vivian. They had teleported to here from the ship and were anxiously awaiting word from Mirta.

Minerva spoke up, "Mirta say that they're jumping now." She waited expectantly, holding her breath. Almost immediately, she smiled joyously, "They made it!" She paused as if listening, "They're parked in orbit behind Aurora, right where they're supposed to be!" The others smiled with her at the news. "Unfortunately, we may never know if they make it or not, once they jump again."

"We're all hoping for the best," said Cassie.

Alex added encouragingly, "You said it yourself, that the math checks out, so ..."

"They're jumping now," interrupted Minerva. They waited for a full two minutes in silence before Minerva said sadly, "Nothing. Absolutely nothing. If they're not all dead or worse, they must have jumped to somewhere else."

The small group sat in silence around the table, not sure what to say or if anything needed saying. They were all thinking the same thing: *Did they make it home again?*

Departure Day Plus One Week – The Captain's Galley (Eridu, Shoomar)

Altair walked into the restaurant and gave his name to the attendant stationed at the entrance. The young man's face lit up in recognition as he said, "Welcome to the *Galley*, Captain Hazeltine! It is indeed an honor to have you here!" He motioned for Altair to follow him as he led the way to the back of the room. Stopping before a cozy booth in a secluded corner of the restaurant, he asked hopefully, "I hope that this will meet with your satisfaction, Sir? It should afford you a bit of privacy."

"This will be fine," assured Altair. "I am expecting someone else to join me, a rather nice-looking brunette woman should be here in a few minutes. I'm early and she's always very prompt. Her name is Athena."

"I'll keep an eye out for her," said the attendant. Somewhat hesitantly, he held out a spare menu and a scribe, "Can I get your autograph, Sir? I mean if you don't mind?"

Altair looked amused as he took the menu and marker from his hands, "What's your name, sonny?"

"Tomini, Sir, with one 'm'."

Altair wrote, "To Tomini, Best Wishes and Safe Landings, A. Hazeltine." Handing it back, he said, "Will that do?"

"Oh, yes, Sir! Of course, Sir! Thank you so much!" He literally dipped his head and bowed as he returned to the front of the restaurant.

Altair laughed to himself as he remembered how he had been treated the last time he ate dinner here. Being a celebrity certainly had its privileges. For the first time in his long career, he felt that maybe it was time to quit gallivanting around the Universe. He had always believed that he would never want to settle down, but his years as a castaway had left their mark on him. Who would have ever thought that life could be just as exciting while staying in one place? And it wasn't like he ever needed to worry about money again, not with the notoriety of being the captain of the first ship to ever return from a Bad Jump. That alone, would be enough. But to have the one and only Bad Jump from Shoomar return with their cargo intact, well now, that was something that legends were made of! Their Bad Jump may have tarnished the reputation of Shoomaran freighters for a while, but their return had not only erased that stigma, but actually ended up enhancing their reputation more than ever. He idly wondered how Allen was getting along. When he had said that they were forever in his debt, he had meant it more for himself than for anyone else. He felt somewhat guilty that he had neglected to tell

Allen about the emergency shutdown override that he would have used to prevent the power supply from imploding. He felt that if Allen knew there was an alternative to the end of his world, he might not have worked as diligently to find an answer. Necessity, after all, is the mother of invention. Without hesitation, he would have dutifully activated the self-destruct command to instantly collapse the force field into a singularity. As its captain, he was more than willing to go down with his ship, but it was a life-saving relief not to have to do so. He reflected on the fact (not for the first time), that if he *were* to retire, he wouldn't be married to his ship anymore. As a middle aged single man, and a wealthy one to boot, who knows what might happen?

Epilogue – Mount Ararat, Shoomar

Ferta had returned to her mountaintop retreat after spending the morning at Shoomar Entertainment Studios. After being fussed over by the makeup artists, she had spent nearly an hour on a holographic set broadcast live throughout the known Universe. As she once more answered the same old questions about her experience, she marveled at how the hostess literally seemed to hang onto her every word. It had been many years since their return, but they still couldn't duck the fame that continued to follow them. Or the fortune. It was only a few months after they had returned that they all agreed it was time to quit while they were still ahead. Not to mention the fact that they were now filthy rich beyond their wildest dreams. In addition to the numerous documentaries and exclusive interview rights to their story, they also shared in the lucrative proceeds from the uncountable action figures and accessories of which people couldn't seem to get enough. They even had a re-imagining in the works with the most popular names in the business playing their parts. She didn't really need to do the interview, since she already had more money than she knew what to do with. But her practical side insisted; after all, when they offer several lifetimes of credits for a couple of hours of her time, who is *she* to deny her fan-base?

She walked over to the counter to grab a soothie as she wondered how her people were doing. Altair was right, she had fallen in love with Mardu and had become emotionally involved with the humans ever since. She sighed for the umpteenth time as she wondered what was wrong with her. Altair seemed to have no trouble settling down with Athena. They were even talking about having a child. Tommi had copyrighted his template for Surf 'n' Turf and Bordeaux (using the original French wine that he had wisely relabeled as "*Pride of Eridu*"). The last time that they had spoken, he had sold over a trillion of them to appreciative customers longing for a new gourmet experience. The others had each gone their separate ways, but they all stayed in touch from time to time. Ferta sipped some of her soothie and sat down at her desk. She pulled up the recording of her interview and decided that she had never looked better. It was amazing what those makeup artists could do! Checking the time, she ran her fingers across the surface of her desk and was rewarded with a holographic image of the Earth floating in front of her. Noting where the shadow fell on its surface, she picked up the notepod lying nearby, and swiped it open as the "Don't Panic!" screen lit up. She sent a notification from her contact list and followed it up with a question: "Are you awake?" While she waited for a reply, she used the console to once more review the events of only six months before. Changing her viewpoint towards the sun, she watched as the sunspots slowly swirled and gathered on the side facing the Earth. Their collision at just the right moment produced a massive flare that reached out and ejected a high-energy burst of radiation. Unlike the many flares in the past, this one was not only a monster, but almost ninety-percent of the radiation it emitted was headed straight for the Earth.

"Hi, Ferta, how are you?" came Allen's voice.

Ferta switched the holographic display of the Sun with Allen's image before replying, "Bored, as usual. I did another interview today."

"I can't believe they still drool over you after all these years," chimed in Minerva, as her face appeared alongside Allen's. "How cool is that! So, how's my mom doing?"

"She's fine, as far as I know. She still on her cruise, of course. Last I heard, she's due at Dystrasyn any day now."

"If you get a chance, tell her I said 'Hi!' and that everything's five-by-five here."

"I will," replied Ferta. "How's Cassie? Is she still seeing that same guy?"

Allen laughed, "Not only, but they just announced that they're getting married in three months."

"Seriously? I want to be there!"

"Don't worry, Cassie's already planning on asking you to be one of the bridesmaids; but don't let on that I told you ... she wants it to be a surprise."

"Mum's the word!" promised Ferta. "And Alex? I suppose she's down in the lab, somewhere, eating pizza?"

"I thought you couldn't peek inside our force-field," said Minerva. "That's cheating!"

Ferta pretended to be offended, "I can't peek and I'm not cheating. Just playing the statistical odds based on her past behavior." She looked back to Allen, "I also assume that Vivian's out on her never-ending quest to hold all of the global governments together?"

"But of course," said Allen. "Since the Final Blackout, she's got most of the planet begging her to take charge as their queen, but she's bound and determined to stick to the plan. In another six months, we should have a unifying body that will, for once, work *for* each other and not *against* each other."

"And how about you, Allen. How's life after the FB? Still basking in the fame of saving the planet?"

"You bet!" said Allen. "Seriously, though, not a day goes by that I don't thank the gods above for providing us with the notepods to communicate and the food and drink dispensers with which to survive. Before the massive EMP that literally fused all of our engines and electronics, no one fully appreciated how dependent we had become on our supply chains and energy grids. Oh, they knew, all right, but it's not the same knowing that you get when it actually happens. Especially since none of our own technology survived the pulse."

"Except for your ACME devices, of course," added Minerva.

"Our devices," corrected Ferta, as she smiled at both of them.

"Yes, indeed, 'our devices'," laughed Allen. "If it weren't for these devices, the world would have fallen into anarchy as the mechanized food delivery systems failed us. Fear and panic would have spread rapidly as the phones and TVs and radios ceased to work and no one knew what was going on. Governments would have been unable to respond, even if they wanted to, since all of their vast resources would have been incapacitated. In less than a year, ninety-five percent of the people on the planet would have died from starvation, suicide, disease, or murder. The rest would have only survived for a few hundred years more." Allen paused for a moment, "Sorry about that, I get a little carried away every time I revisit the original projected timeline. Thanks to your Chaos Machine and 'our devices,' none of that happened. Thanks to your food processors, our society no longer has to fight over food or energy. And, thanks to your notepods and the USBs, the ability to interconnect everyone on the planet has broken down the final societal barriers. You really do love us humans, don't you, Ferta?" Allen grinned, "Well, we humans love you too!"

In her heart, she knew that she had done the right thing by salvaging the Chaos Machine. Instead of simply replacing the quadro-trilithium crystal in the dilator valve, she had swapped it with the one in the replicated nav console in her storage locker. In addition to letting her communicate with Earth using the modified notepod, it would also allow her to keep watch over her people for tens of thousands of years yet to come. She said her goodbyes to Allen and Minerva after exacting promises from them to give everyone her regards. She smiled as she replayed Allen's last remark several times before sighing contentedly, "My people really *do* love me!"